Swoon '64

Also by Jane Kelly

Meg Daniels Mysteries
From Plexus Publishing
Killing Time in Ocean City
Cape Mayhem
Wrong Beach Island
Missing You in Atlantic City
Greetings from Ventnor City

A Meg Daniels Bonus Mystery
A Fear of Seaside Heights

Writing in Time Mysteries
Pretender '56

Widow Lady Mysteries
Widow Lady

Swoon '64

Jane Kelly

Benday Publishing, LLC

Phoenixville PA

Disclaimer

This is a work of fiction. Names, characters, places and incidents either are the product of the author's imagination or are used fictitiously. Any resemblance to actual persons, living or dead, is entirely coincidental.

Dedication

To Carole, Carolyn, Debbie, Denise, Linda. Marilynn
and Suzen

Acknowledgments

Thanks to those who relived the heartbreak of the 1964 baseball season in Philadelphia to help Swoon come to fruition.

Two classmates from my eighth-grade class at St. Athanasius School in Philadelphia shared their memories and knowledge. Debbie Wernert guaranteed that my account matcher her, and her family's, long history with the struggles of the Philadelphia Phillies. Paul Burgoyne shared his recollections of the Phillies' legendary Swoon.

Rick and Beth Kelly read the first draft of Seth's story even before Tracy Shaw took the case. Thanks to all who reviewed later versions: Carole Turk, Carolyn Andersen, Denise Marconi Leitch, Linda Geiger and Suzen Owen.

Thanks also to the Zantal-Weiner family who led me to the best baseball sources online.

Chapter 1

They come to see me because someone remembered seeing an article somewhere, sometime, about some teacher at Wallmann College who tried to uncover the truth of her own friend's disappearance. I knew that she was one of them as soon as I saw her at my office door. She wasn't an undergraduate seeking advice. Wallmann enrolled adult learners, but not many over seventy and I could recognize them all. The desperation on the woman's face suggested she wasn't a student's mother or grandmother appealing a bad grade. Yet, I would have bet the woman had come for assistance. Just not the academic kind I generally disbursed between two and four on Wednesday afternoons.

"Dr. Shaw?"

"Ms. Shaw. No doctorate. But please call me Tracy."

"But you are this Tracy Shaw?" She held up a paperback. She glanced from the author photo to me and back again. She frowned.

"That was taken several years ago, and now I wear my hair up." I pointed to my ponytail as if that, and not the intervening years, were responsible for my more mature appearance. "But yes, it is me. May I help you?"

"My name is Helen Mitchell. A friend told me you might be able to help me."

"Do I know your friend?" I suspected I did not.

"No, but she heard about you." That answer I expected. Either the friend had read my book, seen a news article or watched a five-year-old documentary that ran occasionally on a basic cable channel with a four-digit number and a matching count of viewers.

1

I invited the woman to have a seat because I understood what she was searching for, what I had been searching for only a few years before, any ray of hope to clear away the cloud shading every aspect of my life.

Looking like a woman on one of those 1950s police dramas I watched on TV Land, Mrs. Mitchell sat on the folding chair at the side of the table I'd commandeered to serve as my desk and clutched a scratched patent leather purse on her lap. Despite a relatively slim form, settling onto the seat required great effort and a fair amount of grunting. Her breathlessness might have been the exertion of climbing three flights to the cubicle I called my office or it might have been the stress. A lot of visitors are nervous when they first tell me their stories. Mrs. Mitchell was when she began hers: "My brother, Ralph Barker, died in 1964."

I'm not a professional investigator. I don't know how to ask the questions that drive people to the point. I wait.

She pulled a newspaper from her purse. "I think this article could be a lead." She unfolded the paper and pointed to a headline.

I took the three-day-old Philadelphia Inquirer from her hand and laid it on the desk. Mrs. Mitchell jabbed the paper with an enlarged index finger.

I checked out the spot where her fingertip landed. "This article about Mikey Sawyer, the sports agent?"

"Yes, he was arrested in a brawl at the ballpark the other night."

"And this relates to your brother's death?"

"Ralphie hung himself because the cops accused him of killing a neighborhood boy, Seth Timmons. Seth disappeared on his way home from a party with Mikey Sawyer when they were in the seventh grade together."

A lot of people must have been at the party or it would not have been called a party. "Yes?" I prompted but didn't push. She'd get where she was going.

Mrs. Mitchell poked at the headline. "Sawyer says he has a life-long problem of taking sports too seriously. The murder the cops harassed my brother about happened on September 30, 1964."

"I don't understand," I said although her tone indicated I should.

"That was the day the Phillies lost their last chance at clinching the 1964 National League Pennant."

I fought to control my skepticism. "Mrs. Mitchell, you believe Mikey Sawyer killed his classmate over a baseball game?"

"I know my brother, Ralphie, didn't kill that child. Maybe Mikey Sawyer did. I remember him. He's the same person, the kid who was in school with that poor Timmons boy. Seventh grade. You know boys. Maybe they got in an argument. In a fight like this." Once again she pointed at the article.

"Why do you feel so strongly that your brother was innocent?" Aside from the fact that most sisters would.

"Ralphie was different. He was what we called slow in those days. It was all he could do to get himself dressed in the morning. Where would he get a gun? Where would he hide it?"

A gun? Did she imagine that Mikey Sawyer, a seventh-grader in 1964, had been packing heat? In the twenty-first century, we'd grown used to news of kids brandishing weapons but in 1964? A story like that would have been unheard of, at least unheard of by me. I'd have to check with my Aunt Julia who had actually been alive in 1964.

"How would Ralphie even know he was supposed to dispose of a murder weapon after he used it?" The distraught sister's question was more of a plea.

I understood what she was saying but not what she wanted me to do with the information. "Mrs. Mitchell . . ."

"Helen," she interrupted, "call me Helen."

"Helen, I am sure there were quite a few people at the party with Seth that night."

"I don't know about them, but I do know about this." Once again her finger hit the newspaper.

"This article doesn't give me a lot to go on." The story was straightforward: an altercation, an arrest and an apology including Mikey Sawyer's statement that he had 'a history of taking sports too seriously.' All charges were dropped. "I don't see . . . ."

She leaned forward to grab my gaze from the clipping. "When Ralphie committed suicide, the police stopped the investigation. They closed the case. His death gave the cops an easy out."

Now it became clear why Helen Mitchell had come to me. There were organizations that worked to free the unjustly convicted. There were organizations that worked to solve cold cases. Helen's plight did not fall into either category. I was her best chance.

I stared at the hands she clasped so tightly on her lap. The skin on the back was spotted and her fingers were crooked, but her hands provided only one clue that her life had not been easy. Deep lines in the mottled skin drooping towards her jaw appeared even more pronounced with despair dominating her features. The concealer she'd applied not only failed to hide the deep, dark circles under her eyes, it emphasized the cracks in her skin. Her makeup tried to mask the wear and tear on the woman, but no cosmetics could have hidden her sadness.

"I want to clear Ralphie's name. Can you help me?"

Chapter 2

"Can you?" Alex asked.

"There's always something to be done." I took a glass of red wine from my housemate's hand.

"Okay. Let me rephrase. Should you? Do you have time?" He plopped on the couch beside me.

"I'm only teaching one class this summer, and my research is complete." Each term my class revolved around a writing assignment linked to a real crime from what I called recent history and most of my students called the Dark Ages. "I suspect the murder of Seth Timmons could make a good case study even if it turns out that Ralphie Barker is the perp."

"But I can hear in your voice that you are already hoping for a different resolution."

"I'm not sure I buy Helen Mitchell's theory, but I might uncover an alternate solution unless Seth was killed by some passing sociopath who left the area and never returned."

"Didn't the cops pursue that angle?"

"From what Helen said they never looked at anyone but Ralphie. Maybe another suspect was hiding in plain sight." I threw my feet into his lap. Alex, displaced by what he considered a tragic break-up and I considered the best thing that ever happened to him, paid for the use of my guest room with foot massages. Considering that I was housesitting, and aside from utilities living for free, the price was fair.

"So you'll help her?"

"I have the time." I made another excuse.

"You have a soft spot. That's what you have. What's

wrong with taking some summer downtime and having some fun?" Alex dug deep into the soles of my feet. "Like driving to the beach every weekend."

I had a feeling Alex pictured himself in my passenger's seat on weekend trips to the Jersey Shore. Considering himself a Center City resident temporarily displaced into my neighborhood, he didn't own a vehicle and was willing to ride in my old car—the one he called disreputable—only when he approved the destination.

"I can't just turn my back on the poor woman. You didn't see her face. All these years and the pain is still fresh."

"Is she going to pay you?" Alex suspended massage activity while he waited for a response.

"We didn't discuss money," I murmured but apparently not low enough.

Alex heard me.

"Ouch." I yelped as he dug his thumb deep under the ball of my foot. Therapeutic? Maybe. Pointed? Absolutely.

"Alex, she did not look as if she had a dime to spare."

"And you do?"

"I'm fine. I tucked away a lot of money to get me through my career change. Okay, some. Some money. But investigating won't cost me anything, well, won't cost me much. I wouldn't want to take her money even if I could, because, as I've told you before, I am not a professional investigator. I don't even know if it would be legal to take money. Which I don't need. Because I'm doing okay."

"Pulling down that lucrative adjunct salary?"

Alex knew the income I earned as a part-time instructor at a small college paid for food, gas and utilities and only food, gas and utilities. He also knew the modest size of the savings I'd stashed away to support myself through this phase of my life as I tried to make a move from marketing to teaching.

"At least you could ask your grad assistant to do some of the research for you."

"I am my grad assistant. Adjuncts do not get assistants. I do all the research myself."

"Well, if you decide to investigate this case, don't tell me stories from the past as if you heard them this morning. I'm sick of repeating them and, then, having someone say, 'You know my granny told me the exact same thing happened in 1967.' Then, I discover it happened exactly once, in 1967."

I changed the subject. At least it appeared I did. "Do you know anything about Mikey Sawyer?"

"The big shot sports agent?"

"Yes."

"Honey, I'm gay. I don't know anything about sports."

"Number one, that comment plays on a gay stereotype and is inappropriate. Number two, you just defied the stereotype because you knew who he was."

"Not from the sports pages. He's a player around town."

I met Alex's eyes.

"No, not gay. He's nice looking and all. He's a little old for me." He cleared his throat. "A lot old for me." Alex focused on my right foot. "But I wouldn't be excited to discover he played for my team even if he were younger."

"Why not?"

Alex squirmed and contorted his face as if someone had passed three-week-old milk under his nose. "He's too smooth. As my granny would have said 'full of himself.' He tries to look like he's having fun, but I bet you he doesn't know the meaning of the word fun. I get the impression he is always working some angle."

"Where did you meet him?"

"Oh, I never met him." Alex grabbed my left foot. "But, I've seen him out and about at some of the more posh events I attend, usually on business. Plus, I keep my ear to the ground. Whenever you need information about what's going on in Philadelphia, I am your boy. Inside this brain," he stopped massaging my foot to indicate where his brain resided, "is a huge cache of information much of it involving the intricacies of the social scene of the City of Brotherly Love."

"So, are you going out tonight to update your databank, possibly even about Mikey Sawyer?"

"Of course. I am going out tonight. It's Tuesday."

"It's Wednesday."

"Of course. I am going out tonight. It's Wednesday." He patted my leg. "But I won't take a step outside the door until your feet are in tip-top shape."

That was the last thing I heard him say. When I awoke, my wine glass was on the coffee table beside Alex's note: *I am on the case.*

Chapter 3

My only class meeting on Thursday was an evening seminar where the final group of students would present profiles of the characters they created based on the known facts of a 1956 murder. My part was done. No prep required. I would spend the evening sitting back, listening, and giving advice on edits—generally reminding them that music was on records, the channel changer was on the TV and the news was on the doorstep. Until then, the day was mine. I could do whatever I wanted. What I wanted was to help Helen Mitchell discover the truth about her brother, even if the truth was not what she hoped to hear.

I felt a kinship with Helen. After all, she came from my current neighborhood. Maybe not from a nearby block but from the section of Philadelphia known as Germantown, an area rich in history that I'd been drawn to by a house that had everything I was looking for: large porch, high ceilings, wide windows and free rent. Admittedly, the chance to housesit was the big draw although I liked the idea of traveling the same streets my ancestors, four generations before, had walked. I hoped to learn more about them but my forebearers weren't going anywhere. On the other hand, Ralphie Barker's sister was alive but getting up there.

So I walked to the commuter train, took a seat by the window and enjoyed the way the weather looked, which was as gorgeous as it felt. Spring was finally taking hold. With blue skies overhead and bright sunshine warming me, I strolled from Suburban Station to Philadelphia's main library where I had a decision to make. I could walk to the Art Museum to look at Eakins's paintings of scullers exercising, continue to the East River Drive to watch scullers exercising, or, I could exercise. Then, I remembered pain I felt not knowing the reality of my best friend's disappearance. I climbed the library's wide marble stairs to the room that housed the newspaper collection.

In 1964, the Inquirer arrived on Philadelphia doorsteps in the morning and the Bulletin followed in the afternoon. Seth Timmons had died overnight on the night of Wednesday, September 30, 1964. Doubting that the story could have made it in time for the morning runs, I began my research with microfilm of the Evening Bulletin from October first. I found a blurb below the fold with a variety of other stories, most on the Johnson/Goldwater presidential campaign. The article simply stated that a man walking his dog that morning had discovered the body of a young boy along the Wissahickon Creek. By the Bulletin's final edition, the story, now above the fold with Hilda, the hurricane threatening the Gulf Coast, revealed the body had been identified as that of Seth Timmons, 12, a student at St. Margaret's School. His cause of death was given as two gunshot wounds.

The media circus began on October second.

The front-page articles were long on speculation and short on facts. Seth Timmons, age 12, of Germantown failed to return home from a gathering at the home of Mrs. Marcia Taylor, whose full address was included. Shot twice. Gun not found at scene. A gash on the back of Seth's head and some minor scratches indicated a struggle. The child had been sexually assaulted. To me the sexual assault ruled out a classmate, but what did I really know about twelve-year-old boys, currently or in 1964?

No other details of the crime were given, but plenty of theories were offered. The person the police sought was certainly a sex maniac recently upset by a dramatic life event or released from a mental hospital or, I wondered, both. Experts speculated that the perpetrator, most likely acting alone, spotted Seth and seized the opportunity to lure or force the seventh-grader into the park where he was molested and killed. Not necessarily in that order.

The photo of an angelic young boy with pale hair and dark eyes looking shy, and maybe a little apprehensive, appeared to be a close-up clipped from a class picture. The caption said the shot was taken at St. Margaret's Catholic School where Seth was a new student making a fresh start after relocating to Philadelphia from the St. Louis area following the sudden death of his father.

A history of the Timmons family began with the parents' childhood in Philadelphia, their courtship, their marriage and, because of Mr. Timmons's promotion, a move to the Midwest with their four-year-old son. The article was speckled with quotes from both Susan Timmons and her father, owner of a manufacturing company in the Kensington neighborhood. I figured the writer wanted the readers to understand that Seth was not just some out-of-towner, that his parents had deep roots in the city.

I realized the reporter's job was to draw people out, but I was horrified by the idea of a news person venturing into Susan Timmons's house on the saddest day of her life. Quotes from the grief-stricken mother were prefaced with "sitting next to a photo of Seth in his little league gear" and "clutching his baby photo in her hands." How could the writer do it? I felt bad asking questions twenty, thirty years later.

Or was what I did, calling all that anguish to the surface after so much time, worse? Did my questions unearth feelings that were better left undisturbed? The reporter did not bring the pain to the surface, it was right there, raw and immediate. When I showed up, I dredged up feelings that might have been buried for years. Maybe *mine* was the shocking behavior, not the reporter's. I came up with two rationalizations to combat my feelings of guilt. One, my investigations were conducted only at the request of a concerned party. Two, I doubted that type of pain was ever truly buried.

Comforted by my justifications, I continued through the microfilm, then stopped and reversed to check the byline. Ellie Shields. I wondered if the writer was still alive and if she had any memory of the case or, even better, her notes. I recorded her name and moved on.

An article on page three bore the headline: *No Cause for Celebration*. In a smaller font underneath, the paper noted: *Local Boys Gathered to Watch Loss*. Two classmates who attended the party commented in the laconic style of preteen boys. The hostess's son, Sonny Taylor, said, "It's sad." Mikey Sawyer said, "It's too bad." Not exactly profound but what could anyone expect from a twelve-year-old?

A picture of Seth's seventh-grade class at St. Margaret's demonstrated how vulnerable Seth was. He was seated in the front row among the smallest boys in the class, the ones still waiting for the growth spurt that identified the boys in the back as teenagers. Seth appeared to be a child.

The following day the account of Seth's death was still on the first page. More details about his wounds appeared, including the revelation that he had been sodomized with an object found at the scene. I didn't know Mikey Sawyer, but he'd lived a lot of years since 1964 without, as far as I knew, any touch of scandal. Not that the rich and, in his case, quasi-famous couldn't hide their peccadillos. They could. I was sure they did. But still. Could someone capable of an act so vile have lived such a public life without some innuendo making it into the rumor mill? Then again, was I really on top of what was in the rumor mill?

Seeking relief from melancholy, I scrolled to the sports section where I expected to find sad stories of less tragic proportions, but the coverage of the Phillies's fate was concise and unemotional. I checked the *Daily News,* according to my Aunt Julia the preeminent paper for sports in Philadelphia, but found no accusations, name-calling or mention of subsequent riots. Clearly, the newspaper was from a different century. The city had been numb but would not give up all hope until the season's last National League game was played.

Sunday's papers, with so many sections to fill, offered plenty of room for speculation about the Timmons case and even some space for a few facts. The police concluded Seth encountered someone he recognized and they believed they knew who that someone was. The cops focused on a "close neighbor" quickly and were not afraid to say why. He was a single man. He lived in his sister's basement. He worked as a custodian at Seth's school. And, most damning of all, he had a criminal record. Police had interviewed him but had not as yet made an arrest. I imagined anyone living nearby would have been able to identify Ralphie Barker.

The next day's headlines not only revealed the suspect's name but that he had taken his own life. A hazy headshot showed a man with a wide face and matching features twisted into a contorted smile, one more suggestion that Ralphie Barker was not a good man. I couldn't tell where the picture came from but I suspected if his relatives had been asked, they would have provided a more flattering photo. The only statement by a family member came from his brother-in-law who stated that Ralphie had been very depressed. If he made any attempt to say why, the papers didn't print the explanation. According to an unidentified cop, the case would most likely be closed since they had a considerable amount of evidence against Ralphie Barker.

13

In the afternoon paper, an article ran under the headline. "Victim's Mother Shocked." "Mr. Barker appeared to be such a kind man," Susan Timmons was quoted as saying. That article was brief.

Goldwater was in town on a campaign stop but the local press had time to return to St. Margaret's where the principal, Mother Constance Mary of the Assumption, claiming no knowledge of his police record, fought back tears as she insisted Ralphie was a valued and conscientious employee. The students interviewed, however, recalled threatening behavior on the part of Ralphie Barker. "I didn't think anything of it before," one boy was quoted as saying, "but now I realize how lucky I was to get away."

By the time I got to the day of Seth's funeral, my neck hurt so much that I sent a long profile of the victim to the printer but stayed in my chair to read the page one story that ran with a photo of a sobbing Susan Timmons. "Mother Cries Last Good-Bye to Seth." Also on the first page a photo of Ralphie Barker, apparently taken at the school where he worked, was accompanied by commentary from psychiatrists who had "not examined Mr. Barker but . . . ." Each expert concluded Ralph Barker was a deviant and a predator. Those who professed to know Ralphie were uniformly surprised by these accusations. A psychiatrist, explaining that was the usual response by family, friends and neighbors when maniacs showed their true colors, got the last word.

I could see why Helen felt her brother had been railroaded. He certainly hadn't been given a fair shake in the press. Although it did not include Ralphie's name, an editorial condemned the suspect and those like him. I checked the writer and recorded the name, John Whittaker, next to Ellie Shields's.

I returned the microfilm and found myself humming "I Want to Hold Your Hand" as I walked down the library's majestic staircase on my return trip from 1964. Then, my mood shifted from curious to sad. I wondered if Seth Timmons liked the song, if he liked the Beatles, if he liked music. Then, I grew even sadder. Had Ralphie Barker even known about the Beatles? What did he know about the world he lived in? If he was not guilty, how had he felt about being accused of something so horrible? Confused? Disappointed? Embarrassed? He had to be so afraid. If he understood. I knew how the world saw Ralphie. I'd have to find out more about how Ralphie Barker saw the world.

Chapter 4

"Aunt Julia. Got a minute?"

"Hold on. I'll pull over."

"I'll call you back when you're not driving."

"Not driving. Biking."

I heard a lot of clanking and then her voice came back on the line.

"I bought a bicycle. I'm training."

Apparently, that was not going to be a problem for my aunt; she sounded great. I was impressed. Not that sixty was that old, but Aunt Julia's usual idea of exercise was similar to mine and involved a lot of walking to the kitchen for snacks. "You're not out of breath or anything."

"I'm only about fifty yards from my car. And, I'm not on the way back."

That explained her perky condition.

"So, what year?" She asked.

"How did you know?"

"When you call in the middle of the day, the topic is generally a year when I was alive and you weren't."

Aunt Julia was right. She was my go-to person when I investigated cases from years before I was born—which meant most cases I investigated.

"1964."

"Pivotal year. Beatles were on *The Ed Sullivan Show*. Nothing was the same after that." The development seemed to make her happy.

I'd ask her about that later. In the meantime, I had a specific question. "If I told you that in 1964 a twelve-year-old boy shot his seventh-grade classmate in a fight over a baseball game, would you believe it?"

"Did the shooter live on a farm?"

"No."

"Was his father a cop?"

"Not that I know."

"Was his father a hunter?"

"I have no idea."

"Well, if you find out the kid's father was a hunter/cop who lived on a farm, I'd say it might not be surprising. Otherwise, I'd wonder where he got the gun."

"What if the kid lived in a nice, middle-class neighborhood in Philadelphia?"

"I would have been shocked. In 1964, I wasn't out of seventh grade that long myself. As I recall, at that age my classmates were still playing *Spin the Bottle*. Well, some of them had moved on from kissing games to first base, but my point is they seemed to be innocents. Maybe I have on rose-colored glasses, or maybe I was just completely out of it, but I feel relatively certain that in my day kids did not bring guns to school or even knives. If there were guns in their homes, I never heard about them. Of course, I wasn't going through the neighbor's drawers. I can't say your scenario couldn't have happened."

Even if unlikely, it wasn't impossible that Mikey Sawyer got hold of a gun and shot Seth Timmons. But what could have caused such hostility between them? A baseball game? And what about a sexual assault by a boy that young? I had to admit it could happen. It had happened in the 21st century and could have happened in the middle of the 20th.

Aunt Julia interrupted my silent ruminations. "Is that it for now? I don't want to lose my momentum. I want to ride the Schuylkill River trail as far as I can. Someday I'd like to bike the entire thing."

I briefly considered joining Aunt Julia. Depending on how successful her attempt was, she might be passing close to the spot where Seth Timmons had been found, but I'd already dismissed the need to visit the site. The wide shot in the newspaper made the area appear desolate, but there would be no way to determine how isolated the locale was in 1964. Yes, the Wissahickon Drive would have been right across the small creek but did the same trees protect the spot's privacy? How much had they grown? Even if I waited months and cycled by in autumn, how could I know how thick the foliage was at the end of September 1964? The answer was simple. I couldn't. I wished Aunt Julia luck.

"Thanks. I'd like to raise my personal best above a hundred yards."

"I thought you'd only traveled fifty."

"If I quit now, I'd have to get back to my car. Both ways count, you know."

Chapter 5

Some days I come home from school elated, confident that I have succeeded in unearthing hidden talents in my students. That Thursday was not one of those days. After hearing a lot of presentations where 1956 suspects called each other on cell phones or cranked up their gramophones, I was depressed and considering yet another career change as I climbed the front steps.

"Miss Shaw coming home from school?" The voice came from the porch of the house next door. With tall trees shading the speaker from the glare of the streetlights, all I saw of my neighbor was the blue dot that was the tip of his electronic cigarette.

"Hi, Harry." At that point, I'd said all I had to say to him, not because I didn't like the man, but because he and I had a wall, a porch railing and a flight of stairs to the street in common and not much else. Sixty years of smoking left Harry Wirth with a bad case of COPD that had forced his retirement from the Philadelphia police force over two decades before. All he could do was suck on a battery-powered cigarette which he did for hours, day or night, listening to the Phillies even when the game was playing on his TV.

"Just like I did with my father," he would tell me. "Of course, back then I had a candy smoke." Although, when Harry turned fourteen, his father encouraged him to switch to the real thing.

I was tired, looking forward to cheap wine, warm bathwater and a soft bed, but Harry would certainly know about September 30, 1964. I stopped to ask the question and prompted a frenzied light display by the cigarette's bright blue dot.

"Don't even mention 1964. I don't want to get all hot under the collar. I'll never get to sleep." That's what he said but I knew he wanted to talk. He always wanted to talk about the Phillies.

So, I asked. "I know the basics. The Phillies blew the pennant by losing ten in a row. What's your take on what happened?"

"What happened? Heartbreak, that's what happened. 1964 was supposed to be our year. We'd been waiting forever. Phillies hadn't won a pennant since 1950 and we needed another shot at a World Series; the last one didn't work out so well for us." His tone indicated he still felt the pain, but then his bravado returned. "Phillies go back to 1883. They were my team. I could never be an As fan. You don't even know the Athletics. Come and gone, fly-by-night, Johnny-Come-Lately, team."

"When were the A's founded?"

"1901." Harry sounded outraged.

Seemed like a long time ago to me, and relatively close to 1883.

Not to Harry. "Not even the same century as the Phillies. Upstart American League."

I felt no need to argue.

"Anyway, the A's had been gone for ten years. Good riddance. Enjoy Kansas City."

For someone who didn't care about the Athletics, Harry packed a lot of emotion into his statement.

"Like I said, 1964 was going to be the Phillies's year. Before that, a successful season meant our boys didn't finish in last place. We didn't have many successful years. Some were worse than others. 1961. Well, I can't stand to speak of that team either. Twenty-three consecutive losses. The Phillies's version of a record. But then comes 1964. A miracle. At last, our team is in 1st place. Twelve games to play. Six and a half games out in front. Even

Philadelphia fans could see what that meant. You know what that meant?"

I knew it had to be good.

"Phillies needed to win three games to clinch the pennant. You know what that meant back then?"

I knew that also had to be good.

"It meant they were going to the World Series. No playoffs in those days. You win the pennant, you go to the Series."

"And?"

"Lost ten in a row. Won the last two but it was too little, too late. One of the worst September swoons in history. City was devastated."

I could hear in Harry's voice that he was too.

I told him about my research. "I didn't find any news of riots or even vandalism in the papers."

"Wasn't the same back then. People knew how to behave. Besides everyone was too heartbroken to riot."

"From what I read, even after the tenth loss the team still could have tied for the pennant."

Harry responded with anger. "A tie. Who needed a tie? That title was ours. In the end, the Phils did tie." He paused for effect. "For second place. Second place." The blue dot bobbed up and down. With eyes accustomed to the darkness, I could see the faux cigarette was hanging from his lips. "We had to wait sixteen years to go to the Series." He then launched into a complete review of the 1980 baseball season.

By the end of that story, Harry was in a better frame of mind remembering the Phillies's win. I was still unconvinced that the 1964 loss could have contributed to Seth's death, but Harry's reaction convinced me that the night of the party was arguably one of the worst nights in sports history. At least for Phillies fans.

Chapter 6

The next morning interest in helping Helen and her brother woke me in a way that a desire for coffee never could. I was up and at my computer early. Newspaperman John Whittaker passed away in 2003. Ellie Shields, on the other hand, was not only still living; she was still working. From what I surmised, she had approached retirement around the same time newspapers approached hard times. Maybe that was why she'd made a move to the Internet. I found her blog on a local news site along with a picture of a well-tanned woman who, despite heavy wrinkles, appeared younger than Ellie Shields should have.

The topics Ellie's blog covered ran the gamut from making jam for your book club to making accusations against crooked politicians to making sure that certain predators never walked the streets of Philadelphia again. Keeping criminals in jail was a major theme that she managed to work into her blogs on lighter topics. Men convicted of horrific crimes should never get another chance to sit on a beach, see the autumn leaves or decorate a Christmas tree. "If only," one of her blogs stated, "all these deviants had the good grace to kill themselves like one vicious murderer I remember from early in my career who saved the family of the victim the anguish and the people of Philadelphia the expense of a trial." I speculated that she was referring to Ralphie Barker.

I considered posting on her blog in the hopes that others would chime in with information about the death of Seth Timmons, but I wasn't ready to go public. Instead, I sent Ellie Shields an e-mail including a short version of my spiel describing how I taught a course on writing where students wrote fictional accounts based on aspects of a real crime highlighting its relationship to the era. I explained that I was considering using 1964 and the Seth Timmons murder. I put 1964 first as if the year constituted the more important factor in my decision. I didn't bring up Helen Mitchell or her visit.

It turned out that Ellie Shields was not only alive and working, she was online. A reply e-mail came back immediately: *I know who you are. I will never forget Seth Timmons. What do you want to know?*

I thanked her for getting back to me and, although I was fairly sure what her answer would be, I asked if she believed Ralphie Barker was guilty.

Ellie Shields wrote: *He admitted it, didn't he?*

I wrote back: *I don't think he ever said he did it.*

Ellie Shields wrote: *Cops said hanging himself said it for him.*

I wrote back: *Is that what you believe?*

Ellie Shields wrote: *Are you in Philadelphia?*

I was shocked. I could not recall another instance when a potential witness asked to meet with me.

Chapter 7

Watching Ellie Shields charge through the tables at McGillin's Ale House, I assessed her as feisty. Her build was wiry, which was exactly how I would describe her dark gray hair. She looked tan and athletic and leaned forward when she walked as in a race she aimed to win by getting some body part across the finish line first, even if her feet trailed in second place.

She wasn't much for small talk. I didn't expect that she would be. Like a conscientious reporter, she had barely let her posterior hit the chair before she began shooting questions at me in rapid-fire succession. *Why was I interested in the Seth Timmons case? How did I get interested in the Seth Timmons case? Did I feel that Ralphie Barker was innocent and, if so, why?*

I grew apprehensive. "Ms. Shields. . . ."

"Ellie," she interrupted in her gravelly tone. "Call me Ellie."

"Ellie, I hope I am not going to see my name on your blog."

"Can't promise anything." Her lips formed a smile, but she wasn't smiling. She waved at the bartender who seemed not only to know her but what she wanted. "Been coming here since it opened," she digressed.

"It opened in 1860."

"Sounds right," she smirked.

I got her point. She was old, wise and experienced.

Her digression was brief. She got back to my concern. "Why don't you want your name to appear?"

I had to think through the reasons as I voiced them. "Number one, I don't like having my name appear

24

anywhere."

"It will help your book sales," she shot back.

"My book is five years old. It doesn't sell a lot."

"My point. Maybe it would. Still in print?"

I nodded.

"Online?"

I nodded.

"So what's the harm in selling a few? You haven't written anything else."

"The harm would be that I ask people to talk to me about things from their past. If they are worried that their story is going to end up in the public domain, they won't talk."

"They talked to me."

Yeah, and they didn't tell you the truth. I chose a more tactful response. "I need people to loosen up in a way that they wouldn't for a policeman or a reporter. I have no official status at all. I'm a nobody and I need to keep it that way. That is why people talk to me. I cannot be perceived as someone looking for a conviction."

"Too late, sweetie." She took a long gulp of the drink that appeared before her. "That is how people see you."

"People who know me. Hardly anyone knows me. You know who I am because I called you."

"Not true. I know who you are and that you've solved a few of these old dogs."

"Only because you're interested in Philadelphia crime."

"Anything ever happen with that old boyfriend of yours, the one from the book?"

"Friend. Friend who was a boy," I corrected her. "I intended the book to make that clear." And, I believed it did.

She shrugged. "So you say. I never saw anything about his return. Did you ever find him?"

"Not yet."

"It's been what? Ten years?"

"Close to."

"And you expect him to waltz back into your life one day?"

"I'm an optimist."

"You must be if you're looking to prove Ralphie Barker was innocent."

"I'm not trying to prove anyone is innocent. I just wanted to ask you a few questions. Off the record."

She took a slug of her beer. "Why would I share information with you, if you won't share with me?"

"I never said I wouldn't share. I just don't want you to publish anything until I have a chance to finish my research." I leaned across the table. "If you write about Ralphie Barker now, the topic could get picked up by any number of sources." Unlikely, but I flattered her. I'm not above pandering. "Sometimes I do uncover the truth when doing research for my course. If I do, I'll give you the story. I'm not looking to make a name for myself." I leaned even closer and talked even lower. "If you start writing about a decades-old murder, the people involved will worry that something is up. I won't get anywhere. If you keep our discussions confidential, I will share whatever information I get. You can write the story. You can get the scoop. But you have to let me do my work first."

The woman took no time to consider my request. She raised a finger and wagged it at me. "You promise that I get to break any news. If you find out that Ralphie Barker wasn't the killer, I get the story first."

I held out my hand and she shook it. Now I had just one major question to ask. "What makes you think I might find out that Ralphie Barker was innocent?"

****Ellie Shields****
October 4, 1964

Rumor had it that whatever happened inside this house had everything to do with Seth Timmons's murder. Ellie was glad to see that Jack Grady was on the scene, even though he was no longer the official spokesman for the Police Department. That job had been kicked up a few levels when the story got so hot. But Grady would talk and, more importantly, talk straight.

She needed to get his attention, to get him alone, to get an exclusive. That shouldn't be hard. Jack responded to flirtation. Sure, he played the happy family man but she knew the role was a struggle for him. He liked a pretty girl. So, she used that knowledge. If she were heterosexual, she imagined Grady would be the first man she would go for. Even she could appreciate how handsome he was. Those baby blues were extraordinary.

"Jack, got a minute?"

The cop stared at Ellie with those eyes as if he didn't recognize her. That wasn't like him, but this incident had gotten to all the cops. Every so often, a case came along that shook even the toughest investigator. She'd seen it before and recognized that the Seth Timmons murder was one of them.

Undeterred, she went ahead with her questions. "I hear you've got a body in there. I hear some guy hung himself."

Jack stared at her but didn't answer. Not even a nod.

"This guy who lives here, this Ralphie Barker. Is he the guy? Is he the one who killed Seth Timmons?"

Grady wasn't responsive. He was studying the scene as if watching a mystery that he didn't understand unfold.

"Grady." She called him back to reality. "Is this the guy?"

He squinted at her as if just realizing she was standing there. "Has to be. Knew the kid. Did you notice what street you're standing on? Seth Timmons lived on the next block. This guy has a record, a morals charge. He has to be the one." The Grady she knew surfaced. His voice grew strong. His syntax, formal. "I am, of course, disappointed that we didn't get to conduct a full investigation."

"So the case is closed."

"That's not mine to say but, off the record, I am fairly sure that it is. I mean, when you have a suspect like this who kills himself, why would you look anywhere else? No, this suicide ties this one up nicely. I don't think you'll see much more time being wasted when the facts make it so clear."

She leaned close hoping to distract him with her cleavage. She wasn't above using what she had. That was what made her good: she did whatever it took. "What can you tell me about this guy?"

His eyes never stopped scanning the scene but he answered quickly. "Not much to tell. Led a sad life."

Ellie swore she heard sympathy for the perpetrator of the crime in Grady's tone. That was a first.

"The department will be making a statement. There will be more, but not yet." Grady shook his head. "I've got nothing else to say."

But he did. Ellie knew it. Jack Grady, however, would never say it. He was a reliable source who would slip her information early, but, unlike some cops she knew, never a juicy tidbit that wasn't sanctioned by the department. And, never any personal feelings. Maybe that was all he was holding back. Feelings. Everyone on the case harbored strong emotions about this crime. No gum-cracking bravado when it came to the murder of Seth Timmons.

Grady walked away. Ten minutes later he reappeared, leading a young woman to a police car. Ellie confirmed with a neighbor that the woman was Helen Barker Mitchell. A nurse, the man thought. He didn't really know her. She and her husband worked odd hours. Kept to themselves.

Ellie viewed her as a pretty girl. A little overdone maybe. Too much hair. Too much eye makeup. Too much bosom but Grady didn't seem to notice. With one hand, he guided her gently towards the back seat of his plain, unmarked car. With the other, he pushed aggressive press aside to clear the way. When the press's flashbulbs blinded her, Grady covered her eyes with his free hand. Demonstrating a courtesy Ellie had not seen before, he held the door open for her politely, as if he were taking her on a date, not to the station for questioning. He leaned down to say something. Ellie couldn't read lips but she could read manner. Grady was being kind. The woman nodded but stared with wide eyes at the crowd in front of her house.

Ellie thought Grady asked the dazed woman if she was doing okay. She didn't know what the woman answered but Ellie knew. She wasn't. She never would be. Even if she didn't realize it yet, Ellie did. This woman's life, as she knew it, was over. She was no longer Helen Mitchell, nurse, wife and good neighbor. From here on in, she was the sister of the monster who killed that sweet little boy.

Ellie didn't feel the woman really comprehended what was happening. Family members rarely did. Anyone willing to listen would hear her protests about what a wonderful boy her brother was, how he would never hurt a fly. Blah, blah, blah. Perpetrator's families were all the same. Just once she'd like to hear a mother say, Kid did it. I'm sure. He's scum. Always was. *She doubted that this would be the time.*

*****

The waiter slid another beer in front of Ellie as she finished her story. She grabbed it and gulped half the liquid down. "I never thought that Barker was innocent. I never thought much about him at all. Cops said he was guilty. Brother-in-law said he was depressed. Then he offed himself. Barker's part in that drama was obvious. I focused my stories on the kid and his mother. Heartwarming and heartbreaking stuff. Human interest. I didn't consider Barker human."

I asked her if I'd read her stories correctly, if she had referred to Ralphie over the years.

"I might have used him occasionally as an example of a monster. Never considered the case anything but open and shut—until your e-mail made me take a hard look at the crime, from the perspective of a wizened, old pro. Then, it hit me like a brick." She leaned forward and her gaze held my eyes captive. "Ralphie Barker handed those cops what they needed. Now, I'm not saying the guy was innocent. What I'm saying is the cops had no clue who killed that little boy. What they did have were citizens living in fear, politicians demanding answers. Nowadays anyone who watches cop shows on TV knows those forces drive investigations, but back then not only was I naïve, the country was. Wasn't going to be for long. The first Kennedy assassination set change in action. Other assassinations and Vietnam knocked the innocence right out of the national psyche." She seemed to lapse into quiet contemplation of the national psyche.

"So you do have any information that points to anyone else?" I called her back to Seth Timmons's case. "What about the people at the party that night? Any suspects there?"

Ellie drained her glass and waved across the room at the bartender in a fashion that made me wonder if she had attended the Rosalind Russell School for Hard-Boiled Working Dames. "There never was anyone else. Ever. After I got your e-mail, I thought about this a lot. I wasn't so focused on Ralphie Barker that I missed other clues. The cops were so focused on Ralphie Barker that they never found any other clues." She shook her head. "Now, I feel ashamed and embarrassed. Five years later, I would have known where the real story was, but what can I say. I was green and maybe a little yellow." She stared at me with an intensity that made me squirm in my seat. "You can't be either of those things and get the true story."

I nodded and made some noise. Even I wasn't sure what the sound resembled but I knew what it said. "You recognize that I am both of those things but I will take your advice and try to be neither." Looking back, I think it sounded a lot like "Aaargh."

Chapter 8

Just because Ellie Shields never suspected Mikey Sawyer, didn't mean I was giving up on Helen Mitchell's theory. Before I directed my attention his way, however, I did a search to determine if sexual assault would rule out a twelve-year-old. Sadly, I found it wouldn't rule out an eight-year-old.

I began gathering information on Mikey Sawyer who'd been twelve years old in 1964. He'd made my research easy. The sports agent not only raised his clients to star status, he'd established himself as a public figure. In news articles and profiles of him or his clients, he came across as an arrogant blowhard but, if you discounted his recent brouhaha, nothing indicated he was prone to violence or any form of sexual unorthodoxy. He'd had one long marriage that produced two children and innumerable rumors of infidelity, a second marriage that produced a bitter trophy wife and a vow never to remarry. Even with sixty in the rearview mirror, he played the field.

One magazine article stressed Sawyer's loyalty to his hometown. He'd been born in Philadelphia. His father left shortly after his birth and his stepfather bailed as he entered his teen years. He credited the hard-working single mother who put him through a private high school and a state university with imbuing him with the confidence required to carve out a top spot for himself in sports management, a feat he accomplished without ever straying from his Philadelphia roots. His wives, yes. His roots, no. I wondered if reluctance to leave the town where he'd made himself a celebrity motivated him more than loyalty.

I hadn't asked Helen if she had suspected Mikey back in 1964, if anyone had. Maybe she was privy to some info Ellie Shields never heard. Had the cops ever looked at any of the kids during the original investigation? From what I read in the newspapers and Ellie Fields confirmed, the police had never looked at anyone but Ralphie Barker. I pulled out an 11 by 17 printout from the library to check out an unread article containing comments by a police investigator in the Seth Timmons case, the spokesman Ellie Shields mentioned. Detective Jack Grady said that he had interviewed the kids at the party, but found no indication that they had any relevant information to offer.

Outside my front window, trees danced to the lilt of leaves rustling in the gentle breeze. The sounds of the gorgeous evening were disturbed only by an occasional car, the crack of bat hitting ball, and the cheers of fans. I hoped, for Harry's sake, Phillies fans. I moved to the porch with an ulterior motive.

"Hey, Harry, how you doing today?" I said *you* but I meant *you and the Phillies*.

"Third inning and I'm still doing okay, although the Mets have two guys on base. The Mets! What kind of name is that? Why should New York have two teams anyway? Damn Yankees should be enough for any city. Not that I could root for them. But the Mets? Upstart organization only created in the 1960s."

To me, and a lot of fans, that was more than a lifetime ago, but I didn't argue. I changed the subject back to the weather. "Wonderful day today, wasn't it?" I settled onto the wide railing that separated our porches.

"What a beautiful day. This is the way the weather used to be, but not the way baseball used to be." He jabbed his e-cigarette towards the broadcast blaring through the window. "If they're not careful the boys of October will become the boys of November." Harry did not approve of the expanded season that the playoff system required.

"More games. More suffering."

For the next twenty minutes, I listened to Harry reminisce about the way baseball had been played in perfect weather in a perfect world. But only between plays when Harry was happy to drown out what he called the piffle of the announcer. Harry was not a fan of modern-day announcers or modern times for that matter.

I waited for the commercial. "Speaking of the old days, I was doing some reading and found a comment about a cop named Jack Grady." Since Harry was not fond of the press, I didn't mention Ellie Shields. "You happen to know him when you were with the department?"

"Sure. Grady didn't live far from here when he was on the job. Where'd you see his name?"

"I was reading about a young boy from around here who was murdered."

"Seth Timmons?"

"You remember that case?" My tone went beyond surprised towards shocked. Harry had seen a lot of cases in the thirty years he'd been on the job.

"Not likely to forget it. Kid was one of our own, didn't live that far from here. Sad story. Lucky they caught the pervert that killed the poor boy before he found another victim. At least the creep had the sense to off himself." Harry took a deep drag on his electronic cigarette and seemed to spit out the smoke at the memory of Ralphie Barker.

If I encountered this attitude fifty years later, I could only imagine the mindset Helen had been up against when trying to defend her brother in 1964.

"Grady worked that case. Was he a good cop?"

Harry didn't like my question. "As far as I'm concerned, all cops are good cops, except like the really dirty ones, but there aren't many of them. It's a tough job."

"I just wondered about your opinion of Grady."

"I always found him to be a nice guy. Outranked me so it wasn't like we would hang out and exchange war stories. Reputation was that he did what it took to make the collar. A lot of people thought that was good."

"And some didn't?"

Harry didn't answer. "I don't pay attention to gossip. He must have been okay. They let him teach at the community college."

"I took criminal justice courses there."

Harry appeared puzzled. "Why?"

"I was interested in crime investigations." I didn't explain that I was interested in a specific investigation involving a friend.

"Did Grady teach you?"

"I wonder." I didn't remember any names. "What did he look like?"

"He was a handsome guy, at least that's what the ladies told me. What did I know? He was a sharp dresser. He struck me as kind of a dapper type. He had lots of black hair, back then anyway."

"When did you go to school?"

"About seven or eight years ago."

"I ran into him around that time, I think. He was up there, maybe close to eighty by then. Don't know if he was still teaching, but he still would have had those blue eyes. The ladies always commented on his big blue eyes. I've to admit that even I noticed them and I ain't gay or nothing." With that, he tilted his head to hear what was going on in New York. "Damn Phillies. In the end, they always break your heart."

Chapter 9

Harry may not have been willing to gossip but he did point me in Jack Grady's direction. Not exactly intentionally. He knew where the ex-cop lived, at least when Harry last ran into him. "I couldn't believe he lived in a dump like that. Hope he got out of there." Selfishly, I hoped that he hadn't. Or, to be kinder, that he had moved but left a forwarding address.

I wasn't familiar with Grady's area, but after cruising by the corner a few times, I found a parking space on the single, dead-end block of Luckinbill Lane, a street that in no way resembled what I heard as a lyrical, bucolic and fortune-filled name. Whatever Luckinbill Lane had been, it was now a dingy strip of cement with a dilapidated warehouse on one side and an odd assortment of residential and commercial structures on the other. According to Harry, Jack Grady lived in an apartment building that I identified by its odd blue tile façade, not the worst style on the street. That was not to say that it looked good. None of the windows were broken, but several had wooden planks in place of glass. Sheets and old blankets appeared to be the preferred window dressing, along with cheap souvenirs, dead plants and the occasional live cat.

I approached the man sweeping trash from the sidewalk into the street.

"Do you work here?" I asked in what I considered a very sweet tone.

"No. I do this for fun." He didn't seem hostile, just tired.

"So you do work here."

"Yeah. I'm the doorman. Uniform is at the cleaners. What can I do for you?"

He seemed happy to take a break to tell me that Grady was not at home and, without a single question about who I was or why I wanted to see him, give me directions to the Biding Time Tavern. The description he provided suggested that the Tav, as he called it, was an establishment that had once served the neighborhood's elite. Unfortunately, the local elite were now defined as those who had never been convicted of a felony. And, since the Biding Time Tavern considered itself quite egalitarian, everyone, felon or not, was now welcome.

I walked down Luckinbill Lane and saw the bar as soon as I turned right. The windows, high and masked with Venetian blinds and neon beer signs, offered no opportunity to see inside. It required every ounce of courage I possessed to discover what lay beyond the Tav's solid wood door.

What I found was another door. I took a deep breath to work up my nerve and inhaled a sample of what lay ahead. Smoking might have been banned in the bar for years, but the odor persisted, garnished with the stench of spilled liquor and stale beer. I pushed the flimsy plywood door open and stepped into a dimly lit room, narrow with no space for tables, only a long bar along the wall to my right. From what I could see the drinking establishment looked as good as it smelled, which is to say not very. As my eyes adjusted to the light I saw that the place had one thing going for it. The bar served a diverse population, if you dismissed one commonality among the customers. Evidence of a hard life was etched on every face I saw reflected in the mottled mirror that ran the length of the bar.

No one seemed to care whether I was there or not. I'm not sure anyone at the bar even noticed me. Actually, I'm fairly sure that no one did. The man I identified as Grady didn't. I ID'ed him by the process of elimination. I counted on the fact that since Harry last saw Grady, the ex-cop had not gained a hundred pounds, lost his hair or evolved into a woman, an African-American or an African-American woman. That didn't mean he hadn't changed. I found it hard to see the detective Harry described as a dapper thirty-something in the shabbily dressed eighty-something man sitting at the bar. Except for the eyes. They were notable for their color and, unfortunately, the sad expression in them. Not that I'd seen them except in the mirror. Even after I introduced myself, the ex-cop didn't even glance my way.

"Should I know you?" Grady kept his eyes on his beer as he took a gulp.

"I took your class at the community college." I might have. I figured if I couldn't recall, neither could he.

He turned his head slightly to look me over. "I can't say I remember but there isn't a lot I do remember these days."

"I wasn't a star student."

"I wasn't a star teacher." He turned his attention back to his drink. "Teaching was just a way to keep myself out of the bars. And then I asked myself why I wanted to stay out of the bars." Grady drained his beer without looking my way. "You got a question you forgot to ask in class?" He downed a shot and signaled the bartender for another.

I gave him my spiel on my course, *Writing in Time*. I explained how I have the students write fiction based on real crimes. "Actually, one crime. We get a lot of different twists on the same event."

"Too lazy to let the kids pick their own topics?"

He hit upon the exact reason but I wasn't about to admit that. I played dumb. "Why would that be lazy?

"If you let them pick, you'd have to check every fact. Remember, I taught. I learned that lesson the hard way."

"Good point." I nodded as if his idea was news to me.

He seemed pleased by the idea that he'd taught me something. The deep crevices that ran from the corner of his mouth to his jaw spread with his smile until he looked like a clown. A very old, very tired, very sad clown. His eyes never brightened.

"Anyway, when someone told me about the Seth Timmons case, I did some research."

Beside me, Grady seemed to miss a breath.

"When I mentioned this case and your name to my neighbor, Harry Wirth, he suggested I try to talk to you." Not a lie, an embellishment but a typical one when doing this type of work.

"Harry Wirth. I remember him. How is the old guy?" He chuckled. "Younger than me, but still an old guy. I hope he's doing okay."

"He's doing well but he'd be better if the Phillies were better."

Grady snorted. "They are being reliably bad this year."

I had the feeling he was happy to hear about Harry Wirth but happier for a lighter topic of conversation. I didn't let that continue. "Harry thought you'd remember the Timmons case."

"Unlikely I'll forget." He grabbed the shot before the bartender got it to the bar and emptied the glass. I speculated that he was trying to drive the recollection from his mind. "I don't understand why you're bringing it up now." He signaled the bartender and a replacement shot appeared while I delivered my next lie—but a lie only by the omission of Helen Mitchell's visit. "This particular murder interests me because it happened not far from where I live."

"You live in Germantown?" He sounded surprised. We exchanged addresses.

"Very posh. Chestnut Hill."

"No way. I rent next door to Harry who still lives in his parents' home." I explained the location of my house.

That I was not only a true Germantown resident but proud of it seemed to tear the wall down between us. He waved at the bartender and ordered a beer for me.

"Seth Timmons." He spoke the name with wonder. "I never thought I'd hear that name again. I guess I never wanted to hear that name again." He took a swig of his beer. "Seth was a cute kid, a good kid. He didn't deserve what happened to him. I mean no one would, but, from all we heard, Seth was an exceptionally nice kid. Kind of shy. Small for his age. Made him vulnerable." Grady took a long drink.

"The cops had a prime suspect right away, Ralphie Barker."

"Guy was a weirdo. Neighbors knew him. Had a prior, and no alibi. He was right there. Who else would we look at?"

I would have liked to come up with some suggestions but I didn't argue. "You were at the murder scene. I saw your name in the paper. You talked to the press. Did you interview the kids at the party?" I didn't specify Mikey Sawyer.

Grady emptied another beer glass. I wasn't counting but any tally would be high. "I could talk about the party myself. I stopped by the Taylor house that night. Are you aware that I was the last person known to have seen Seth alive?"

I shook my head and sipped from the beer the bartender slipped next to the shot for Grady. I didn't think the newspapers had offered that information, but I could have missed it.

"If you paid attention in class, you would know that makes me the prime suspect." He made a noise that I took to be a chuckle.

I ignored the remark and got to the point. "I'd be interested in hearing anything I could about Seth's last hours."

"He watched a baseball game, drank some soda and ate some potato chips." Grady shrugged. "Beyond that, I have no idea. I saw him when I went to pick up my son. The two went to school together. I volunteered to walk Seth home too."

An odd detail to be omitted from the newspaper accounts. Did Grady keep his kid's name, and his, out of the paper?

"Did anyone indicate that something unusual happened at the party?"

"Not to me and everything seemed okay when I arrived. It made sense for me to talk to them. No formal interview was needed. I was there. I didn't want those kids traumatized any more than they were."

"Any bad blood between the boys?"

He had a sharp reaction to my question. Shock? Concern? I wasn't sure. The expression was gone as quickly as it surfaced. "Not that I saw but I wasn't there long. Phils choked. My kid was devastated."

"How was Seth?"

"Seth didn't say much but he seemed happy. He'd just moved to town. I remember wondering if he was a closet St. Louis fan, but he was smart enough to keep his mouth shut."

"How long was the walk to Seth's house?"

"A couple of blocks. It didn't take me long in those days. Today I'd probably drive. Or ask someone else to drive me. And insist we stop to use the men's room on the way, which reminds me . . . ." He downed the whiskey before slipping off the stool and disappearing towards the back of the bar. I wondered if he had disappeared full stop, but after a few minutes, he emerged, still adjusting his zipper. The bartender had another beer and a shot waiting for him. I didn't have to prompt him. He picked up where he left off. "Our house was across the street from the Timmons's, not quite as far down the block. Seth lived maybe four or five houses closer to the corner."

"Did you walk Seth to his door?"

I saw the muscles in his jaw tighten, his eyes narrow.

"If I had, the whole thing wouldn't have happened. My kid ran home and I walked a few houses more to the front of Seth's. I saw him walk up the steps. The door was five feet away, just out of sight. The kid turned and waved. Everything seemed fine. He was on his goddam porch." His eyes filled with tears. He snorted and cleared his throat before he could continue. "How could I have known there was a perv waiting for him? I didn't hear anything. No scuffle. No scream. No conversation. I believe I heard the sound of a storm door opening but nothing else." He sounded as if he were testifying to his own conscience explaining that he had no reason to suspect danger. "I swear I heard that sound, but maybe that is wishful thinking. I was walking away."

Grady left the beer but downed a shot. "I gotta get out of here." He moved with amazing speed for a man his age. Sure, I had to dig out a bill to cover my beer, so he had a head start, but I had to hustle to catch up with him as he pushed the outside door open. Apparently, he had not yet taken on the frailty of advanced old age. I tried to imagine what such a handsome man might have looked like had he lived a clean life.

Grady staggered into the light, and, for an instant, I worried he might topple over. I extended an arm for support, but he regained his balance before I could reach him. "Times like this I wish I still smoked."

He looked to me. Hoping for a cigarette? I gave him a smile.

"You know, I think about Seth a lot. About those last few steps, the steps that I didn't take, the steps that would have let me see the front door. How much of a hurry could I have been in? I should have waited, walked a few more measly yards and watched the kid get inside." He wiped his eyes. "You'd think a cop would be tougher than this, wouldn't you? Must be the whiskey. I can handle my beer."

I felt surprised that the pain, even at the loss of the young boy he'd known, remained so close to the surface after half a century. But the emotion he felt wasn't alcohol-induced regret. Grady lived with the guilt that somehow he had caused Seth's death.

"Miss Shaw," he appeared to have controlled his emotions, "don't tell anyone I cried, okay?"

"Of course not." I tried to make my sympathetic expression reassure him. "Your reaction is completely understandable. It was a horrible crime."

"A crime," he repeated. "A horrible, horrible crime."

"Over the years, did you ever consider that the police didn't get the right man?"

"I never questioned what we concluded in that investigation. Nothing about that boy's final hours suggested what was about to happen to him. Theory was the perv waited for him."

"So he knew that Seth was out at the party?"

"He lived one block down. He could watch. We actually passed his corner on our way home." He pulled a paper napkin from his pocket and blew his nose hard. "I know you're interested in that party. All I saw that night was a bunch of kids eating chips, drinking soda and watching a baseball game. Pretty routine except that the Phillies broke their hearts."

"Do you know what happened to the kids who were there?"

"You mean when they grew up?" Puzzlement drove the pain from his face.

I nodded.

"Why are you asking about them?" Grady didn't even try to hide his defensiveness.

"I'd like to speak with them. I found a couple of names

but I'd like to talk to everyone who was there."

"They don't need to relive that night." He sounded protective as if he were talking about kids and not retirees.

"I told you. The get-together was like thousands of others that night." He waved off my question.

"But those kids could provide a unique perspective."

"Why would you want to bring up such painful memories?" His question sounded like an accusation. "If you want, what did you call it, social context, ask anyone that age."

He made a valid point that I ignored and plowed ahead. "From the newspaper stories, I know that the party was at Sonny Taylor's house and that Mikey Sawyer was there."

"Of course, I told you that." He sounded frustrated.

I scowled as I tried to recall any mention of Mikey Sawyer.

His voice grew soft. "People might say he was my stepson, but I couldn't have loved that boy more if we shared DNA." He reacted to my puzzled expression. "Mikey Sawyer is my son."

Chapter 10

I was shaking as I walked to my car. I felt stunned but believed I'd hidden my reaction to the news that Mikey Sawyer was the stepson of Jack Grady, the detective on the scene. When I set out on my investigation, I expected that I'd be putting a grieving sister's mind to rest, confirming that justice had been done but now I had questions. Even if Mikey Sawyer hadn't killed Seth Timmons, Helen's was not a far-fetched scenario. Sawyer's stepfather, a cop with a gun, not only investigated the crime, he was the last to see the victim alive.

"That doesn't prove anything." Alex brushed off my conclusions when he returned from work and found me in the back garden waiting with a bottle of wine and two glasses.

"Have a drink." I held his glass aloft. "My theory will sound better."

Alex settled onto a chaise lounge and loosened his tie. "You don't actually have a theory, you know. All you have is a suspicion that something isn't right."

"That's why we need refreshments, to get our imaginations going." I toasted him from the chaise beside his.

"Why didn't Mrs. Mitchell tell you that Mikey Sawyer's stepfather was on the case? Is it possible that she didn't know?"

"Mikey had a different last name." I found it hard to believe she wouldn't have shared that information if she knew it. "I don't think the cops were feeding information to the sister of the perp."

"They all lived on the same street. The victim. The perp. The cop. Back then people knew their neighbors," Alex protested.

"Not all of them. The Mitchells lived a block away from the Timmons and Grady families. They might never even have seen them. I haven't seen the occupants of twenty houses on this block. Ellie Shields said Helen and her husband worked odd hours, kept to themselves. Helen didn't have any children. She wouldn't have been out walking a baby and without a kid in school, she wouldn't know those kids or their parents."

"Maybe her friends didn't have kids either, so she had no one who knew to tell her."

"I think after it happened she didn't have any friends, full stop. Wait until you see this." I pulled out a printout of the editorial by the late John Whittaker. I didn't make Alex read it. I gave him the basics. "The writer contrasted predators, and the reader would know that he was talking about Seth Timmons's killer, with men who did what they were supposed to, such as Robert "Bob" Timmons, Seth's father." I summarized for Alex how the editorial went on about men like the successful young businessmen who worked hard to support their families and to inculcate them with sound values, the type that made America great. "You know. The right kind of men." Bob Timmons put in long hours to earn his promotion so he could provide the best of everything for his family. His devotion to this duty was the reason he barely noticed the growing pain in his stomach and, when he did, he ignored it until the prognosis was grim. Bob Timmons lived only six weeks after the diagnosis of his cancer. "Until the very end, he put providing for his family first." I paused, going for a dramatic emphasis. "If I were alive and old enough to read in 1964, I would have been tempted to write a letter to the editor suggesting that perhaps taking care of his health would have been taking care of his family. I might have been tempted but I wouldn't have risked the wrath of the public for saying anything that could be perceived as negative about Bob Timmons."

"Or anything positive about the man who murdered his son." Alex got my point.

"Yep. The article concludes by asking, and answering, the question 'What was this maniac doing while Bob Timmons was building his family and career?' According to the writer, he had been living a life of leisure, taking easy jobs, mooching off his sister."

"Yeah, from what you told me, Ralphie Barker had been living the good life." Alex sounded sympathetic to my opinion and to Ralphie.

I tried to remain objective. "Ralphie was tried and convicted in the press, but that doesn't mean he was innocent. Even the news that Mikey Sawyer's stepfather was the lead investigator on the case doesn't convince me that Helen's notion is right. I can't believe that Mikey Sawyer killed a classmate because he rooted for the Cardinals and that his father, a well-respected cop, covered for him."

"So, what happened?" Alex asked.

"No clue." I looked to the sky. "Storm clouds are gathering."

"Is that a metaphor?" Alex didn't look up.

"No, it's a weather forecast. We'd better drink fast."

"I'll drink. You talk. Fill me in on what you know."

There are only so many ways to say *something isn't right here* and I used all of them. "You know what made me really sad when I went to the library?"

"I'm trying to think of a library joke but I'm not coming up with one, so tell me."

"From the day after Seth was found until the day of his funeral, his story was plastered all over the newspapers. His and Ralphie's. Front-page articles, up there with a presidential campaign, a hurricane slamming the Gulf

Coast and an ongoing review of the local magistrate's court which appeared to be very big news in Philadelphia. Fighting for column space every day were stories about every angle of the Timmons case. Then they buried Ralphie in a private funeral and Seth in a very public one, and the frenzy was over. Seth and Ralphie disappeared. The candidates campaigned, Hurricane Hilda left a trail of damage in Louisiana, and the court drama continued, but not a word appeared about Seth and Ralphie. The whole episode was over as far as the press was concerned, but the suffering was just beginning. For Susan Timmons. For Helen Mitchell. Even for Jack Grady, the man who walked Seth home."

"Are you sure you should be working this case? You are beginning to sound like kind of a softie."

I considered his comment before answering. "I think only a softie would do it."

Giant raindrops were slamming onto our heads. I still had no theory about what did happen as we ran inside, but I was convinced that I knew what didn't happen. Despite all my proclamations of objective reasoning, my gut told me Ralphie Barker did not kill Seth Timmons.

Chapter 11

I called Helen Mitchell at home to set up a meeting for Monday. She picked up on the second ring.

"I'd like to know more about Ralphie. Can you help me?"

She sounded more than willing. "Of course, you come over here and I'll make lunch."

"Let me take you out." I hoped Alex didn't overhear that invitation. He would not be pleased. Not only was I not taking a fee from Helen, I was spending money on her.

"Oh." She sounded delighted. "There is a wonderful little restaurant on my corner. I'll walk down and meet you there. Would noon be okay?"

When I pulled up at 11:45 I spotted Helen standing in front of her favorite place. Her smile was visible even from halfway down the block. Mrs. Mitchell had dressed for the occasion. Although the impression she projected was still closer to the worn-out woman who came to my office, I did see traces of the young woman Ellie Shields had described as a little overdone. She accessorized her red stretch pants and white t-shirt embroidered with red flowers, with red patent leather sandals. Her bag was large, with wide rows of red and white straw. After I parked and walked closer, I saw that bright red nails and lipstick completed the look.

Her smile disappeared when she saw me. "You look as if you are here to tell me my brother is as guilty as sin." She sounded more angry than worried.

I really had to work on my facial expressions. Strangers would call out to me on the street that things were not that bad. I didn't explain that to Mrs. Mitchell. I told her that I wanted to get together simply because I needed additional information. "I'd like to learn more about your brother."

Helen appeared surprised and cautiously optimistic as she led the way into the Sunshine Grille. The restaurant was, as she promised, small. Once we stepped inside I understood not only the restaurant's name but the grin on Helen's face. Everyone in the place turned to greet her. When the groups at several tables waved, she made an effort to straighten her back and lift her arm to wave back. If I weren't mistaken, Helen looked proud to have a guest in tow.

My forced smile masked my real thought. The diners might have been cheerful but the environment wasn't. Would I be able to eat in such a depressing place? Yes, I concluded, when I was blinded to the dinginess of the room by the sunshine of the radiant smile of the waitress who rushed to the door to greet us. Maybe the grill was named after her, or at least her attitude.

"Helen, we haven't seen you in here in a dog's age. How have you been?"

"Fine. Just fine, Mandy. Thanks for asking. This is my friend, Tracy Shaw. She's looking into Ralphie's case."

The waitress nodded knowingly as if Ralphie Barker had been arrested last week. "I'm happy for you, Helen. Maybe, after all these years, she can make it come out all right." She smiled at me. "Why don't you two take that table over by the window? It's the nicest one we have."

Not only the nicest table, the only. Every other seat had an occupant.

"What can I get for you?"

I ordered a salad that promised to include as much cheese as a pizza. Mrs. Mitchell ordered meatloaf and a baked potato with butter, melted cheese and sour cream which it turned out was her usual. And she had survived to close to eighty years. I changed my order to match hers.

As soon as the waitress stepped away, I took the lead. "I don't know if this will help at all, but you never know what might come to the surface when there is time to chat."

"What?" Mrs. Mitchell pointed to her ear. "Sometimes in crowded spaces I have trouble hearing. Speak up. We're among friends."

So, I spoke up. I had the feeling Mrs. Mitchell wasn't the only one hanging on my every word. "When I spoke to you the other day, I didn't ask you a lot of questions about Ralphie. I don't feel as if I know him. I thought that you could tell me about him. What he liked. How he spent his time."

Her face lit up. One thing about investigating the past: people are thrilled to talk about things that no one has asked about in decades. The truly shocking part is that sometimes what they want to talk about is how they committed a crime. I didn't expect a confession from Helen and I was right. She did, however, love talking about her brother.

"You said that Ralphie was slow?"

"Today he'd be diagnosed. Not then. My family thought he was an angel from the time my parents brought him home from the hospital. It was just the two of us. I was four years old when he was born and I loved him to pieces. He was beautiful and he was sweet. He never cried or complained. My father called him 'Gurgle' because that's what he did all the time. He smiled and made happy noises." Lost in memories, she stopped but only for a moment.

"I remember all happy times. The family didn't realize that Ralphie had a problem. We felt he had an easy-going disposition. My parents realized that he was late doing things, but eventually he caught on. He was just a little different, and as he grew up all the other kids knew it. The teachers too. They weren't mean to him. They didn't pay any attention to him at all. The system just pushed him along. He didn't learn much or participate in any school activities. He had no friends, so my mother got him a puppy. Skippy. Everywhere he went that dog went too. He'd come home with a frown on his face but Skippy, his pet, his best friend, would make him smile."

Speaking of frowns and smiles, our food arrived. Mrs. Mitchell smiled. I was responsible for the frown. I didn't remember that meatloaf was gray. The color must have looked right to Mrs. Mitchell. She dug right in. I picked at my potato while I waited for her to continue.

"I have to tell you about the miracles in Ralphie's life. There were two. At least two that I know about. There might have been more. Ralphie didn't like to brag much about himself. He was that kind of person. Was." She appeared to focus on cutting her meatloaf but I felt she was really focused on controlling her emotions.

I ate in silence. I loved the potato chock full of things allegedly bad for me but didn't have the courage to face the meatloaf although Mrs. Mitchell had several bites and still appeared to be in good health.

"The first miracle," she said as she took a bite.

I had to wait until she finished chewing to hear what happened.

"In fourth grade, Ralphie had a teacher, the only one who cared about him, who tried to work with him. She was a musician so she got the idea to have Ralphie sing spelling words so he would remember them. She sent a note home with him that very night. It said, 'I did not know that Ralphie sings like an angel. I am the director of the church choir at the First Baptist Church. Will you give him permission to come and sing with us?' Well, we were flabbergasted. I never heard Ralphie sing. My mother never heard Ralphie sing. The first time we heard him was when he had a solo at that church. Come that very first Christmas, he had a solo. His teacher was right; he sang like an angel. Even after his voice changed. That just made him sound like a bigger angel, a more important angel. We weren't Baptists but my mother and I went to church with him every Sunday just to hear him sing. He could be so inspirational. He loved to sing 'You'll Never Walk Alone.'"

Across the table, I smiled to encourage her to go on.

"He never had any friends at school, but those people from the choir, they treated him real nice."

"That must have made a huge difference in his life."

Helen beamed. "He seemed happy." Then the joy on her face vanished. "Until he went to high school."

Anyone who had ever attended high school could imagine how that might work out.

"The kids in his elementary school and even junior high mostly ignored him. He didn't have any friends, and he got teased sometimes but he didn't have any enemies."

I knew what was coming next: high school and bullies. My conclusion turned out to be true, but there had been a second miracle yet to come.

"So there was this fellow named Walter. Tall kid. Left back a ton of times. He didn't understand what was going on in class any more than Ralphie did. But he was the tallest, heaviest, strongest kid in the class and, aside from Ralphie the slowest, and by that I mean the dumbest." Her expression apologized for her choice of words. "He didn't like kids making fun of slow people, so he didn't like kids making fun of Ralphie. Walter became my little bother's protector. After that, no one messed with Ralphie. They were never friends like you think of your friends. They didn't go out together on weekends or anything like that but Walter looked out for Ralphie, brought him things like comic books, magazines and records. Probably not always the right sort of books, but I don't think my mother ever checked. She was so happy to see he had a friend. I have a picture of the two of them. When you come to visit,

I'll show you. At their high school graduation." She stared into space. Conjuring up the image of the two friends? "Ralphie was so proud to be a high school graduate." She smiled, remembering. "But even after that, Walter would come around with things for Ralphie. He did that right up until the day he went to jail. Walter that is. Walter went to jail. Got in a fight there. Got knifed and died. Ralphie was really sad."

I was feeling really sad too. Not just about Walter but about the whole story, about Ralphie's entire life. "What did Ralphie do when he got out of school?"

"He went to work at the Baptist Church. He swept all week and sang all day Sunday. That was his life. Until my mother died."

"He lived with your parents?"

"My mother. My father went away to the war when I was ten and Ralphie was six. He never came back."

"Oh, I'm sorry." This was one depressing story.

"Don't be. We got over it. Wasn't like he got killed or anything. He didn't even have to go into battle. He was one of the last people drafted. They sent him to basic training somewhere down south and he met a girl there and got married. My mother used to fantasize about turning him in for bigamy, but she didn't want us to be the children of a criminal."

She seemed completely unaffected by her father's desertion. Of course, it had happened seventy years before. She had time to get over the loss of a father, yet not of her brother. Ralphie, however, she saw as blameless, as a victim, as someone who never hurt anyone. She still grieved for him, not herself.

"So did Ralphie come to live with you after your mother died?"

She nodded. "Of course. What else could I do? I fixed up the basement and found him a job he could walk to. That's how he ended up at St. Margaret's. I tried driving him back to the Baptist church on Sundays but it was just too much. I felt horrible that Ralphie was so alone, but I didn't know what else to do. Ron, my husband, wasn't happy about the situation, but he hadn't been happy since the day he found out we couldn't have children. Blamed me. He found himself another wife and guess what?"

I could have guessed but I let her tell me.

"They never had kids. No matter. He was a bad penny. I'm well rid of him." The pain in her eyes told a different story. "Me, I made a bad mistake after Ralphie died and Ron left. I worked at a hospital and believed this hotshot doctor when he said he loved me. I gave the baby away. What else could I do? I lost my job over the whole mess. By the time I got another position, my baby was part of a family. There was no hope of getting my child back."

"Did you ever see him?"

"Her. And, no. In those days, we didn't do that. I don't know what happened to my daughter. I used to hope that she might come looking for me, but she never did. Why would she? She had a wonderful mother. At least that is what the nuns in the home told me."

It wouldn't have mattered if we were eating at LeCirque in New York. I didn't have any appetite. If my calculations were correct, Helen's mother died, her brother committed suicide, her husband left her, her lover jilted her and she gave her only child up for adoption in the space of a few years. How did this woman keep on going while getting buffeted with such bad luck? A hangnail slowed me down.

The restaurant appeared to be full of people with similar bad luck. I heard the term juvenile diabetes from the next table. I saw extreme disability at another table. No one in the place looked as if they'd had an easy life. I felt like a spoiled brat. I finished my meatloaf.

"Helen," I didn't know how to broach this question, "did you know anything about the police who interviewed you after Ralphie died? Did you recognize any of them?"

"No. And, I am sure I would remember because I could have used a friend that night. I never thought to write the names down. There were so many policemen, some of them in uniforms and some of them in suits. Some were nicer than the others, but I have no real recollection. I don't think I could have told you the day after it happened. I was in such a daze."

"Do you know if any of them investigated Seth's murder?"

"I know that I should have done what you are doing now, asked all these questions, but my husband kept questioning what good it would do. He said we had to move forward." She plastered a fake smile on her face. "Well, he certainly did."

I felt a little relieved when the waitress interrupted. "Ready for your pie?"

"Sure am," Helen said, her smile turning genuine.

"You got it." The waitress turned to me. "You going to join her?"

"What kind do you have?"

The waitress turned to Helen with a look that conveyed puzzlement and shock.

"You see, Tracy," she leaned across the table as if warning me about a house policy, if not a rule. "We always have apple pie a la mode, Ralphie's favorite dessert. To me, a meal isn't finished until I've had my pie a la mode. It's my way of remembering Ralphie."

"Well then." I smiled at our server. "I'll have apple pie a la mode."

Chapter 12

"The most amazing thing is that she eats all this pie and ice cream and is still skinny. She's around eighty and doesn't move all that well, so how much could she be working out?" Alex speculated.

"More than we are and the owners left us a veritable fitness center in the basement."

"Maybe tomorrow." Alex considered the possibility.

"Yeah, tomorrow. I'm kind of comfortable here."

I settled onto the couch with my glass of wine and told Alex about my lunch date with Helen Mitchell, except for the part where I picked up the check. "She made a real effort to look nice for our meeting. Lots of makeup, but tasteful. The customers and the staff in the restaurant seemed to know her and like her." I described the depressing details of Helen's favorite restaurant. Not only the physical environment but the other customers. "But you know what else I saw there, Alex?"

"Roaches?"

"Don't be glib. I am being serious. I saw love, incredible amounts of love. And not only because of the way the waitress and the other customers treated Helen. I saw a woman with a group of kids who appeared to be mentally and physically challenged and you know what they were doing?" I answered my own question. "They were laughing and so happy to be with each other. And I watched a couple. I think the woman must have had a stroke. Her husband had to guide her to a booth at the slowest pace imaginable, but he didn't seem to get impatient. He was so kind and so gentle. He had to encourage her and move the food to her mouth. And then

57

you know what happened?"

He shook his head. He probably had a wisecrack on the tip of his tongue but was smart enough to hold it there.

"The waitress helped him feed her. The waitress."

"I get your point. You and I are extremely lucky and just as petty to complain about our little problems."

He did get my point.

"So what did Helen say about the night her brother died?" He shifted gears.

"She didn't want to talk about it. She said we had discussed such happy times, she didn't want to recall the bad days."

Alex froze. "They were the good times?"

"In her eyes, I guess anything is compared to the night she found Ralphie hanging in her basement."

"There is no doubt about it." Alex voiced his conclusion. "We are world-class whiners and possibly the most shallow people on earth."

I waited for the punch line, but none came. For once, Alex was serious and apparently believed his assessment. I didn't accept that we were that bad but given the comparison between our lives and Helen's life, I couldn't argue.

"So what's next?" Alex asked.

Next from me was a sad expression accompanied by a long sigh.

He read the combination of distaste, discomfort and fear on my face. "The little boy's mother?"

I grimaced as I nodded. "If I am going to continue, and I feel obligated to continue, I will have to talk to Mrs. Timmons." Partially to let her inform me; partially to inform her of my actions.

The part I hate most about any investigation is talking to the victim's family, even if they come to me. It's a lot harder when I approach them. Yes, they like reminiscing about the good times, but then we always have to move

58

on to the reason we are talking at all. I couldn't postpone making the call much longer. I had to reach out to Susan Timmons.

I decided that before I contacted her I should read the detailed profile of Seth Timmons and his family I printed out at the library. It had started on page one and continued for four columns on page three. Running under the headline "Illinois and Penn Neighbors Agree" and then "Friends Recall Kind Boy," the article repeated how in the summer of 1964 Seth had moved with his mother from the Midwest after his father died so that the new widow could be closer to her family.

Unlike in the other articles, Ellie Shields included quotes from the Timmons's neighbors in their St. Louis suburb explaining what a nice boy Seth was, how close he had been to his father, how it pained them to see such a wonderful family destroyed. Mrs. Timmons claimed that Seth was such a thoughtful son that he wanted to move from the only home he remembered to Philadelphia so that she would be happier. The article quoted the grief-stricken mother. "When his father knew he was dying, he had time to say good-bye. He told Seth to take care of me. My little boy took that instruction very seriously."

Mrs. Timmons said that her son was quite excited to go to the party because after such a short time in Philadelphia he had not made any friends. I, and most everyone else who lived in the twenty-first century, knew that made him a perfect target for a pedophile. The question remained: was Ralphie Barker that pedophile?

Ellie and the other reporters covering the case found no shortage of Philadelphia classmates willing to comment on Seth and, consequently, get their names in the paper. I tried to shake off my cynicism as I read comment after comment about how nice Seth was, how cute Seth was, how smart Seth was. Admittedly, several students commented on how shy he was. No one claimed to be his friend, not even the boys who said they attended the party that night. This time Marcia Taylor, who hosted the gathering, spoke for her son. "Sonny is so upset. He wanted the get-together to be special for Seth because he was the new kid in town."

Mikey Sawyer was allowed to speak for himself. "He was a nice kid. I believed that he really had become a Phillies fan, so we were all sad that night." The reaction of a true sports fanatic. A truly insensitive sports fanatic. I reminded myself that, at the time that Mikey Sawyer chose those words to remember his slain classmate, his priorities were those of a twelve-year-old, not necessarily a sociopath.

Chapter 13

I didn't reach out to Susan Timmons immediately. I couldn't handle much more unhappiness and Helen's story had depressed me enough. On Tuesday I told myself I couldn't distract myself from preparation for the evening's class. On Wednesday I told myself I needed to be in an upbeat mood for office hours. Of course, on Thursday I told myself I had to focus on that night's class. By Friday I ran out of excuses. So, I made the call. I was surprised, and a little nervous, when Susan Timmons agreed to see me so readily.

"Are you with the police?" She asked without any indication of what the right answer would be.

I went with the truth. When I assured her I was an independent researcher, she said it would be fine if I stopped by. I'm not sure if it mattered what I said beyond "I'd like to ask you about Seth." I sensed that she wanted to talk about her son. I made an appointment for that afternoon.

The house where Seth Timmons had lived and where Susan Timmons still resided, was on a street of red-brick, semi-detached houses in Germantown but not close enough that I could walk. I circled the tree-lined block three times and made two attempts at parallel parking before an SUV vacated a space that I could pull into. After I climbed the steps onto the porch of the Timmons house, I was aware that I was standing on the spot where Jack Grady last saw the young victim. "This is where Seth disappeared," I whispered.

I always pause at significant sites in the hopes that I will feel something, sense some truth to resolve the mystery. I developed the approach after my friend, Mitch, disappeared. I would go to a spot we had visited or a place someone claimed to have seen him and wait for some message, some clue as to what had happened to him. I never felt a thing. Yet, I still employed the tactic, despite consistent results i.e., none.

The Timmons porch was no different. The collection of wooden slats, ravaged by cold winters and hot summers, revealed nothing but it did support Grady's story. The front door was out of sight of the street, five feet back from the front wall of the home. I understood Grady's mindset, what could possibly happen? Unless Grady was lying. My instinct said no. I'd seen his grief. But what if the guilt developed because he left Seth earlier, told him to run on home, he'd keep an eye on him? But what if he didn't watch? Maybe Grady couldn't admit, to himself or to his community, that he'd done something irresponsible, something that had fatal repercussions.

Disappointed at receiving no inspiration, I rang the bell. The door opened quickly, too quickly like in a movie when you know the actor has been waiting on the other side for a cue.

"Mrs. Timmons? I'm Tracy Shaw."

I'd seen newspaper photos of Susan Timmons but didn't recognize the woman from fifty years ago in the eighty-year-old woman in front of me. Photos didn't convey how small she was, short with tiny bones. Age might have contributed to her diminutive stature, but she was undoubtedly genetically petite. Her solemn look was in contrast to her bright yellow pants and daisy covered t-shirt that might have come from the preteen department.

"I called. About Seth. I was asked to look at his case." The passive voice was carefully chosen in the hopes she would not ask who had made the request.

"Why would you do that now?" Her tone was puzzled

not confrontational. "Seth's been gone for fifty years."

I could have equivocated and told her that her only son's death would be a class assignment. A way to give my students one story to research so I could evaluate how they used the era in their story. But why would she want her tragedy reduced to a class project? I told her about my visit from Helen Mitchell.

She indicated that I should follow her and led me into a pretty, lovingly decorated living room that was, as reporter Ellie Shields had recorded decades before, dominated by photos of a young boy. Celebrating his first birthday. Posing with proud parents. Sitting on Santa's lap. Modeling his little league uniform. Dodging ocean waves. Brandishing an American flag. Holding his Easter basket. Toting a school bag. Smiling, always smiling.

There were also pictures of a happy family, proud father, adoring mother, grinning baby. I focused on a shot of the Timmons at the Grand Canyon. Seth was still young but the family had progressed to using color film. Within a few years, the tan and healthy family in the brightly colored clothes would be gone. Only Susan Timmons would remain.

When I see photos like these in victim's homes, I feel real pain. So many of the pictures are the same. Sure, the settings are different, the faces are different, the eras are different but in one way they are all similar—showing happy families without the slightest fear that some horrible fate would befall them. That's how the Timmons looked. Feeling blessed. A loving couple, an adorable child, with a long happy future ahead of them. But now, fifty years later, Susan Timmons was the only witness to her family's existence.

Mrs. Timmons sat on a hard chair and pointed at the couch. I sat at the end closest to her. Just because the cushions were soft and plush did not mean I felt comfortable. As I said, I never did in the home of a surviving loved one. At least in this house, I didn't have to speak first.

"I didn't know that Ralphie's sister was still alive. The cops said Ralphie Barker killed my Seth. Have they changed their minds?" Mrs. Timmons simply sounded curious, not angry, not apprehensive.

"I haven't spoken to the police. When Ralphie's sister came to see me, she suggested another line of investigation. She insists her brother was innocent." I waited for an angry retort but got none.

Mrs. Timmons shook her head. "It must be hard to face that kind of truth about someone you know, someone you love. I didn't believe that Ralphie killed Seth either. Until he hung himself. The cops told me that was as good as a confession."

"So you accepted that theory?"

"I never heard any other. It *was* hard to believe." She stopped and took a short breath. When she spoke, her voice quavered. "All of it was impossible to believe."

"So you accepted what the police said."

"That was the only thing I knew to do."

"How well did you know Ralphie Barker?"

"Not well. We were neighbors but we were so new to the neighborhood I hadn't gotten to know anyone. It was summer but I only remember seeing him once on the street. After school started, I did see him on a few occasions when I went to meet Seth." Her gaze drifted to a school photo where two boys in the first row held a banner: St. Margaret's School. "I wanted to walk with Seth to and from school, you know, just until he made friends to walk with. He didn't want to hurt my feelings so he never told me that he hated the idea, but I understood. After all, Seth was in the seventh grade. So I would only go part way with him then I would hang back and try to stay out of sight. In the afternoon, I would wait across the street so any classmates who noticed me would think it was a coincidence that I ran into my son. That's how I saw Ralphie. He worked there, at the school. He was some sort of custodian, maybe a handyman. He seemed nice. I mean he was very quiet and kept to himself. I assumed he had problems. Not that he was bad but that he was slow."

"You knew Ralphie's sister and her husband?"

"They lived down the street. Next block. I didn't know Mrs. Mitchell. That was Ralphie's sister's married name. Oh, you know that. You met her. I only knew who she was because I saw her with Ralphie one time, and I saw Ralphie at school. I didn't know many people who lived on the other side of Rittenhouse Street. I heard Mrs. Mitchell and her husband were medical people who worked odd shifts. I imagine that's why I never saw them. I don't know if Ralphie ever went out alone. Like I said, he was a little slow in the head. The time I saw them together, his sister seemed very protective of him." Her intonation was sympathetic. "I appreciated that he was kind to Seth at school. He was having trouble making friends, being the new kid and all."

Mrs. Timmons chose one of the many pictures from the table beside her, one showing Seth's big toothless grin. She smiled back at her son as she spoke. "Seth was always one of the smallest boys in his class. I guess he got that from me." She looked at the array of photos. "Just before, you know, the end, he had a little growth spurt but I didn't take any pictures in the last few months after his father died. Not that there was a big change. He was still not as tall as most of the kids in his grade and being short is not easy for a boy. Some kids gave him grief, but Ralphie Barker defended Seth. I saw him set a couple of students straight one day when I went to pick Seth up."

****Susan Timmons****
September 1964

Things would get better. Susan had to believe that. Seth had only been in school a few weeks and he was still reeling from his father's death and their move. He would make friends. He always had. At school. In the neighborhood. But, it broke her heart that he was having trouble finding new friends. Back in Illinois, he had tons of kids to play with, to laugh with. Once they moved to Philadelphia, the little boy who had always had a grin on his face rarely smiled. His expression was solemn as she watched him walk across the school playground. Searching his face for some clue as to what was bothering him, she didn't notice the boys moving towards Seth until they jumped in front of him. She fought to hold herself back as they crowded him. His face grew even sadder as he realized the kids were trying to block his way. Sonny Taylor and Mikey Sawyer. After less than one month of school, Susan knew the names of these two and not for a good reason. After much prompting, Seth had finally admitted that the kids in his class were giving him a hard time. Sonny Taylor was the ringleader but she'd heard Mikey Sawyer's name as well.

Now the two boys kept blocking Seth as he tried to make his way to the gate. She wanted to step out from her hiding place and run across the street to slap the boys aside but she bit her lip and let Seth deal with their taunts. Bob had made her promise she would not let their son become a mama's boy and she'd sworn to let Seth stand on his own. Watching the action unfold in the schoolyard, she found keeping that vow more difficult than she ever could have imagined. She felt proud watching a determined and calm Seth try to maneuver by the two boys, but his tactics couldn't deter his bigger classmates.

"Hey, Bethie. Is that your name Bethie?"

Susan felt a pang of guilt. She had picked Seth's name because it was unusual. In all of his school years, he never encountered another Seth. Back in the St. Louis suburbs, where he had been a cool kid, having an unusual name had made him seem even cooler. Now that he was the new kid, the odd man out, his name was no longer an asset to work in his favor, but a weapon to be used against him.

"Beth. That's a girl's name, isn't it?" Sonny Taylor taunted him.

Seth didn't correct him. He simply swerved to avoid running into the boy.

"Bet there ain't no baseball players named Seth, eh Mikey." The Taylor boy teased.

Mikey Sawyer stuttered and Susan knew why. The kid was a Phillies fanatic. She might not know a lot about baseball but she knew a lot about Seths. Sonny forgot that Seth Morehead once played for the Phillies, but Mike Sawyer would never forget a fact like that. "No baseball players ever named Beth." Mikey threw the retort at Seth's back.

She watched and wondered how mothers could let their sons become so cruel. That Mikey was a nasty kid. Susan could see it on his face. She didn't even have to hear his words. "Why don't you go back to Illinois, you little twerp?"

Sonny was worse. In the few times she had seen him, she developed a fear of some invisible essence, a poison gas that he gave off. He was big for his age with a foul mouth that was far advanced for his years.

She breathed a sigh of relief as Seth made it past the bullies. Not that they stopped harassing him, but they didn't follow. She hoped they were losing interest. As Seth walked with a steady gait across the playground, she fought her urge to run to him.

But Sonny wasn't finished. He jumped in front of Seth one more time and bent down to stick his face into the smaller boy's. She heard the tone even when she couldn't make out every word. "They like runts in Illinois, don't they, Mikey?"

Mikey, who was not quite as tall but just as threatening as Sonny, took a spot on Seth's other side. Just close enough to be threatening.

It was all Susan could do not to charge into the playground, grab her son and hug him, but she knew he had to stand on his own two feet, that her help would only give his classmates ammunition to call her son a mama's boy.

Slowly Seth bobbed and weaved to make his way to the street. Mikey hovered over him, continuing the jeering. "Yeah, go back to Illinois and root for the Cubs, those losers."

Susan felt relieved that the kid didn't realize that their Illinois home was in a suburb of St. Louis, home to the Cardinals that were challenging his Phillies.

Susan could see that Seth was upset but was proud that he remained composed even when the two boys leaped in front of him once again.

Sonny blocked Seth's way to the gate. Mikey backed him up. "You gonna cry, baby?"

At that moment, a large hulking figure stepped between Seth and the two bullies. "Leave him alone." The man's register was deep but his speech was slow and halting. The short sentence suggested that although he appeared to be in his late twenties he was not functioning at that age.

Mikey and Sonny began to make noises like a barking dog. "Here, Ralphie, Ralphie, Ralphie." Sonny started and Mikey echoed.

The big man was undeterred. "Go. Get out of here." He took a menacing step towards Sonny and Mikey.

The two bullies kept laughing and barking, but they backed away. After calling out a few more taunts, they turned and ran, barking like the mean dogs they were.

The man turned and spoke to Seth in a comforting tone. Susan stepped forward to listen. With the bullies gone, there was no reason to hide. "They think that's funny because my name is Barker and they are barking like a dog."

"I know."

Once again Susan was overwhelmed with a feeling of pride at how sympathetic her son sounded.

Ralphie shook his head. "But I don't think it's funny." He placed a hand on Seth's shoulder, leaned down and spoke in a calm tone. She moved up to the schoolyard gate but still strained to hear his words. "You let me know if they are mean to you again."

Seth nodded and looked away, anxious to flee from the man and the scene. He spotted his mother at the gate. "My mom is here. I've got to go."

Seth ran, but because of embarrassment not fear. Susan saw no sign of the smile of joy Susan had grown used to before the events of the last few months. She held back the hug she wanted to enclose him in and simply patted his shoulder. The bullies might be lurking nearby, watching.

All the way home, Seth stared at the sidewalk and provided monosyllabic answers to her questions about his day at school. When they got home he ran to his room, but fifteen minutes later he was back at the kitchen table, eating cookies. Susan not only loved her son's resilience, she admired it.

*****

"You know how when there's something wrong with a person, you feel it. A warning bell goes off?" Mrs. Timmons asked.

I nodded my understanding.

"I didn't hear one with Ralphie." She grew pensive. "He touched Seth's shoulder like a coach would. Not creepy. He played the authority figure and helped Seth with those jerks."

I was puzzled. "If Sonny Taylor and Mikey Sawyer were picking on Seth, how did he end up at a party with them?"

"At Sonny's house?" Mrs. Timmons reinforced my puzzlement. "I know it seems odd, but Mrs. Taylor invited Seth over to watch a baseball game. Seth loved baseball. Here is his little league photo." She exchanged the photo in her hand for one of her son in his uniform. She passed it to me to admire. I smiled. The boy's enthusiastic grin was contagious.

"After what you witnessed in the schoolyard, didn't you worry about his going over there?"

Her tone asked me to understand. "I viewed the invitation as a sign that the boys were coming around, that Seth had passed some initiation rite and was now making friends. I guess I let myself hope that was the story." She pulled a tissue out of her pocket but didn't use it. "You know that the party was at the Taylor house. I had met Marcia Taylor. I ran into her once with John Lockwood, a friend of my late husband. They grew up together. He was in our wedding. He was going to be at the Taylors and I had no doubt that he would look out for Seth. And, it was such a big night. The Phillies were supposed to clinch the National League Pennant with that game. I remember Seth saying it was going to happen. They had already lost nine games; they couldn't lose a tenth." She took a deep breath to gain control of her quavering voice. When she spoke, her tone was again strong. "I wanted my son to feel part of things, so I was thrilled when Marcia Taylor asked Seth over. It was an accident that he even got to go that night. I ran into Mrs. Taylor, Marcia, that day at the grocery store. She was kind of a character. Dressed a little flashy. Actually, dressed a lot flashy. And, she was a chatterer. She told me all about how she wanted to do something for John's daughter, Linda, who had a crush on Seth."

I smiled at the photo in my hand. I could see the appeal Seth would have for a preteen girl. "Did you tell Seth about the crush?"

She smiled. "No. He would have been embarrassed. He might not have gone."

"What did you tell him?"

"Just that he'd been invited."

"Was he happy?"

"Happy? He was over the moon." Her face lit up at the recollection.

"Not scared?" After all, aside from Linda, he wasn't walking into a friendly crowd of classmates.

"He didn't act it and he wasn't a kid who hid his emotions." Her smile sweetened. "I didn't tell Mrs. Taylor but Seth had talked to me about Linda. My parents invited John Lockwood to a get-together they gave for me when I returned from St. Louis. He brought Linda along. You know what?" She pulled herself out of the chair walked slowly to a bookcase lined with photos. "You can see her in this photo, the last one I have of Seth."

I traded the photo of Seth for a picture of a young woman, a preteen boy and an older man. I assumed I was looking at Susan Timmons with her son and her father. "You can see Linda in the background."

Mrs. Timmons was exaggerating. I could barely make out the image of a young girl standing about five feet behind the posed group. Her side was to the camera and I could see long blond hair hanging halfway down her back. In dark shorts and sleeveless shirt, she could have been a hippie several years before hippies came on the scene. She had turned her head and stared into the lens as if responding to the click. Somehow she appeared both wise and serene. And, above all, cool. No wonder Seth was smitten.

"I saw the look on Seth's face when he heard that they

would be in the same grade. I think he was happy she was going to the Taylors. But he would have been excited even if Linda didn't show up. Seth hadn't been invited anywhere since we moved to Philadelphia."

"Is that why you let him stay out so late on a school night?"

Pain and doubt overwhelmed her smile. "The game didn't begin until 9 PM. On a school night. I know how that sounds. What kind of mother lets her son stay out so late when he has to get up in the morning? Normally, I wouldn't have but the pennant race was all the entire city talked about that week. He would have watched at home. I wouldn't have sent him to bed. That was the do or die night for the Phillies."

"Were other kids going?"

"I understood it would be a small group. Turned out it was just Marcia and John and three kids, Linda, Mikey and Sonny. I thought a get-together away from school would be great. He had a shirt but I ran out and bought Sethie a . . . the . . . the Phillies hat, the hat they found with the body." She took a deep breath. "I asked for it back but the police told me his baseball cap was evidence. I didn't see what it mattered since there would be no trial but they would not let it go." She shrugged to show how defeated she'd felt. "I guess it's better to have souvenirs of happier times." She looked at me expectantly, waiting for a question.

"According to the newspaper, you didn't report Seth missing until almost 4 AM."

"I dozed off." Tears welled in her eyes. "I can't believe that I could sleep while Seth . . ." She reached into the pocket of her slacks and pulled out another tissue although she hadn't used the first. "I tried to watch the game so I could talk to Seth about it, but I am not a baseball person. I changed the channel and then I fell asleep. It shouldn't have mattered. The phone was right beside me. Seth said he would call so I could go pick him up. I would have heard the phone. If it ever rang."

Was that yet another source of Grady's grief? His offer to walk Seth home was the reason the phone never rang. He must have realized that too.

"But I never heard a thing. No call. No scream. No scuffle on the porch. I just woke up. The test pattern was on the television. You're probably too young to know what that is, but when you saw one on the screen it meant the shows were over and it was the middle of the night. I went into the kitchen to look at the clock and felt so confused. I don't think it occurred to me that Seth hadn't come home until I went upstairs. I expected to find him sleeping in his own bed, but he wasn't there. Or in any bed. Like a fool, I kept moving his covers as if he would materialize. I even checked under the bed and in his closet, but he wasn't there."

She still sounded puzzled at the events of so long ago.

"I ran through the house, every room. I opened every closet. I went upstairs, downstairs calling Seth's name. I could not believe that he wasn't there."

After so many years, her expression said she still found it hard to believe.

"I went outside and checked the yard but there was no sign of him. I told myself that the boys must have decided to sleep over at the Taylors'. At least I tried to, but I couldn't convince myself that was true. Can you believe that I let my son go to the Taylors' house and I didn't know how to reach them?"

Her eyes begged for forgiveness that I understood she would never grant herself.

"I tried to remain calm but my hands were shaking too much to use the phone book. I tried but there were so many Taylors listed and I was getting more and more frantic. The operator couldn't understand me any better than I could understand her. So, I asked her to connect me with the police. I still remember how uneasy the cop at the other end of the phone sounded. He shouldn't have understood what I was saying but he did. Perfectly. I heard all this whispering and then he said he would send someone over. That was when I knew. His tone was so strange, full of pity. I didn't want to believe it but I couldn't deny that something was very wrong."

Her voice that had grown more and more agitated, reflecting her emotions from fifty years ago, grew calm.

"It seemed like hours that I just sat on the couch feeling numb and waiting for the news that I knew would be bad."

She sat for a moment lost in the past before she spoke again.

"Turns out that not long before I called the cops had gotten another call—from a guy who was out walking his dog, although what he was doing walking his dog at 3 AM I can't tell you. He had found something, someone, a boy. He went home and called the police. Luckily one of our neighbors, a policeman, the policeman who walked Seth from the Taylors', heard the call on his scanner. He got there and could identify Seth. I felt better knowing that Detective Grady was with him so that people weren't looking at my little boy as just some body to be handled." She sobbed while I watched. At last, she used the tissues already in her hand. With what appeared to be well-practiced moves, she used one to wipe her eyes and one to blow her nose. "You know what I hope?"

I shook my head.

"I hope that Lockwood girl kissed him. I'd like to believe that he experienced a kiss before he died." Her smile was sweet. I found myself matching her hopeful expression.

Chapter 14

Alex, unduly influenced by Grace Kelly's portrayal of Tracy Lord in *High Society*, has a belief that Tracys are, by edict, tall (I am five-foot-five), blonde (I have brown hair) and no older than twenty-nine (I am). Not only do I fail to meet his physical requirements for a Tracy, I do not even possess what he sees as a Tracy personality, always elegant and unfailingly unapproachable. I am the one on the street that out-of-town visitors ask for directions and out-of-luck lunatics target for insults.

"That is not worthy of your name," Alex said when he found me lying on the couch eating Frosted Flakes from the carton on my chest.

"I deserve some rest. I've been busy with school," I rationalized. "I'll be getting dressed later to meet Aunt Julia for lunch."

"Are you seeing Mr. Wrong tonight?" He sneered at the crumb he pulled from the ponytail that curled around my neck.

I'd encountered Mr. Wrong, aka Marcus Landon, at my eighth-grade reunion. Ever since I made the mistake of telling Alex I didn't remember Marcus from grade school, he had been convinced that Marcus is a spy, a criminal or worse. He refused to define worse.

"Get over it, Alex. Why on earth would an international spy choose to crash my elementary school reunion? What could possibly be gained?"

"Maybe he was escaping down the turnpike with foreign agents close on his heels."

"On the Pennsylvania Turnpike?"

"Every car chase can't take place on the streets of

75

Berlin or the hills above Monte Carlo." His tone added *silly*. "Anyway, he came to accept that he could not outrun them."

"Then?"

"He picked an exit at random and pulled into the first hotel he stumbled upon. He spotted the party going on, made himself a name tag, and hit on the prettiest girl in the room."

"And when Kimmy Pollack turned him down, he hit on me?"

"I will not dignify that comment with a response." Alex sneered.

"Don't think that *prettiest girl in the room* suggestion is going to win me over. I do not understand what you have against Marcus? You've never even met him." I shoved a handful of Frosted Flakes in my mouth.

"I'd be happy to meet him if he ever showed up."

Okay, Marcus hadn't helped his standing with Alex by canceling a few times. "Those were dates that he initiated. Why ask in the first place if he is planning on not showing? He intends to come. Things happen."

"Uh-huh." Factoring in his sarcastic tone, Alex really said, *You poor delusional idiot. You believe that, don't you?*

"We're on for tonight. He's driving up from DC."

"From Langley?"

Learning that Marcus lived in Northern Virginia had prompted Alex to imagine a James Bond life at the CIA for my would-be date.

"He works for Commerce. That's why he travels all the time."

"I didn't know the Department of Commerce had so many emergencies. What? Does someone need to place a rush order for an American flag? Oh, wait. Aren't most of them manufactured in China?"

"He didn't always cancel because of work

emergencies." Only on two occasions. I didn't mention those. "There was the ice storm in February, the freak blizzard in March and the flooding in April."

"Conveniently arranged, I would guess, by the folks at Langley."

"The CIA does not control the weather." I let a short, but loud, sigh express my exasperation.

"Or so they want you to believe."

I shook off his suspicions. "Today it doesn't make a difference. Given the blue sky this morning, I think we'll be able to get together."

"We'll see." Alex picked up a decorating magazine and flipped through the pages. He wasn't reading. He wasn't even looking at the pictures. He was expressing doubt with the snap of each page. "I am simply playing my role here. Every single woman needs a gay gal pal to guide her."

I could have argued on Marcus's behalf. I couldn't dispute that our choice of dates had proven unlucky, but Marcus could not control the weather. Maybe he couldn't control his work schedule either. Why would Marcus continue to follow up with me if he didn't want to see me?

My phone vibrated. I smiled expecting a text from Marcus confirming our date. I was half-right. The text was from Marcus. Short and apologetic. I kept the grin plastered on my face as I pondered my options. I didn't condone lying but I did not want to tell Alex that Marcus was canceling yet again.

So I wouldn't have to deal with Alex's reaction, I considered deceiving him, getting dressed up and taking myself to dinner. Then he asked: "Message from lover boy?"

I nodded.

"Why can't he make it tonight?"

I wasn't born to be a liar. The truth, at least as I knew it, flew from my mouth. "Emergency business trip. South

America." I set the phone down without replying to the text. "That's okay. I'll work on my investigation."

Alex dropped the magazine. "Let me provide assistance." I heard no tinge of recrimination in his voice. Pity yes, but no hint of *I told you so*. He jumped up and plugged his phone into the speakers. Soon the sounds of the Beatles filled the room. "'Yea. Yea. Yea.'" He sang along. "1964, Right?"

I nodded.

"Atmosphere for you to tell me all about your investigation."

In that moment, I confirmed why Alex was welcome in my spare room. No one had a bigger right to say *I told you so* and he would, eventually, but I loved him for not saying it right at that moment when it would have hurt most.

"What's new? I'm all ears. I'm very interested." He really wasn't. He was trying to make me feel better.

I didn't say *thank you* but I felt it. "Mrs. Timmons told me what she knew about the current whereabouts of everyone who attended the party. The newspaper said that Marcia Taylor had been the hostess and her son had invited two friends from school: Mikey Sawyer and Seth Timmons. I hadn't seen a word in the newspaper about this guy that Susan Timmons mentioned. John Lockwood. He brought his daughter, Linda. He's retired and splits his time between Florida and the New Jersey shore. The former detective, Grady, told me that he had attended the party for a few minutes when he picked up his stepson Mikey. I think that is the entire guest list."

"What next?"

"I want to talk to all of them."

"Do you know if they are all alive?"

"Not yet. Mrs. Timmons's information is old so it's possible not all of them are still with us. However, I should start with my prime suspect and the one person I am certain is still alive and living in Philadelphia. Mikey Sawyer."

Alex whistled. "How are you going to get to him?"

"Not a clue."

"Let me think about it too," Alex said before, still humming Beatles classics, he disappeared out the door and into his non-stop social life.

Chapter 15

I too had a social life left on my calendar for that Saturday, although mine would stop after my lunch with Aunt Julia. She tried to think of a 1964 restaurant where we could meet but decided on Ruby's which was, she claimed, more 1957. "But the 1950s hadn't completely disappeared by 1964. If we were talking 1967, I'd have to rethink. But in 1964, I was still eating hamburgers and drinking milkshakes. As a matter of fact, I am still eating hamburgers and drinking milkshakes. Let's go to Ruby's but come to my apartment first. I have something to show you."

The pile of photo albums I spotted when I entered Aunt Julia's book-lined, memento-stuffed apartment confirmed my suspicion that *something* involved 1964.

"People were different in 1964. Most people. That was the year the fifties ended for me although I didn't understand that at the time." She laid a book on the table beside me. "I dug out some pictures. Here I am in 1963 and 1964."

I studied Aunt Julia in her neat page boy. She stood in a line of girls, all with similarly neat hair and all in shirtwaist dresses.

"Notice our little heels. I had a pair to match every outfit. What you can't see are the stockings or the garter belt. I can't believe that I ever took that much time getting dressed." She shook her head, screwed her features into a look that shouted *What a waste of time!* "Although I loved that particular shirtwaist. I wore it every time it came out of the wash, which was something back then because I had to iron it. Or at least my mother did. I don't remember that part. I just remember the good times I had in that dress. I only gave it up when the print started fading." She took a moment to mourn her long-gone item of clothing. "Anyway, here is the same group five years later."

"Not a shirtwaist in sight," I said.

"Not a dress in sight."

The women, no longer the sweet innocent girls of the earlier photo, had grown their neat hair into long unmanaged manes. Instead of smiling in a rigid line, the college students were strewn all over the grass in a selection of cut-off jeans and bell-bottoms. The heels and stockings were gone. Actually, the shoes were gone.

"You were a hippie?"

"I had different groups of friends. Some were, some weren't, some pretended to be. Most of us looked a bit like hippies in those years. I did—although my handbag usually matched my shoes in some way. Some habits die hard."

"Do you have a picture of my mother?"

She went back for another album and opened to a shot of her older sister in a neat sheath.

"The sixties didn't really resonate with my mother, eh?"

"She was older, not to mention more mature, well-behaved and responsible."

I stared at her. Those were not the words I would have used to describe my mother in her current stage of life.

"That's why she needed a mid-life crisis. Why maybe she deserves one." Aunt Julia grew defensive although I'd said nothing. I just couldn't quite accept my parents as separate entities, with separate lives and separate life crises.

Aunt Julia moved on. "I think 1964 is an interesting year to work with. Maybe the world would have changed for me in that year no matter what because of my age, but there were far stronger forces at work. A lot of bad stuff lay ahead, but we had that little bit of breathing room before we realized that the Kennedy assassination would not be our generation's only shared trauma."

"Before you had to clarify which Kennedy assassination." I paged through her photos. So much fun. So many smiles. This would have been Seth's world if he had lived. Who knows how that world would have been for Helen Mitchell and Susan Timmons if their lives hadn't changed, been changed by Seth's killer.

"You're thinking about what Seth and Ralphie missed, aren't you?"

I nodded. "If Seth and Ralphie came back a couple of years later, they wouldn't have known their world, would they?"

Aunt Julia agreed. "Although I suspect Ralphie would have found it a kinder place than the one he left." She let her gaze linger on her photos. "Painful in a lot of ways, but more open and understanding." She paused. "At least in some quarters." She took the album from my hands. "I know that Alex bemoans the fact that you don't get paid, but I think you do. Just not in money. You can't help the dead but you do help the living. Not many people get a chance to make a real difference." She piled the old albums on top of a tall stack of similar books. "Now let's eat."

Chapter 16

"I bet that Seth's parents took him to places like this," I said as we settled on the red leather bench in our booth.

"If he was anything like the rest of us, I bet he loved hamburgers and hot dogs and milkshakes. You might think he wasn't old enough to be part of his time, but he was. Given what you told me about Ralphie Barker's developmental issues, Seth might have been more aware of the world he lived in than his accused killer was."

We ate a meal that Seth might have eaten and talked about the world where he grew up. At least Aunt Julia did.

"Harry already told me about the 1964 Phillies, so you can skip that," I explained.

"Oh my God. If President Kennedy hadn't been shot the year before, the 1964 Phillies would have been the biggest disappointment of my young life." She shook her head. "After the game you talked about, the entire city was so sad. People were in shock. A friend of mine still talks about how everyone walked around like zombies. The Phillies only had to win one game out of ten to win the National League Pennant. One measly game out of ten and they didn't do it. But to torture their fans, after losing ten in a row, they won the next two—just enough to keep hope alive that by some odd combination of wins and losses across the League they could still get into the World Series. I remember we had to wait until Sunday before we were forced to give up."

Everyone of a certain age seemed to recall the trauma of the Phillies's swoon.

"But you don't want to hear all that one more time. So, tell me more about the players in this investigation."

I told her about Helen Mitchell who had brought me the case because she believed in her brother's innocence. I described how the murder had ruined Helen's marriage, how she still lived in Germantown, how sad she remained even fifty years later. My eyes misted over when I told her about Susan Timmons and her small family that had disappeared in the course of a single year.

"And the suspects?"

"I don't have any. Mrs. Mitchell suspects one of the kids but I don't. Not really. I mean they were just kids."

Aunt Julia's face said you never know. "Today we read about the horrible things that children are capable of. Just because I didn't hear about that type of behavior in my peer group doesn't mean it wasn't happening. I didn't know about it, but people kept so many secrets back then. Bad behavior was covered up."

"So people weren't as naïve as they appeared?"

"Well, some people were. I certainly was."

"When I read all those newspaper articles, the entire population of 1964 seemed that way, so vulnerable and optimistic as if the Kennedy assassination the year before had been an aberration, the kind of tragedy that happens only once in a lifetime. If only they'd known what was coming."

Aunt Julia and I both knew how it all turned out. Despite a landslide in 1964, Johnson would leave the presidency after one term, assassinations would become all too familiar and Vietnam would escalate into a conflict that would claim the lives of boys like those in the class picture of St. Margaret's seventh grade.

"The bottom line? I can say I don't think a kid like Mikey Sawyer was capable of murder, but I can't say he wasn't. I'm sorry."

I was also sorry although I wasn't as interested in indicting Mikey Sawyer as I was in exonerating Ralphie Barker. "I just want someone to convince me that Ralphie couldn't have done it." I ordered apple pie a la mode in his honor.

"As a survivor of that era, I wish I could help. But there are some positive things about being from that era. For example, if I were a 21st-century type, I'd ask how you could have dessert after a milkshake. But, this is 1964. So, I'll suggest you might want a root beer float with that pie. You'll need your strength."

"For?" I asked.

"You haven't been to the cemetery yet." Aunt Julia held the same conviction about gravesites as I did about crime scenes. We each believed we would find not only inspiration but some sort of supernatural enlightenment. We never did.

"Seth was never there," I countered with my usual argument.

"Actually, in this case, Seth was at his gravesite. Not even a year earlier. To bury his father." She pulled out a sheet of paper. "I took the liberty of locating both Seth's and Ralphie's graves. They are not in the same cemetery so we might not be able to get to both. Let's go to Seth's first."

I agreed, assuming it would be easier to find Seth's. Given the circumstances in 1964, I wondered if Helen even dared to put a headstone on her brother's burial place.

Chapter 17

Seth's gravesite was hard to find. Even the correct *section* of the cemetery was hard to find. I made a quick left just as Aunt Julia shouted, "Turn right."

I backed to the intersection of three small winding roads and followed her direction. "We've been here before. I recognize Thomas Smith's grave." I pointed to a tall monument.

"Common name. There could be two of them. I would bet there are two of them. Keep going."

"Three of them?" I asked when we circled back to the same spot again. I pulled the car onto the side of the road. "Let's walk. It's a gorgeous day."

"It's a shame the residents have to miss it."

Aunt Julia was right. A light wind and a bright sun made the day comfortably warm. The Timmons's gravesite was in an older part of the cemetery where tall trees with new leaves offered occasional shade. More importantly the breeze rustling the leaves provided a comforting soundtrack for our visit.

"It's gorgeous here." Aunt Julia stopped to read an inscription. "Looks as if the father died in World War I and the son in World War II. The son was born the same year the father died. I wonder if Francis Junior ever met his dad."

I had similar thoughts as I passed headstones, so I tried to avoid looking and imagining unhappy histories. Seth's short life was sad enough. "I think we're in the right area. I bet it's the one with the little angel."

"Good guess." Aunt Julia beat me to the spot.

I read the inscription that went back three generations.

Malcolm and his wife Margaret, their son Robert and his son Seth. Born 1951. Died 1964, before he reached his thirteenth birthday. Only months after the death of his father.

"It looks to me as if Seth's mother added the angel to the top of the headstone. It's much newer than the base stone." Aunt Julia crouched to study the monument.

"Hanging around is not going to tell us anything about what happened to Seth." I sounded so practical.

Aunt Julia did not. "I cannot imagine the pain she felt. Seth's mother. Coming here twice in six months to leave the people she loved the most. Her entire family. Bringing her husband here never imagining in her wildest dreams that she'd be back within a year to bury her young son."

We stood in silence for a moment, until Aunt Julia spoke. "Doesn't look as if anyone's been here lately."

The cemetery maintained the grave, but the Timmons's gravesite was free of the ornaments decorating nearby headstones. Flags. Toys. Flowers, real and plastic. "It's been over fifty years. Seth would be in his sixties now." I stood at the grave mourning all that Seth's killer had stolen not only from his victim but from Susan Timmons.

Aunt Julia verbalized my thoughts. "Susan Timmons might have been a grandmother. Even a great-grandmother."

I envisioned Susan sitting alone in her apartment with fifty-year-old photos instead of an ever-expanding collection of pictures showing generations of loving family. I was right that I never found any answers at gravesites, but Aunt Julia was right too. I did find something. I found motivation.

Chapter 18

When Alex returned from his afternoon outing, he located me in the garden rereading the newspaper articles about Seth Timmons's death. The weather kept me from falling into despair. "Beautiful day." I greeted him.

"And promises to be a beautiful night." He leaned on the back of the chair next to mine. "That is why we are going to the Phillies game."

"I didn't know that you liked baseball."

"Don't be ridiculous. I hate the game and the uniforms are not tight enough for my taste, but if you are going to talk to Mikey Sawyer you have to get to know his world. We are spending tonight in Sawyerland."

"But it's Saturday night."

"And it will still be Saturday night when the game is over and I drop you like a hot potato. Now I have to go find an outfit that will take me from the game to the games if you get my drift."

I got it.

Alex selected one of his uniforms for the outing: a combo of shiny loafers, pressed jeans and shaggy-collared shirt that said *he was really above it all and had been since prep school days* when he'd bought these clothes. Somehow the look worked for him and had, he assured me, since high school.

It would have been too easy if Mikey Sawyer had shown up in the seats next to ours at the Phillies game. It also would have been very unlikely since our seats were out beyond first base. I bet Mikey Sawyer didn't even know that our section existed. If he was somewhere in a crowd of almost thirty thousand stalwart fans that showed up for the game, Alex and I didn't spot him although Alex kept an eye out for fights.

"I appreciate your coming here, and I don't mean to be a defeatist, but I feel certain that security squelches any altercations in the boxes before they become physical." And, that is where I was pretty sure Mikey Sawyer was. "Do you actually believe that Mikey Sawyer would sit out in the stands with the rest of us? The last time he ventured into general admission, he ended up in court."

Always the optimist, Alex proposed a plan. "Well then, let's take a walk and look."

I figured the effort would be futile and I was right. I could have called our stroll around the ballpark a total loss but the Schmitter, a cheese, steak and salami concoction I'd grown to love at McNally's in Chestnut Hill, was great. One sandwich—well one sandwich and a wide array of snacks—made me forget about my missed date with Marcus.

Despite Alex's best efforts at the ballpark, I had to resort to a different method to get a meeting with Mikey Sawyer. Even I was shocked that I came up with one that worked. I was even more shocked that the strategy that worked was honesty.

The next Wednesday morning, while I waited in the expensively furnished reception area of the center city office with a panoramic view of Philadelphia's skyline, I couldn't believe that I was actually there. It had taken me Monday and most of Tuesday to convince Mikey Sawyer's assistant to present my request to her boss. Once she did, at 2 PM on Tuesday, I was given an early appointment for Wednesday morning.

I arrived half an hour early and spent my time studying the sports mementos that covered what was a very large and well-appointed reception space. I was studying a poster of the 1964 Phillies—better known to me as Exhibit A, proof that Mikey Sawyer cared deeply about the lost championship—when I heard the tiniest click. I turned and saw that Sawyer's door was open and the sports agent was striding across the plush carpet wearing a broad smile. He followed my gaze to the Phillies photo. "I've been told an agent shouldn't keep a picture of a bunch of losers in his office, but I loved those guys. They broke my heart but I loved them. He offered a warm handshake and a booming greeting. "Mikey Sawyer. Pleased to meet you."

I wasn't impressed. Number one, I detected not one ounce of sincerity in the greeting. Number two, Mikey Sawyer was too old to call himself Mikey. He didn't even look deceptively young for a man over sixty. That is not to say that he wasn't handsome. He was. Very, but not in an elegant way. He wore the right clothes, cut his hair in the right style and, yet, I had an inkling that at any moment he might spit out dese, dems and dose. Even when he didn't, he gave the impression of making an effort to avoid saying something that didn't match the opulent office space.

Mikey led me to his office where I took a seat on a small leather chair and tried not to stare as I determined if my host had plastic surgery. In his line of work, I bet it paid to look young, but I didn't think that was exactly what the skin-tightening around his eyes had accomplished—maybe because his deep tan accentuated the creases that did remain.

"How can I help you?" Mikey had settled into a trendy black chair at a shiny black marble top desk loaded with the latest electronics, mostly in black. He flashed a smile that he needed to employ more carefully. If the bright sunlight streaming through his floor-to-ceiling office windows hit his face, the glare on his overly whitened teeth might have blinded me. Although his tone suggested that I could not be more welcome, the seating suggested that I might not want to linger. I gave up on trying to make myself comfortable and answered his question. Or, tried to. I managed to tell him that I was a teacher before he interrupted me.

"I assume you are a sports fan."

I had no idea why he would make that assumption, but I didn't disabuse him of the notion that we had something to bond over.

"I was at the Nats game on Saturday night." I hoped he didn't want to discuss the game in detail, or even who won. When Alex and I failed in our search for Mikey, we focused on the food stands, ate too much and went home early.

"What about that play . . ." He went on to describe an elaborate series of actions that made not only headlines but history yet had somehow eluded my attention. "Not good for the Phils but amazing."

"Amazing," I repeated. Just to be sure he didn't ask for elaboration, I changed the subject

"This is an impressive collection." I nodded at the photography that covered the walls. Baseball. Football. Basketball. Hockey. Pictures of men playing men's sports. I tried to look enthralled with all the sports memorabilia around the office and then focused on a baseball on his desk.

Mikey handed the ball to me. "Johnny Callison hit that to me in 1964. Check out the signature." His enthusiasm made it easy to see the twelve-year-old boy in the man.

I didn't know current Phillies, let alone past teams, but I knew to express not simple admiration but reverence for this artifact.

"You must have been thrilled."

"Thrilled doesn't even begin to explain it, but I'm willing to bet you didn't come here to look at my baseball." He placed the relic carefully on its brass holder and studied it proudly before decorating his face with sadness. "I understand that you were interested in Seth

Timmons. Poor kid. He and the perv who killed him have been dead for over forty years. Man, fifty now."

"You sound pretty sure that perv killed him."

He stared at me with eyes devoid of emotion. "That's what the cops said. I had no reason to doubt them."

I tried to keep my expression blank, my mouth shut and let Mikey talk.

He did. Smugness replaced innocence. "My stepfather was on the job, so I got the inside dope. Anyway, the guy killed himself. That was tantamount to a confession. Why are you asking about this now?"

"I noticed the story about the altercation you were involved in the other night."

His laugh was dismissive. "'A long history of taking sports too seriously.' That's what I said in my apology."

"Exactly. That's why I wanted to talk to you about Seth Timmons."

His eyes narrowed as he stared at me. Then they filled with amusement. "You think I killed Seth Timmons because the Phillies lost the pennant in 1964? It wasn't exactly his fault, you know." His sarcastic grin faded and his tone turned sincere. "You do know everything that happened to him, don't you?"

I nodded.

"It would take a real pervert to do something like that to a little kid. If I thought you believed that I was capable of something like that, I'd throw you out of my office. Via the window."

"I am certainly not making any such accusation." I shrugged off his concern. "I am looking for background, for a twelve-year-old's perspective. You were a kid. Would you even have known about things like that?"

"When it came to things sexual, we were babes. We would talk about stuff but we didn't even know what it meant. And what we did happen to understand, we never actually did." He smiled.

"And the things that were done to Seth?"

The smile disappeared. "My father explained it to me but I don't think I really understood for another ten years."

"It was a different time." I tried to smooth the way for my next question. "Did kids in your day have access to guns?"

"Cap pistols. I am not kidding. That was it. Today there are guns everywhere. In my era, only the cops had guns and they didn't leave them lying around or even let anyone know where they were hidden, at least in our house. I guess hunters had guns too, but we city kids couldn't get our hands on them. Not that we tried to."

"I was wondering what happened at that party. If anything took place that could, in any way, have predicted what would happen to Seth? You were one of the last to see him."

"Hardly a party. Just a few people watching a baseball game."

"Wasn't it unusual for Seth to be included? I heard that as the new kid in town, he was kind of an outcast."

"Hardly an outcast. Boys that age always give new kids a hard time. Especially because his name was Seth. If he had been cool, maybe a bigger kid, we all would have wanted to be called Seth. But he wasn't. So the guys picked on him for his name. Not me. Even if I didn't like a Phillie called Seth Morehead and was glad when the Phils traded him, I realized that Seth wasn't always a loser's name."

"What about kids like Sonny Taylor?"

"I don't understand why you want to know." He tried to keep his tone polite but I heard antagonism in his words.

"I told you. I am a professor." I inflated my rank–for clarity's sake I assured myself. "I am looking at Philadelphia crimes."

He leaned back in his chair and let a knowing

expression cover his face. "You don't think I checked up on you? You are a teacher but you have a sideline. Don't try to scam me, Ms. Shaw. Someone asked you to look at this specific crime. Look at me all you want. I have nothing to hide. If you like, I'll tell you about the 'party.'" He used air quotes to mock me, but his tone grew serious. "It wasn't much of a party. My eyes were glued to the television set but I know that Sonny Taylor acted like the jerk he was pretty much the whole time."

****Mikey Sawyer****
September 30, 1964

Most of the time Mikey was happy to hang out with Sonny. Better to be the bully's friend than his target. Usually, they had Taylors' rec room to themselves, but not tonight. With a crowd to perform for, Sonny was getting on his nerves, showing off for everyone else in the room. Mikey wanted to watch the game but Sonny couldn't settle down. A major disaster was unfolding on the screen and Sonny had to tease Seth, flirt with Linda and do anything he could think of to take his mother's attention away from Mr. Lockwood.

Mikey couldn't believe that Sonny was so naïve about the ways of adults. Naïve. That was the word his mother called his step-dad. She was amazed that a cop could be so gullible. That was her other favorite word. He didn't catch on sometimes, just like Sonny. Mikey knew what was going on between Mrs. Taylor and Mr. Lockwood. He also understood that Mrs. Taylor would not let anyone, even her son, get in the way of what she wanted from the man. Her clothes told the story but Sonny didn't realize how trashy his mother looked. That was one of the ways Mikey's mother described her. "That trashy-looking woman who wears all the leopard spots and zebra stripes." That and "desperate for a man." Mikey figured wearing animal prints gave some sort of signal to men. He certainly understood the message Sonny's mother was sending to Mr. Lockwood.

Didn't Sonny notice that up on the couch his mother moved closer and closer to Mr. Lockwood until she was sitting up against him? How could Sonny miss that his mother slid her hand down the guy's leg? Even if he hadn't understood what that meant, Mr. Lockwood's reaction, moving her hand away and nodding at the kids, told Mikey what was going on. But not Sonny. Poor dumb Sonny.

Sonny was pretty naïve about the ways of kids too. He kept saying really stupid things to impress Linda, but she wasn't impressed. Even a dumb girl would not have been impressed and Linda was smarter than most of the girls in their class. The more Sonny tried to get close to her, the farther away she moved until she got off the floor and settled in a recliner. When Sonny sat on the floor beside her, she waited a couple of minutes before getting out of the chair and settling back on the floor on the opposite side of the room, next to Seth.

Mikey couldn't help noticing but he had more important things to worry about than Sonny Taylor's feelings for Linda Lockwood. All through the baseball season, he had been excited and now here it was, the most important game of the year. The Phillies's last chance to clinch the pennant. Each play took on an exaggerated importance. "Yes. This is it. We are going to turn it around now," he said to no one in particular. No one bothered to agree.

He didn't expect any response from Linda. She wasn't interested in the game. She was interested in Seth. He tried to ignore their conversation but now they were sitting right next to him.

"You lived in Illinois. In Chicago?" Linda asked as if Chicago was the most interesting place in the world.

"No. Downstate."

"Doesn't that mean near St. Louis?"

Seth nodded at the screen. "Yeah. We lived on the other side of the river in Illinois."

"But close." Linda persisted.

"My father worked in St. Louis but our house was in Illinois."

Mikey felt a new appreciation for how smart Linda was. She might have uncovered a secret. Was this new kid secretly rooting for the wrong team, for the Cardinals, the team with the power to steal the pennant from the Phillies?

"My dad used to take me to see the Cardinals play. But now I'm a Phillies fan."

Mikey didn't understand how you could change your allegiance like your underwear but he didn't have time to get involved in some stupid argument when the most important game of his life was playing out in front of him. But, unfortunately, Sonny had heard. "You are a Cardinals fan?" Sonny grasped a baseball bat and tapped it on the rug in front of him.

"No." Seth's one-word answer managed to convey that he understood he'd made a mistake professing any affection for the Cardinals.

"But you went to games?" Sonny asked.

Mikey might not have been ready for a fight but he enjoyed hearing the fear in Seth's voice as he tried to explain away his attendance at Cardinals games. That was what a Saint Louis fan deserved.

"My dad rooted for Saint Louis when we lived there but only if it didn't hurt the Phillies."

Stupid kid. Any game they won hurt the Phillies.

"I root for the Phillies. My parents are from Philadelphia." Seth kept explaining.

Mikey tried to ignore what was going on around him and focus on the game. He yelled at the television screen.

"Oh no. No. This can't happen," he cried even though this happened time and time again. *Richie Allen made his fortieth error of the season. Jim Bunning, pitcher of a perfect game, was sent to the showers. And, Kurt Simmons, once a Phillie and now a Cardinal, was the one who was going for a perfect game. So much was happening in St. Louis but the people in the Taylors' basement seemed oblivious.*

Beside him, Seth was still trying to win Sonny's favor. "We always went when the Phillies were in town." Nice try, but it didn't satisfy Sonny.

"Well, you better not root for them tonight."

"I am rooting for the Phillies. I told you. I read that even if they lose this game they can still tie for the pennant."

Sonny was interested in what Seth had to say only so he could ridicule it. "Tie. Who wants to tie? This pennant is ours. We earned it all season."

All Mikey wanted to do was watch the game. He was sick of all the stupid fighting going on around him. "They're not going to lose this game. Do you hear me? They are not going to lose this game."

But Sonny didn't care. He was on his feet, waving his baseball bat. That worried Mikey. He knew how Sonny could get when he was riled up. And Mikey knew that Sonny was getting riled up because of Seth. "Why don't you go home, you dirty little Cardinal-loving shrimp?"

Thank God, Mrs. Taylor stepped in. If she hadn't, the whole place could have gone nuts and Mikey did not want to miss the game. She didn't tell Sonny to stop. Not that it mattered. He never saw Sonny take orders from anyone, even his mother. She tried to sweet-talk him. "Sonny, Seth doesn't root for the Cardinals anymore. Do you sweetie?"

Mikey glanced at Seth who was shaking his head with exaggerated motions. At least, he knew enough to be nervous, even if Mrs. Taylor did not see just how mean

Sonny could get.

"See, Sonny Honey, you and Seth are rooting for the same team. Now, put that bat away. You kids watch the TV."

Sonny tightened his grip on the bat before he backed off and returned it to a box in the corner. Before he turned his attention to the screen, however, he gave Seth a look that Mikey had learned to fear. It appeared to him that Seth had learned to fear it too. The new kid probably didn't even realize that he pulled back from the bully.

When Linda spoke to him, Seth turned away from Sonny. Mikey knew that was Linda's plan. She was like him. She understood Sonny. She spoke to Seth in a soft voice. "My father said you moved back here after your father died." She acted all girly and sweet with Seth. Mikey had always liked Linda but he had never seen her act that way before.

"My mother works in my grandfather's company now. That's why we came back."

"My mother died when I was born." Linda's voice grew even softer.

Mikey pulled his gaze away from the television and looked with annoyance at Linda and Seth. How could they be talking at a time like this? He ignored them and turned back to the TV. He saw that Sonny had too. He screamed at the Phillies, "That's it. That's better." He seemed happy again.

Mikey glanced at Seth. The kid was smiling too but not because of the game. Linda was the root of his happiness.

*****

"Any sense of hope was fleeting. That game was bad news but the real sadness didn't really hit me until that Sunday. Up until then, there was a possibility we could get into the series, but that day the Cardinals clinched the pennant and we knew that there was no way."

The real sadness? That was what made him sad? Even now as a grown man?

"I shouldn't have gone to the Taylors' that night." Mikey appeared more frustrated than sad. "People talking and moving around. They made it hard to watch the game."

That was it. That was his main regret about that night?

"It wasn't easy back then. Black and white games on small screens. Kids today don't know how easy they have it."

Did he remember I came here to talk about a boy whose life ended forever not a team whose pennant hopes ended for another year? I decided to remind him of the reason for my visit. "Sonny didn't like Seth." I made more of a statement than a question.

"Sonny didn't like anyone. He was a bully. He and I only got along because of baseball. He didn't know as much as I did about sports, but he was fairly knowledgeable. If the others hadn't been there that night we might have gotten to talk about the game."

"What did *you* think of Seth?"

Sawyer shrugged. "I suspected he was a closet Cardinals fan. But that didn't make me the only one who didn't take to him. Nobody likes the new kid, except the girls. I don't think that made him any more popular with Sonny."

"Sonny liked Linda?"

"Maybe." He leaned back and stared into space as if he could see the Taylors' basement all those years before. "He liked to tease her. I guess that was his idea of flirting. But, it was never gonna happen. Sonny's mom wanted to marry Linda's dad. I was a kid and even I could see that. She didn't want Sonny falling for his future stepsister."

I nodded but it didn't matter. Sawyer didn't see me. He was still gazing into the past.

"Sonny's mother was always bringing boys around for Linda to make sure she didn't get interested in Sonny." Sawyer chucked. "As if that was going to happen. But she believed her son was irresistible." Another chuckle.

"Did she hope you and Linda would hit it off?"

He shook his head vehemently. "Never me. I was too friendly with Sonny. As an adult, I finally understand that the woman knew how to cover all the angles."

"That's why she invited Seth?"

He turned his eyes to meet mine. "Sonny wouldn't have asked him. Social suicide."

"He didn't want anyone at school associating him with the new kid?"

"Kids are mean." Sawyer grew thoughtful or wanted me to think he was growing thoughtful. "I was no exception, but Seth's death had an incredible impact on me. My stepdad and I were the last people to see him. Did you talk to my stepfather?"

I nodded.

"He changed after that case. I think because he knew Seth, saw him that night, felt like he should have waited until he saw him close the front door behind him. Then, because he was nearby when the call came in, he caught the case and, as the first detective on the scene, ended up being the spokesman, the one who worked with the press."

"You and he ever talk about the night Seth died?"

"You mean now?"

I nodded.

"He and I don't talk at all. Like my mom, I got tired of picking him up off the floor. I can't believe that she, who lived a clean life, was the one who died while that man, that drunk, took all sorts of chances and lived on. Lives on." He pulled a baseball out of his desk drawer and tossed it from hand to hand.

"Do you believe that Ralphie Barker killed Seth

Timmons?"

He kept throwing the ball but met my eyes with a gaze that I read as direct. I was tempted to cross his name off the suspect list. "Who else would have?" He caught the ball with dramatic flair, a gesture that let me see the twelve-year-old boy behind the man.

"Someone at the Taylor house that night?" No need to mention I'd speculated he might be the one.

"Well, I didn't. Besides. We were kids. In those days, kids didn't have guns." He dropped the ball back into the drawer.

"And Sonny? You never saw him threaten Seth?"

"Sonny acted like a bully but he was all hot air—and sad underneath. He kept waving this bat at Seth but I never worried he'd hit him."

"Because of that underlying sadness?"

Sawyer regarded my question with disdain. "No. The bat was signed by Johnny Callison and Bobby Wine. Sonny wouldn't hurt that bat."

Chapter 19

I called Helen Mitchell from my car. I didn't have answers for her but I still had questions. Helen sounded delighted to hear from me and suggested meeting again at her favorite restaurant. I claimed to have just eaten. Not because I felt any disdain for the restaurant. I was curious to see her home. I still had time to drive there and get to campus in time for office hours.

When Helen described her life following the tumultuous times after Ralphie's death, she was very much alone in life, but back in a good job. How had she ended up in such a rundown setting? The houses on the street where she had lived when Seth Timmons was her neighbor were spacious and gracious. The paneled lobby, wide hallways and worn marble floors suggested her current residence had also been, a very long time ago. What had gone wrong to make her live out her life in such a drab setting?

After she buzzed me in, I climbed two flights to her apartment door where she greeted me warmly. Her bright turquoise outfit contrasted with the large beige room she invited me into. Bland but neatly maintained, the living area shared none of the grunginess of the public space. Outdated furniture, unlikely to come back into fashion, was unaccessorized except for pictures, many pictures, most of a boy from infancy through young manhood. In that respect, and only in that respect, the room reminded me of Susan Timmons's home.

I tried not to stare at the eight by ten portrait of a nursing school graduate, ready to take on the world, proud of the cap perched on top of her tight curls and of the career she had chosen, but Helen noticed my interest.

"Pretty girl, wasn't I?"

"Very." I agreed, able to see a natural beauty through the colorization that made her lips and cheeks appear ridiculously red. I waved a hand at the photos on the walls and tabletops. "Ralphie?"

She nodded.

Two houses. Two shrines linked by one tragedy.

"And this must be Walter. Ralphie's friend." I studied a photo of two boys in graduation gowns. Maybe because I'd heard about him Walter looked like trouble to me. Ralphie, on the other hand, appeared innocent and joyful, thrilled to be posing with his friend at graduation. I glanced at the other pictures and did not see any smile so broad, at least after Ralphie passed the age of two. The joy slipped from his eyes as Ralphie morphed from a beautiful baby into a shy child, an awkward teenager and then a bland-looking adult who stared into the camera without emotion.

I followed Helen's direction and settled onto a couch that was surprisingly more comfortable than it was attractive.

"I am sorry that I don't have any results to report. But now that I know the basic story of your brother's life, I thought you could tell me more about why you are convinced he was innocent."

"Aside from the fact that he was a gentle man who could never hurt anyone?"

"Any specifics will help."

"Well, my brother liked girls, not boys."

"People hide things." I used a gentle tone.

"I was with Ralphie for 27 years. He wasn't sharp enough to hide anything for 27 minutes let alone 27 years."

"And he liked girls?"

"He had a huge crush on Connie Francis."

Well, that was one good counter to the argument that he sexually abused Seth.

"He would sing that song of hers *Where the Boys Are* all the time."

Well, maybe not.

"Of course, he would change it to *Where the Girls Are.*"

Okay. That was better for Ralphie's defense.

"After I told him people wouldn't like that."

Better to discount the entire Connie Francis angle. "Did he have any real girlfriends?"

Mrs. Mitchell shook her head. "He might have if he met someone like him, but even then he probably would have been too naïve. He looked at pretty girls and giggled about pretty girls. Always girls. Never did I see him look at a male person in a sexual way."

"Little girls?"

"Never a child."

"What was his police record? The press indicated that there was a morals charge?" I didn't say Grady had confirmed that for me.

"Public urination when he was just eighteen. He didn't even know doing that was illegal. You remember I told you about Walter. Well, Ralphie saw Walter urinate against a wall in an alley and he thought that was okay. So, he did it too. No one saw him but a cop who called what Ralphie did indecent exposure."

That scenario seemed believable. Both that Walter would relieve himself in a public place and that Ralphie would copy him.

"One of the articles that I read said that Ralphie had frequented the area where Seth's body would be found. Is that true? Did he like walking along the Wissahickon?"

"Sometimes he and I would take a stroll along the bridle path but I never knew him to go without me. He would walk to work at the school and back but aside from that he didn't like going anywhere on his own. He was always afraid of being out without me." Remembering her relationship with her brother brought a smile to her face and threatened to bring a tear to her eyes.

"Do you think he asked Seth Timmons to go with him?"

"At 11 PM? I suppose it's not *impossible*, but it would have been highly unlikely. Ralphie never went out after dark and, if for some reason he wanted to, he would have waited for me. That night I worked the second shift and a couple hours of overtime but I was home by midnight. He was in his apartment and asleep."

"You know that for sure?"

"The overhead lights in his apartment were out, the television was off and his nightlight was on. That's how it was every night. I always peeked in his window when I got home. Never did I find that he was out."

"If you were at work, how did you know what he did at night?"

"That's what the cops asked in '64. They didn't want to hear how well I knew him, how much I talked to him, how I heard all the details of his life. They didn't want to hear anything I had to say about Ralphie." Tears filled her eyes to the brim but didn't spill over. "When they came to talk to him, they were so mean. They scared him."

"He told you about the cops' visit?"

"He didn't understand why they wanted to talk to him, how they could think he would do anything. When I got home, that night, he was in a panic."

*****Helen Mitchell*****
October 2, 1964

Ralphie must have heard her come in. She had barely dropped the brown paper grocery bag on the kitchen table when she heard the banging on the door from the basement. She turned the lock and Ralphie burst in.

"Helen. Help me. I'm scared. Help me."

"Tell me. What's wrong?" She put a hand on his shoulder to calm him. It didn't work. She moved towards the open door. "Is someone down there?"

"No. No. They left." He paced around the room. "I never do anything bad. I don't. I told them. I am a good person."

"Who was here, Ralphie? What happened?"

"You have to help. You have to help me."

"Ralphie, look at me." She grabbed both his arms and held him in place. "You know I always help you. You know I always will. Right?"

He stared at her with eyes wide open in terror, but she didn't know if he could see her. He shook his head back and forth and made a groaning sound she'd never heard before.

"Calm down. Tell me. Please, Ralphie. Please."

Her plaintive tone seemed to call Ralphie back to reality. "The police came here. Today. Here. The person who hurt Seth hurt him real bad. They think I hurt Seth."

Even as she wondered why the cops would talk to Ralphie about the murder, she knew. That damn morals charge. Public urination that wasn't even seen except by a passing police cruiser. If only she'd known that he'd seen Walter relieve himself in public before he'd copied the behavior. If only she'd known to tell Ralphie that was wrong. She felt responsible. She felt guilty. She felt sick but asked her question with a calm that she did not feel. "What did you tell them?"

"I told them Seth was a nice boy. I told them he was my friend."

"I imagine the police are talking to everyone who knew Seth." She lied. She understood what the police visit had been about but she tried to appear nonchalant, unconcerned, hoping Ralphie would sense and react to her mood. She gave him a quick hug. "I can see why you would be upset, but don't worry." She hoped her brother didn't see the slight quiver of her hand as she struggled to light a match. "Don't worry, Ralphie. I am sure they are talking to everyone who works at Seth's school." Unable to make the flame meet the tip of her cigarette, she dropped it unlit into an ashtray.

"But they said I hurt him. Why would I hurt him? He's a nice boy. He might be the nicest boy in that school."

Helen hoped Ralphie hadn't said that to the police. She knew what those cops were getting at. She'd read the newspapers. Better they think that Seth was just one boy among hundreds to Ralphie.

She had to reach up to wrap her arm around her brother. Such a gentle giant. She took his elbow to guide him back downstairs to the basement, to the apartment she and her husband had made for him. Ron was due home at any moment and he would be tired after a long week at work. He never wanted to see Ralphie at night, even when Ralphie was in a calm and happy mood, let alone in this condition. She knew Ron was lying in wait, looking for an excuse to throw her brother out of their home.

Ralphie slumped on the worn sofa. She settled onto the cushion next to him and wrapped her arm around his heaving shoulders as he wept.

Her heart ached at the thought of him waiting alone in his dreary apartment for her to return from work. She'd thrown an old bedspread over the couch to give the illusion of décor but the trick didn't work for her. Not that decorating mattered to Ralphie. He told her he found everything about the place pretty. Helen found it depressing but the beat-up couch, the worn hook rug and the used single bed were the best she could do with the money she squeezed out of the household budget. Ralphie was so proud that he had paid for the television out of his *own pocket. She was so grateful he could. Without the small portable TV, what could he have done down there alone night after night?*

She could barely understand her brother when, gulping for air, he tried to speak. "They said that I did funny things to him. I didn't know people did those things. Why would anyone hurt Seth so bad?"

"I don't know, Ralphie. I don't know." She paused, afraid to ask but she felt she must. "You didn't hurt him did you?"

*****

"The look on his face." She stared at the floor as she shook her head. "I can't forget it. He was so devastated that I even asked. But I had to, didn't I?" Her eyes met mine, to plead for agreement. "I never believed that he would hurt anyone but I had to ask. Although, I never doubted him and not just because of my feelings. Ralphie wasn't smart enough to fake it. He didn't hurt Seth. I know that."

"What did your husband think?"

"He thought the time had come to move to a place where he wouldn't be known as the pervert's relative. I haven't seen him since Thanksgiving, 1964."

I didn't know what to say.

Luckily, she spoke. "He wasn't as convinced of Ralphie's innocence as I was."

I wanted to be, I was trying to be, but I wasn't convinced of Ralphie's innocence either. Not yet. I wished Helen had more than belief in her brother to offer as proof.

"I should never have left him alone that other night."

I understood what night she meant, his last night

"The newspaper that morning didn't give his name but basically identified him. He didn't know that. He never looked at a newspaper but I told him to be careful, that some of the neighbors may not know the truth yet, that he had not done anything wrong. I was afraid someone might try to hurt him. I never even thought that he might hurt himself. I am still shocked by it." She sounded frustrated with her earlier self. "I was worried about leaving him alone and didn't want to go out, but my husband insisted. Said I was being crazy, that no one would hurt Ralphie, although the way he said it made me think that he wouldn't mind it if someone did. *He* had plans and *we* were going to stick to them. Once a month his mother had Sunday dinner for her boys, all six of them. I hated going. The brothers would sit there and get drunk and then I would have to fight with Ron to give me the car keys."

"I understand why you would want to go along. I would have worried about his driving."

She shook her head. "I didn't worry about him. If something happened to him, he would have deserved it, but I never could have forgiven myself if he drove into someone else."

"So that's why you went?"

"One reason. The real reason is that I was becoming scared of Ron, of my own husband. If he wanted me to do something, I did it. And when Ralphie got into trouble, I was terrified."

"Of what he might do to Ralphie?"

"Of what he might do to me. Although I was devastated at the time, I was lucky he left. He was a very angry man by the end of our marriage." She waved a hand at the photographs that dominated the room, none of her husband. Her eyes met mine again. "You know why I keep all these pictures of Ralphie around?" She didn't make me answer, she continued. "You probably think I made these displays to remind me of Ralphie, but I don't need pictures to remember my little brother. I keep these images to drive another vision from my mind, what I saw when I heard his TV on too loud and went down the basement steps and found my baby brother hanging from a pipe."

Chapter 20

I was feeling motivated. In truth, I was feeling guilty. What had been so important that I hadn't made time to focus on Ralphie's case? There were other witnesses to talk to. Maybe not witnesses but people who would remember that day.

Mrs. Timmons had said that Marcia Taylor, the party hostess, was a chatterer at thirty. I hoped that she remained a chatterer at eighty. I just needed to find a way to make sure I found the right Marcia Taylor and made her chatter with me. Based on what Susan Timmons said, if I could get Marcia Taylor talking, the hard part would be getting her to stop. I hoped that was my biggest problem.

I stayed up late searching online for Marcia Taylor and was in my car early Thursday morning. The Internet offered no indication that the party host still lived in the same place. When I drove over to see that house, I assumed that unless Marcia Taylor had become a major drug kingpin at eighty, she had moved on and I'd better do the same. The Taylors' former home appeared to be what suburbanites would generalize and call a crack house. I didn't even take the time to try my usual crime scene exercise: envisioning Seth at the 1964 party. I beat it out of the area.

Based on inconclusive data, I drove to an apartment building in Northeast Philadelphia where I believed the right Marcia Taylor lived. At least had lived at some point. As an approach, I selected *accidental meeting combined with a request for an interview*. Not easy but worth a try. Even if I got inside to show up at her door unannounced, I didn't know which door to show up at. I settled in to wait for an opportunity to bump into her; I had nothing to lose but a couple of hours.

I parked down the block from the alleged residence of Marcia Taylor in front of one of the modest twin homes that lined the street. With one obvious exception, where the homeowner found broken toys and rusty tools appropriate lawn ornaments, the houses were lovingly decorated with bright flowers, lush bushes and an occasional garden ornament. The apartment house was not adorned with blooms, foliage, decorations, or architectural detail for that matter. The best I could say? The building appeared clean and solid. Red brick, flat roof, square windows, metal doors, cement path. If a guard appeared to tell me to move away from the minimum security prison, I would have believed him.

I pulled out my cell phone for some imaginary phone calls. No one seemed to notice me, but who knew how many eyes lurked behind those windows? Although technically, since they belonged in their home and I was the one spying, I was the lurker. I felt some discomfort when the first few people to exit the building resembled recently released inmates, but, after an hour passed, so had a wide variety of residents. A couple that appeared to be babies themselves wheeling a stroller. An elderly man with an oxygen mask strapped to his face pushing a walker. A middle-aged woman with a slow gait pulling a grocery cart. But, no one I pegged as Marcia Taylor.

All I knew about the woman was her age, somewhere north of eighty, and her fashion style, if it had not changed since 1964. I was hoping a leopard didn't change its spots, even if those spots were woven into spandex leggings.

Minute seventy-eight. Bingo. I was willing to bet that the elderly woman dressed in tight pants, low cut blouse, oversized jewelry, and heavy makeup was Marcia Taylor. Her pants and her dog's collar were covered with leopard spots.

Apparently, Mrs. Taylor had ventured outside so that her poodle could take care of business. I sprang into action. Well, sauntered into action. I climbed out of the car and wandered up the street with a scrap of paper in my hand. I pulled up beside the woman and waited until the dog finished his business before I spoke. "Excuse me." I smiled politely. Didn't want to overwhelm her with eagerness.

The alleged Marcia Taylor spun around but seemed relieved to see me, well someone like me. And, she appeared happy that I was looking for her address. She didn't question why I couldn't read the wrought iron numbers over the door. If she had I could have used the dangling six as an excuse.

"It's right there." She pointed to the next building, the one she'd come out of.

I took my shot. She could run away, but I was fairly sure I could keep up. "This is awkward. I'm a writer." True, at one time in my life. "I was hoping to interview someone who lives there. I don't suppose you know a Marcia Taylor, do you?"

"Why would you want to interview her?" She did not appear to be put off by the request, just curious.

My lying began in earnest. "I am writing a piece about Germantown in the 1960s. I hoped she might be able to provide some information on a specific story."

"Is that so?" She considered her options while her poodle sniffed around my feet. So far I had the alleged Marcia Taylor fooled. I wasn't so sure about her dog. "A story for the newspaper?"

"If all goes well." A lie? Technically. In my opinion, the article, if written, could be suitable for a newspaper. If I wrote for one. Which I didn't.

I lost the woman's attention to a somewhat disreputable-looking man in his fifties. "Hi, Marv." She cooed.

"Marcia." He nodded but kept his eyes straight ahead.

"When are we going to get that drink?" She teased.

The man didn't break stride. "Soon." By the time he completed a lengthy answer, actually more of an excuse, he was tossing his response over his shoulder. I might not have heard his exact words but I did get the message. Mrs. Taylor did not.

"Wonderful. We'll do that soon," she called after him.

The phrase *when hell freezes over* popped into my mind.

"I guess you date a lot." She turned to me for an answer.

I didn't tell her that, lately, I made a lot of dates. I just didn't go out on any.

"At your age, it's easy. Even for girls like you."

I scowled but didn't get a response together before she continued.

"I got used to being hot, having every man I wanted. You'll never know how painful it is to feel that power fade away."

I was at a loss for words. As Sue Timmons predicted, Mrs. Taylor was not.

"Why do you want to talk to Marcia?"

"I'm not sure I should say. I don't want to invade her privacy."

"But her privacy would be invaded if her name appears in the newspaper."

"But it wouldn't go in the paper if she didn't want it in the paper."

Her face brightened at the prospect of her name in print.

"We wouldn't put a picture unless she wanted her photo included."

Her face lit up like a three-way bulb turned to the max. Her picture in the newspaper. The opportunity seemed to appeal. Time to reel her in.

"I'm sorry. Thank you for your time." I made a half-hearted effort to turn away. "I may have already said too much."

"Not really." She offered a bright smile. "I'm Marcia Taylor."

"Really?" I went for flabbergasted yet delighted. I felt I came fairly close to hitting the mark.

"Pinky's done doing his duty, aren't you, Sweetie." She played the coquette, even with her dog. And, even with me. "Come on in and we can talk over a drink." She plastered a big, phony smile across her face.

"Don't you think you should ask for my ID?" I made a weak effort to reach for my wallet.

"Honey, I've known a lot of bad people in my lifetime. I have a nose for sniffing out evil-doers."

I wasn't really evil was I? Deceitful, yes, but for a good cause. Maybe that was why she couldn't smell the deception in me.

"Are you sure, Mrs. Taylor?"

She was sure and she wanted me to call her Marcia.

Chapter 21

I followed Marcia and Pinky into an over-stuffed, over-decorated living room. Even though the style stopped just short of hoarder, no photos or mementos offered a clue as to what Marcia Taylor had been doing for the past six decades. The only picture I spotted was a portrait of a high school graduate who, while not unattractive by 1950s style standards, wore a smug expression that made her appear exceedingly unlikeable.

If I wanted to be generous, I could call Marcia's décor eclectic. On the other hand, I could say the room contained a hodge-podge of mismatched junk tied together with a lot of leopard skin accents. Seth might have sat on several of the items in the Taylor rec room in 1964. They didn't match what appeared to be newer items. None of those matched each other either.

"I live here alone. Except for Pinky. He's the only male visitor I've had in several months now." She scooped him into her arms and spoke to him nose to nose. "Is that right Pinky? Haven't we been lonely here all by ourselves without a male *friend*?" She turned to me. "Dating isn't easy at my age."

I didn't find dating easy at any age. I hadn't had a male *friend* in much longer than several months, which meant that Marcia was getting more action than I was.

"When I was your age, I had men fighting over me." She wasn't so much bragging as reminiscing, staring into space, petting Pinky absent-mindedly. "And in my day there weren't so many singles. Everyone got married young. You don't know how good you have it. She has it easy these days. Doesn't she Pinky?"

Pinky didn't offer an opinion but Marcia's comments made me feel worse that I couldn't nab one of those singles for a Saturday night dinner.

"Have fun while you can. I did." Her eyes met mine to confirm her meaning. "Of course, I had some hard times too. I liked the bad boys. Always did. How about you?"

"I've liked my share." I saw no reason to explain that those bad boys did not appear to like me back.

"So, let's have a drink for the bad boys."

According to the clock on her wall, noon would soon be behind us, if an hour counted as soon. Why not?

Only after we were seated with mismatched glasses in front of us—coke with a dash of rum in mine, beer in Marcia's—did she ask what I wanted to know about 1964.

"Seth Timmons was killed in the autumn of 1964."

My comment about Seth didn't seem to faze her at all. "I thought that might be what you wanted." She shook her head with marked theatricality. "I felt terrible. I guess you know that he was at our house that night. I was the one who invited little Seth to come out on a school night." She sounded proud when I would have sounded remorseful.

"Did you know Seth well?"

"No. He was new to my son's class. I appreciated how hard being a new kid can be. I moved Sonny when he was younger and I had to work so hard to handle the change. I understood." Marcia painted her younger self as the epitome of empathy. She punctuated her statement with a slug of beer. "I asked Seth's mother if he could come."

"How did you know Susan Timmons?"

"I was dating John Lockwood, a lovely widower from our parish." She took a long drink and licked her lips to make sure she removed every trace of foam. Or she might have been remembering John Lockwood. I was more comfortable with the foam clean-up interpretation. "John and I ran into Mrs. Timmons by accident one day downtown and he introduced us. Susan, you say. I didn't

117

remember that. Anyway, John had been friends with her dead husband. That was why she came back to Philadelphia. Her husband died."

"Was it Mr. Lockwood's idea to include Seth?"

"No. Mine." Again, the pride. "In those days people didn't jump all around the way they do now. Not that many families moved into the neighborhood. Being the new folks on the block was seldom easy, especially for the kids. As I said, I sized up the situation as soon as I noticed Seth at school."

"He stood out?"

"The kid looked miserable. Then I heard a piece of news. Linda Lockwood had a little crush on him." She sat back and beamed.

"So you played matchmaker?"

The coquette came into full flower. "I was being a wee bit devious. Since I was dating John, I liked doing nice things for his daughter."

*****Marcia Taylor*****
September 30, 1964

Wonderful. Linda thought Seth was cute. Marcia could tell by the way she smiled at the new boy and sat near him on the carpet. Linda was a lot more interested in Seth than she was in the baseball game on TV.

Seth was so shy. Marcia wished he would respond to Linda. She wanted John's only child to have a boyfriend. The last thing she needed was her son flirting with Linda. Not that Sonny knew how to flirt. He believed acting like a bore was appealing. John would recognize Sonny's behavior for what it was. And, he would steer clear of him and her.

She knew John wasn't sold on Sonny—even when he was on his best behavior which he wasn't that night. He had been cranky before the Phillies started messing up.

Damn. She didn't want him to come between her and the best thing that had happened to her in years. This guy had some cash. She could tell. His house and his car were modest, but his clothes gave him away. She'd worked in the men's department at Wanamaker's, only for a couple of months, but long enough to learn the tell-tale signs of expensive men's clothing. John wasn't flashy. What he wore might not have been to her taste, but the quality was excellent. This guy had money and class. He wouldn't want some ill-behaved little brat like Sonny embarrassing him.

The good news was that Sonny seemed to like Lockwood. If only he would see him as a role model. Maybe that was all the kid needed, a positive role model. He needed something, anything to keep him out of juvenile hall, a place he'd been heading since the age of five. Maybe earlier. Sonny had given new meaning to the term terrible twos. Marcia felt sure other mothers would have given up on him right then, but she stuck with him, even though he was a trial. Like his father. That no-good lout.

She knew Lockwood would not like the idea of a household that put a tough kid like Sonny in the same home as his proper little daughter. Soon they would be teenagers and she knew what that meant. She'd spent enough time in the backseat of cars to see what could happen if you let two hormone-charged teens alone. She'd tried to find Sonny a girlfriend, but then she realized it would be a lot easier to find Linda a boyfriend. Any boy would be happy to be paired with Linda. Even Seth, she bet, if he could work up the courage.

"Seth tell Linda about Illinois." She smiled broadly. "I bet she'd like to hear about it."

*****

"I got the conversation rolling. Of course, Sonny had

to jump in with some nasty comment. That kid was hopeless. Always bad-tempered. Didn't get it from me." She took a slug of her beer.

"Did your son like that you invited Seth?"

"Sonny was rooting for me to marry John Lockwood. His father walked out on us when Sonny was five. My son knew a meaningful relationship was important to me—for his sake. I wanted to give him a stable home. Sonny trusted my judgment."

"Tell me about that night." I hoped I could direct her chattering back to September 30, 1964.

"Nothing to tell. It was a nice evening." She got lost in a daze for a few seconds before she plastered a forlorn expression on her face. "Except that the Phillies blew it."

"What was everyone doing?"

"I had this great rec room down in my basement. Big, not by today's standards, but in 1964, huge. I had all the latest things. Took up most of the basement. Made a great place to have a get together to watch a baseball game. Especially since I had a color TV, not that the broadcast was in color. Even though the Phillies lost, it was a nice night. John—Mr. Lockwood, Linda's father—and I sat on the couch, that same couch you're sitting on now, well the same under the slipcover. Sonny and Mikey went nuts over the game. Linda and Seth talked a lot, just like I hoped.

"You didn't mention Jack Grady."

"Jack Grady?" She was thrown by the reference to the ex-cop. Her eyes blinked repeatedly. Long, hard blinks. "Haven't thought of him in a long time. I barely knew him. You're right. He was there, but only for five, maybe ten minutes. He didn't come to watch the game. He only dropped by to pick up his kid. No wonder I forgot." She frowned as if she wanted me to see her thinking. "How could I forget that? He walked little Seth home. I can't believe that I didn't bring his name up, but I guess I was thinking about the people watching the game."

"You didn't ask him to stay?"

"I would have but the game was over and the kids were out very late on a school night. Besides Sonny was all in a tizzy because the Phillies lost the pennant. Nobody liked being around Sonny when he was in a tizzy."

I noted Marcia's use of the past tense. Was he different now or simply not around?

She shook her head. "It's hard being a single parent."

"Sonny still lives with you?"

"No." She made no move to hide her disgust. At the idea of a grown man living with his mother or of the reality of Sonny living with her?

"Where is Sonny now?"

"Sonny's had some problems over the years. Drugs. I did everything I could to keep him clean but he got in with a bad crowd."

"Where is he?"

"You got kids?"

I shook my head.

'Don't. They ruin your figure, your marriage and your life."

"Where's Sonny?" I tried my best not to sound challenging.

"He had some trouble raising money for drugs so he's spending a little time in Graterford prison."

Chapter 22

"Those are lovely." Aunt Julia commented when she saw the oversized bouquet of summer flowers on the mantel.

"I put the arrangement in front of the mirror so they would look more substantial." Alex rolled his eyes. "They're from the phantom. He sent them because he couldn't make his date with Tracy last Saturday."

"Wow." Aunt Julia was impressed. Not by the gesture but by how fresh the flowers looked. "They still look great."

Alex answered. "He canceled on Saturday and these arrived today, six days later."

"He was in South America," I protested.

"I guess he never heard of online ordering." Alex made no attempt to disguise the sarcasm in his voice.

"Maybe he couldn't get a connection." I played defense. "By the way, how did you know he sent them?" I answered my own question. "You read the card."

"That little white envelope didn't have a name on it."

"How did the flowers get here?"

"A guy knocked on the door. I opened it. He handed me the flowers. How did I know they were for you? They could have been for me."

"From?" I challenged him.

"Maybe I have a secret admirer." He flung both hands out while he waited for me to agree. When I said nothing he waved them at me with a dismissive action. "Yeah. You're right. Make me depressed about the state of my love life. I guess I wasn't thinking." He shrugged as if to say *what could I do?*

"He had to take an emergency trip. South America," I explained to Aunt Julia.

"Yeah, I heard." Aunt Julia sounded disappointed.

"Don't feel bad." Alex protested, "We went to the Phillies game instead." Alex patted the couch cushion. "Hey, Aunt Julia. Sit by me. I've been meaning to ask. Do you remember Marcus from Tracy's schooldays?" Alex's tone suggested he knew the answer to his question.

"I don't recall many of Tracy's friends. I moved away when she was about five." Tucking one leg under the other, Aunt Julia settled onto the couch beside Alex.

"Hmmh."

I frowned at Alex. "What? Now you think my aunt is lying about her past to provide cover for Marcus's sinister plot to date me?"

"The CIA has long fingers."

"Marcus works for the CIA?" Aunt Julia accessorized the question with a frown.

"No. He does not." I spaced my words in hopes of making an emphatic statement.

Alex rolled his eyes again and began to hum *Secret Agent Man*, one of his favorite tunes since Marcus came on the scene. "He's on a mission."

"He's on a business trip," I corrected Alex. "He had to fly to South America."

"Where in South America?" Aunt Julia, full of interest, asked.

Alex answered for me. "Oh, you know. South America."

"He wasn't more specific?" Aunt Julia asked me.

Alex answered. "He never is. No one in the CIA is."

"He's busy. He's successful. He is not in the CIA," I repeated.

"Can I see his business card?" Aunt Julia asked me.

"Did you ever find that card, Tracy?" Alex supplemented her question with his own.

"I told you I never got one. Why would I? His number is in my phone. That's how I get texts." I made a face that I hoped asked, *Have you no confidence in me?*

"Don't worry about her, Aunt Julia. I'll take her to dinner to keep her mind off her missing paramour. Would you like to join us?"

"I'd love to, but I can't."

She didn't want to explain and I didn't push. Alex did. "A hot date?" He inquired with a great display of anticipation.

"I doubt it." She used a sigh to explain that the date was anything but hot. "I said yes because until I got your invitation I had no excuse." Her tone indicated that she wished she did.

I feared I shared a gene for dating luck with my aunt.

"How did you escape marriage all these years?" Alex asked Aunt Julia a question that, coming from him, sounded more teasing than prying.

"I didn't."

"It didn't work out?"

"It did."

"Oh, I am so sorry. I never knew you were a widow."

"I'm not."

"So you're divorced?"

"I am."

Alex released a theatrical sigh. "At last, I got one right. However, I am confused as to why I got that one right."

"Aunt Julia has the most amicable divorce on record," I offered.

"I got married in my twenties to a guy I met on a trip to Europe. He was from New York where I was living at the time. We had an incredible five years. We worked, saved, quit, traveled. Worked, saved, quit, traveled."

"Sounds great." Alex nodded.

"One day while we were in the working phase, he came home and said he had been offered a great job and he wanted to take it. He wanted to settle down, buy a house in the suburbs, raise a family. But that wasn't what I wanted. Then or ever."

"And that was it?" Alex sounded shocked.

"I wouldn't hold him back from doing what he wanted, although I've got to say I was a bit annoyed. I felt he was reneging on the deal we made, but I guess he'd changed. People do change. He called it growing up, something I had no real interest in doing. When he found someone else so quickly, it confirmed for me that we wanted different things out of life."

"Didn't you leave something out?" Aunt Julia's marriage wasn't something I'd ever heard much about but I did know she'd neglected to mention one important fact.

"He did come back after a year to see if I changed my mind. I hadn't. By then I'd accepted that we'd had an incredible five years, but it just wasn't meant to be. It was after that he found someone." There was a time a statement like that would have been accompanied by a wistful expression but no longer. The story was just a part of Aunt Julia's distant past.

"Did you ever hear what happened to him? Did his marriage last?"

"Over thirty years. Three children. Living in a huge house in Connecticut with money from a high-level corporate job. Who would have thought?"

"How do you know all this?"

"Every couple of years he comes to town and we have lunch."

"How does it go?" Alex seemed cynical.

Aunt Julia shrugged. "How would you think? We laugh."

"Wow." Alex whistled. "Sounds so civilized."

"Yeah, I make it sound that way. There was a time I was really angry, especially when I had to pay all my rent in New York City and all my hotel expenses on the road

125

where I seldom got to go because my rent was so high. I never got to live as well as the two of us did together again. But I didn't come by to tell you my life story. I wanted to let Tracy know I mentioned her case to a friend. Turns out she remembered Seth Timmons's murder."

"Did she think Ralphie Barker was guilty?" I asked.

"According to her, everyone thought Ralphie Barker was guilty."

"Except?"

Her tone suggested an exception.

"My friend went to school at St. Margaret's, but before Seth. Ralphie Barker was the custodian. She told me a story about how she had lost a locket on the last day of school and asked him about it. He promised her if he found it, he would return it. She told him her name and where she lived. One day in July, over a month later, Ralphie Barker showed up at her door. His sister had driven him to her house because he had found a necklace under a floorboard in the lunchroom and he wondered if it belonged to her."

"He went to all that trouble to return a piece of jewelry?" My voice indicated both admiration and amazement.

"Turned out the necklace wasn't hers. It wasn't even a locket." Aunt Julia shrugged. "But that didn't matter. The point is he went to so much trouble to return it."

"How far away could she have lived if she went to St. Margaret's?" Alex the Pragmatic asked.

"Far enough that he had to ask his sister to drive him. Why are you minimizing what he did?" I countered. "The effort he put in was very nice."

"And," Aunt Julia interrupted, "my friend said he was terribly disappointed when it wasn't hers. She felt so bad, she wanted to lie and take it. Instead, she helped him make a poster to put up at school in the fall."

"Did they ever find the owner?" I asked.

"She couldn't remember, but my point is, she said Ralphie was a very nice man. She kept referring to him as sweet. She claimed she never detected anything frightening about him. After everything happened, she thought and thought, trying to come up with one indication that he was capable of the kinds of things they accused him of doing. And, she never came up with one example when his behavior was off. I mean he was slow but never creepy."

"Great." Alex took a long drink of wine. "Now Tracy will never give up."

Aunt Julia smiled. "That's one of her best characteristics. Tracy never gives up."

"Apparently, Marcus is counting on that," Alex offered but both Aunt Julia and I ignored him.

Chapter 23

Alex wanted to drive me to dinner in my car. Even though he feared being seen driving it and kept the top up to minimize the danger, he felt sitting in the passenger's seat would make me feel more like I was on a date. Another effort to make up for Marcus's deficiencies.

"If you look to your right, you'll see the spot where the dog-walker found Seth's body."

Alex looked but we were past the spot in a few seconds. "How did the body get there? You never talk about that."

"The assumption was that he was abducted from his front door and killed where his body was found."

"And no one heard the kid screaming?"

"Even if the perp couldn't subdue and silence him somehow, the temperature was around fifty degrees, so most people would have had their windows closed."

"Do you think he would have gone willingly with anyone at that time of night?" Alex sounded doubtful.

So did I. "I can't imagine he would, but who knows how kids think."

"And, if he did go with someone, most likely he knew that someone."

I agreed.

"And, he knew Ralphie Barker."

Again, I agreed.

"I can see how Ralphie Barker provided an easy solution for the cops." Alex seemed reluctant to break that news to me.

"I know it was easy, but I wonder if it was too easy."

The drive down the Wissahickon Drive to the West

River Drive and on to downtown Philadelphia offered some beautiful sights. I decided to chase sad thoughts from my mind and enjoy the park and river views. After we were seated at one of my favorite restaurants on Rittenhouse Square, we tried to avoid talk of bodies and murder and, most of all, Marcus.

"You know I'm not much of a reader." Alex sounded apologetic.

"Not everyone is." I didn't know where this was going.

"So you know how when your book came out, I bought a copy?"

"Do you think I look a lot older than the book jacket photo? When Helen Mitchell came to my office, she didn't seem to recognize me."

"Your hair was different. You didn't have the ponytail. But remember I bought your book."

"I know you hate my ponytail but until I have a real income again, I don't have the time or money for a salon."

"I understand. But remember when I bought your book."

"At the book party Kathy gave for me."

"Right." He sounded sheepish. "And you signed it for me?"

"I did."

"That was very nice of you."

I waited for Alex to continue but he didn't even though I sensed that he had more to say. "You never read it." My comment was an accusation, not a question.

"I meant to. Really, I did. But I never knew Mitch. He was gone before I met you and I've been busy."

"For five years?" I tried to make myself sound indignant but I understood. Not everyone is a reader.

"But I'm reading it now. Because I want to understand why you do all this for people and now I realize that Mitch is the reason. I get that he disappeared and you were so frustrated trying to find him that you want to help others.

I get that."

"Then you get it all. One day he was there. Acting goofy and laughing, and then he was gone. End of story."

"But the book is over three hundred pages long." His tone was light just for a moment. Then he grew serious again. "And I realize it isn't about Mitch at all. Sure, I am learning some stuff about him, and he sounds like a cool guy, but the book is really about an unrelenting friend. It's about you."

My eyes misted over. I tried to come up with a snappy retort to alter the mood but failed. "I wrote it because I thought it might produce leads to find him."

"Did it?"

"False ones."

"But you pursued every one. You kept going even though you never found him."

"Yet. I haven't found him yet." My search for Mitch wasn't over and probably never would be. We'd been friends before we could speak and our mothers had us share a playpen. "I could never abandon him."

"Of course not. I understand why you couldn't walk away."

"Not only then. Now. I'm only inactive because I just couldn't think of anything else to do, but I will."

"Now, I understand why strangers come to you. I mean I really get it. It's not only about what you can do for them; it's about how you will do it. With heart and understanding and true empathy." Alex's tone was as gentle as I had ever heard it.

We sat in silence for what felt like an hour before I produced a proper response. "I feel as if I just listened to my own eulogy."

Alex leaned back and slipped into his usual cavalier manner. "I'll write it down when I get home. That was rather moving, wasn't it?"

"Lovely but I'm not sure I can live up to it. I hate to

disappoint Helen but I think the cops got it right in '64."

"So you're giving up?" He seemed closer to shock than surprise.

"I can't. Not yet. If I gave up, I'd have to tell her and I can't bring myself to do that. Her life appears so sad." I felt my determination rising. "I'd love to know what Sonny has to say. Even his mother said he had a rotten temper. Sawyer said Sonny inherited it from her. Although even when they were kids, he understood Sonny was full of hot air." I paused. "Who am I kidding? Want to know the real reason I'd like to see him? If I can't help Helen Mitchell, maybe I can find out something for Susan Timmons. Maybe he saw Linda Lockwood kiss Seth that night."

"And he killed Seth in a jealous rage?"

"I never considered that possibility. Maybe I should have but I didn't. My real motive? Seth's mother said she'd like to think Seth was kissed before he died."

He patted my hand. "See you are a closet romantic. Deeply closeted but cracking the door a bit." He wagged a cautionary finger. "Just be careful who you let in." He meant Marcus but did not speak the name. "So, you romantic you, finding out about the kiss could be the reason you give Sonny for wanting to talk to him. That explanation is just weird enough it might work." Alex seemed far more excited by the idea of investigating a romance than a crime. "Where does he live?"

"Near Skippack."

"That's a nice area up there. I wonder what made him move there."

"The State of Pennsylvania."

Alex stared at me. "He lives in Graterford prison?"

"I wouldn't call that living, but some residents get accustomed to it."

Alex affected an extremely pensive look. "I can see how it might be a problem to get to him. You need an excuse to get you through the door, metaphorically speaking. I still think the kissing excuse is just odd enough to work."

My turn to affect an extreme look. I chose dejected. "I don't think there is any way I can get inside to see him."

"But you could write to him." Alex found this prospect energizing. He began a lecture on the topic of prisoner communications. "You can find the address on the web. When you ask him to talk, offer to put some money in his commissary account for his trouble. That's not a bribe. Say you simply want to offer him a small token of your appreciation just for a conversation. He'll call you. Collect. Be prepared, however, the call is gonna cost you. Although depending on the rules, he might not be able to talk very long."

"How do you know all this?"

Alex focused on his salad. "I'd rather not say."

"Do I want you staying in my house?"

Alex shrugged. "I wasn't the one making the calls."

An hour after we got home, Alex appeared in the living room and dropped printouts of web pages in my lap. They came from a website called *PrisonFriends*.

I spotted Sonny Taylor's name at the top of the page. "Can you give me the executive summary?"

"Ostensibly it's a website for finding pen-pals, but for most of the guys inside, it's a dating website. That's Sonny Taylor's profile. Scary looking guy, even without the tattoos."

Since his mother didn't display any pictures, I'd only seen young Sonny in the newspaper and those photos had been blurred and grainy so I couldn't tell what Sonny Taylor had looked like as a twelve-year-old. "It's hard to imagine this guy was ever a child."

"But easy to imagine he was a bully." Alex countered.

The man who stared out from the printout was conveying a clear message: *mess with me and I'll break you in half,* something I was fairly sure he would have no trouble doing, to me or to someone twice my size. His profile said he had been in prison for three years. His picture said he'd spent most of that time in the gym.

"Nice tats, eh?" Alex asked.

"I don't think you need to use the plural. I think it's just one tattoo starting at his neck and ending, well, I can only guess where it ends. He looks like the quintessential intimidator, don't you think?"

"I wouldn't mess with him, but then again, I'm a little bit frightened of you." Alex plopped beside me and grabbed the top sheet. "I think it's significant that he didn't include one shot with even a hint of a smile. You're right. He wants to intimidate. Why does he think that will attract women? *Write to me or you'll regret it.*"

"*You, your family and all your Facebook friends,*" I added.

"He doesn't look bad for his age. I mean he looks *bad* but not the meaning that has to do with aging."

Alex was right. Sonny looked younger than Mikey Sawyer. So much for all that money could buy – which I suspected in Sawyer's case included more than one visit to a plastic surgeon.

"I bet he gets a lot of responses."

"Can we see them?" I asked with an eagerness that surprised me.

"Not that I can figure out."

"I can't believe people look at these websites. I can't believe the prison lets the inmates do this."

"They may not. Sonny-boy may have someone on the outside maintain it for him. Although I would imagine he did write his own profile." Alex speculated.

Along with the basics, name, location, crime and projected release date, Sonny's profile provided information on his favorites. *Music: Schubert.*

"He's lying, right?" I asked Alex.

"How would I know? You have stereotyped the man with the shaved head, big muscles and head-to-toe tattoos as a heavy metal type. Me too. So, he likes classical music. One wrong." Alex signaled with his finger: What's next?

"*Favorite Book: Holy Bible.*" I read.

"He's no dope. He put that there in case the parole board finds it. Looks a lot better than *Skanks on the Skids.*"

"At least Sonny doesn't claim he's innocent." I sounded impressed.

Alex read over my shoulder. "But he does claim to be looking for a meaningful relationship with a woman who is straightforward, loving, genuine and honest." He struck a pose with his index finger held to his chin. "Hmmh. I wonder if that means he's looking for a woman just like his mother, or one who's nothing like his mother. You met her. What was your impression?"

"Let's just say the words loving, genuine and honest never crossed my mind. She wanted me to think she was straightforward but I think she was simply aggressive."

"When you write are you going to say his mother referred you?" Alex asked.

I considered his question and decided it would be better to leave Marcia out of my effort to contact her son.

Chapter 24

I didn't send the letter that night, or any of the next four nights. I spent every spare minute trying to unravel the intricacies of prison telephone systems to locate an option for a stranger wanting calls from an inmate, but not on her home phone that belongs to the nice people who let her live in their house for free. Turns out I wasn't the only one who wanted to get collect calls on a cell phone. Not that Sonny would ever know my number. I located a call-forwarding service. Then, I started to compose my message.

It took me a couple of days and several drafts to find the right tone but early on a warm morning as the sun beamed on the dew-kissed garden and birds serenaded me with joyous songs, I sat down in a charming wicker chair and drafted my letter to a man who would read it on a hard stool in his prison home with little idea of what the day's weather offered. I had no idea what to say. Why should Sonny Taylor help me? I described the basics of my class and explained that if he would share his memories of the era, I would put some money in his commissary account. By the time humidity infiltrated the air and clouds blocked the sun, my letter seemed less than persuasive, so I asked if he could think of anything else he might need and headed for the mailbox.

Clearly, I was offering a bribe in return for his call. Perhaps, however, the offer was not sufficiently generous or specific. Several weeks went by and I hadn't heard from him.

"You could try again under a different name," Alex suggested.

"A second person happens to have the same interest and the same phone number?"

"You could get a disposable cell and a new account."

"You're the one who warns me about running up expenses. I can wait."

I called Helen to tell her that, although the investigation had slowed, I was still working on her case. I was relieved she didn't answer so I could leave a message. I didn't want to hear the disappointment in her voice. I was disappointed myself. I was disappointed in myself. The sound of Helen's voice, somehow ever hopeful, prompted me to take action.

In the garden, I found Alex, who justified calling in sick because he was sick of work. "I'm going over to St. Theresa's High School."

"Sock hop?" Alex asked.

I ignored him. "I'm trying to find out more about the group at the party that night." He knew what night I meant. "The kids went to St. Margaret's School but it closed eight years ago. I called Susan Timmons to get the name of Seth's teacher. I found out that Sister Rita Mary, now Sister Rita Douglas, teaches at St. Theresa's. She taught Seth for less than a month but I'm sure she'll remember. I need to get over there before the school year ends."

"Which means you better hurry. At this point, you should be tracking the end of the school year on your watch, not your calendar."

"I hope not. Colleges break earlier. I don't think the high schools get out for a couple of weeks."

Alex sounded almost excited. "Then you can find out if she taught Linda Lockwood."

"I'm asking about everyone who was there that night."

Alex's voice was animated. "You know when a young girl gets upset, she might confide in a nun."

"Not a Catholic girl."

"Even if she was distraught because the boy who bestowed her very first kiss had died?"

"Talking about a kiss to a nun? I never would have done that." I didn't want to admit it to Alex but I was still embarrassed to talk about kissing with a nun.

His tone switched to exaggerated solemnity. "Yes, but tragedy changes everything." He followed me to the front door. "Don't forget to ask." He called from the porch as I climbed into my car. "I'll check with you when you get home."

I waved and pulled the door shut.

Chapter 25

St. Theresa's occupied an entire city block and dominated the surrounding neighborhood. Built in 1924, the building screamed *Fear All Who Enter Here.* To me the structure's message was clear—*You are here to get an education. Don't even think about having fun*—but perhaps I was reading too much into the three-story building's austere façade. I just didn't feel welcomed by the increasing narrow staircase designed to funnel students and visitors into tall metal doors, blackened by decades of doing their job in the middle of a city of well over a million.

In an era of heightened school security, I was shocked to find one of those doors unlocked. The weight of the door might keep weaklings out, but even I managed to pull it open and step into the cavernous lobby. Maybe the principal thought any wrongdoers would melt under the unwavering stare of St. Theresa and back away. Personally, I would have found a lock more effective than a statue—even an oversized one sporting a beatific smile that challenged others to match her obvious piety.

I slipped by the oversized sculpture and started down a dimly lit hallway where I found myself in front of the office. The door was locked although the area was still lit. I knocked on the glass window, got no answer, and then, amazed that no one stopped me, wandered the marble-floored hallways looking for a staff member or student who could point me to Sister Rita Douglas. I made two turns but it appeared that both the kids and the teachers had cleared out for the day.

The high school felt big, intimidating, unlike the small,

suburban academy I attended. The current student body, not much larger than the one at my alma mater, must have rattled around in the old building. St Theresa's had survived several cost-cutting efforts by the archdiocese but probably wouldn't survive the next round.

When I turned the third corner I saw a human form. The custodian. Well, the custodian or a burglar. The man was fiddling with a lock on a classroom door. I didn't think a burglar would have his name stitched on his shirt, so I approached Hank without fear.

"I'm looking for Sister Rita Douglas. Is she still here?"

Hank didn't look away from his work. "Oh, Sister Rita. She'll be here. She's always here. Talk about a dedicated woman. You'll find her in room 205. Go up those stairs right there." He directed me with a point of his screwdriver.

I started toward the stairs and then remembered. "You know the front door is unlocked. That's how I got in."

The man didn't seem as much concerned as angry as he charged towards the front of the school. He was mumbling something about careless jerks as he passed by me. I don't think he heard the thank-you I threw at his back as I headed upstairs.

In an old fashioned classroom with old-fashioned desks, I spotted a new-style nun identified as a religious only by a small crucifix hanging around her neck. I bet she hadn't worn a bright pink skirt, loud flowered blouse and white pumps when she taught Seth. The little boy never would have seen the thick curly hair that was now mostly gray. It, like any indication of the nun's form, would have been hidden under a bulky habit. Then what should have been obvious hit me: I hadn't seen Sister Rita in the class photo. The students had posed with the parish priests. The nuns, who had worked with those students seven hours a day, five days a week for nine months a year were not included. I felt indignation on their behalf but

Sister Rita did not appear to harbor any bad feelings towards anyone. She hummed a happy tune as she worked, a serene smile on her face.

Sister Rita was pinning a Phillies poster to the bulletin board headed *Have a Wonderful Summer* when she noted my presence. She jumped.

"I am so sorry. I didn't mean to scare you."

"No problem. I didn't hear you. I don't hear too well these days. Can I help you with something?"

"I'm sorry to interrupt."

"Don't worry. I've done this for so many years, I could carry it off in my sleep. I'm just getting the room ready for summer school. When you've been decorating classrooms as long as I have, you get the knack of making a single poster that says good-bye to one class and welcome to the next." A warm smile provided the period at the end of her sentence.

"My name is Tracy Shaw. I'm a teacher too. Well, trying to be. I teach one college class," I said as if she would care and then moved on to something that might interest her. "Seth Timmons's mother told me you were his teacher the year he died. I was wondering if I could talk to you about him."

Sister Rita Douglas appeared to be in her sixties which meant she must have been close to a child herself when she was teaching Seth. I was asking her to think back over dozens and dozens of classes. Nonetheless, she answered immediately. "Seth Timmons. My heavens. That goes back a long time."

"You remember Seth?" My voice conveyed more admiration than shock.

The expression that covered her face was kind not unlike the one carved onto St. Theresa's face. "He's in my prayers every day. Not that he needs them. When you are a teacher, you learn how to spot the genuinely good boys. I was only a very young sister when I taught Seth, but even then I realized Seth was one of them." She smiled at the recollection. "I never got to know him well. He died in the first month of the school year. He was new to the class so I made a special effort to make him feel welcome. He told me about all the friends he had in Illinois and how he missed them, but he was glad he and his mother returned to Philadelphia so she could be near her father. I remember his solemn little face when he told me fathers are very important."

"He sounds like a very nice little boy."

"He was. May I ask why we are talking about Seth all these years later?"

I told her more about my class to explain why Helen Mitchell had known to approach me.

"And you do all this just so your students know more about Seth?"

"It started out that way. Now I just want to find the truth."

"And you believe learning about Seth might help?"

"You never know what will help. I have other questions, but I would simply like to know what he was like. To hear about him from someone who knew him."

"He seemed so sweet. One time," her smile disappeared, "he was very upset because he had gotten a low grade on a test, something like an eighty-five. Other children would have been thrilled. I tried to comfort him, to assure him that he had not done badly. He told me he had to do better because he didn't want to make his mother any sadder than she was. He said his father had told him to take care of her." Her smile returned. "He took the request very seriously."

"He sounds almost too good to be true."

"I am sure he was just a regular kid. Most likely his highly visible gentleness was a reaction to his father's death. Mr. Timmons had died so recently. I don't think Seth had even begun to recover when he arrived at St.

Margaret's. He seemed to be an exceptionally nice boy."
Her eyes glowed remembering him.

"I guess you knew Ralphie Barker as well."

The joy left her face and was replaced with sadness. "I suppose he might need my prayers more than Seth. I pray for him every day as well. Such a tragedy for both families. Seth's mother and Ralphie Barker's sister." She got lost in her thoughts. I hated to call her back but the silence was getting awkward.

"Do you believe Ralphie Barker was guilty?"

"Because I pray for him? It's true, a guilty man would need prayers more than a guiltless one, but I pray that Ralphie was innocent. I never knew him to be anything but a kind and gentle soul."

"Had he worked for the school for a long time?"

"The year Seth died was only my second at St. Margaret's. I recall Ralphie worked there at least one year before I did. Maybe more."

"Did anyone suspect he had a violent side to him?"

"I saw Ralphie around school almost every day. He was always there, in the background, cleaning up, fixing what he could. Ralphie never showed any sign of anger, let alone violence. His disposition was amazing given the way some of the students taunted him, but he never retaliated—in word or deed. No one ever said a single word about him that made me doubt my judgment. I mean before . . . . And I didn't trust a lot of the speculation that went on afterward."

"So you never saw Ralphie behave in a threatening way to any of the children?"

"Never. That's why when it all happened, I was so . . ." She shook her head. "I felt so bad for his sister. I chatted with her on a few occasions when she accompanied Ralphie to school events. Concerts. Plays. That type of thing. I only saw her once after it happened. She had a very small, very private funeral at the Protestant church where Ralphie sang when he was younger. Several of the sisters went. *I* found it hard to believe he was guilty. As I said, I never knew him to be anything but kind and gentle."

The repetition in her description of Ralphie sounded a bit rehearsed. "Did you ever see trouble between Seth and Ralphie?"

"Trouble?"

"Was Seth ever mean to Ralphie?"

A gentle smile covered her face. "I thought I was the only one he told about that. He was such a nice little boy."

*****Sister Rita*****
September, 1964

It broke her heart to see Seth Timmons looking so dejected. All the other pupils had left on their walks home, but Seth remained alone in the empty school. The small boy, made even shorter by the droop of his shoulders, appeared tiny as he came down the tall hallway. She was afraid he might burst into tears before he reached her.

"Seth, are you okay?"

Seth fought back his emotions but he couldn't get a single word out.

Sister Rita knelt and held him in place with a hand on each of his arms. "Tell me." Oops, that sounded too much like a command. She softened her words and her tone. "You can tell me. Why are you upset? I can see that you are."

"I did something really bad."

She could not imagine Seth doing anything truly bad. He was new to the school but she didn't expect time to reveal another side of the seemingly ideal student. She'd only been teaching a few years but she had a sixth sense about children. "Do you want to talk about it?"

Seth shook his head.

"Sometimes it helps when we talk about our problems. I know it helps me."

Seth wouldn't let his eyes meet hers.

"Do you want to sit down?"

That he would do. Seth followed her to the wooden bench just inside the door, the one the older sisters used to keep an eye on the action in the playground.

"Now, tell me. Whatever you did can't be that bad, can it?"

"It was mean."

You can tell me." She pulled a handkerchief from the deep creases of her habit. She was always armed with extras for situations like this one.

"Mr. Barker, he is really nice to me."

"Mr. Barker is a very good man."

"You know kids bark at him."

"Yes, that's not very nice."

Seth's voice shook as he made his confession. "I barked at him today. I wanted the other kids to like me." He held the handkerchief to his nose and sniffed but held back the tears.

"And you know that was wrong to do?"

He nodded and a few tears threatened to overflow his eyes. The little boy blew his nose hard.

Sister Rita leaned down so her head was close to his. "You don't have to do things you think are wrong to make friends."

A single tear ran down each of Seth's cheeks.

"Do you feel sad?"

He sniffled and nodded.

She felt sure he was referring to more than his encounter with Ralphie, but that was all she could try to fix. "I'm sure if you tell Mr. Barker you are sorry he will understand."

*****

"Do you know if Seth ever apologized to Ralphie?"

"I suspect he did. I didn't get a chance to ask but I met his eyes a few days later in class and he nodded and gave me a big smile."

"Do you recall when this happened?"

Sister Rita shook her head. "Sorry."

"Was it just before Seth died?"

"He was with us such a short time." She was right. The event had to have happened close to the date of Seth's death.

"Did you ever observe Ralphie and Seth together?"

"In the same place, probably. Interacting? I don't think so. That was a long time ago but, given the circumstances, I am sure any memories would have stuck with me."

"Did you tell the police about this incident?"

"I didn't speak to the police about Seth or Ralphie. Maybe they would have come to talk to the sisters if Ralphie hadn't died."

"Did you ever consider that this incident might have provided Ralphie with a motive?"

"I prayed that it didn't."

So it had occurred to her. I didn't press. "The other boys who were with Seth the night he died, were they in your class? Mikey Sawyer?" I asked.

"Him I remember. He was a pain in the neck as a kid, but he's been very supportive of our causes."

"Causes?"

"We kept St. Margaret's functioning for a few years after it was scheduled for closure. He was a big part of that effort. Now he helps other schools, including this one. He donates prizes when we have fund-raisers. Tickets. Hats. Balls. Bats. That type of thing."

"So you're in touch with him?"

The nun shrugged. "Me. Other sisters. With his secretary actually and then mostly via e-mail."

"You said he was a bad kid."

"Not bad. Annoying. He had an attitude. His mother had married a policeman. I remember his stepfather was great. I know that eventually there was a divorce, but perhaps having that role model, even for a short period of time, saved him. He tried to work with the boy, keep him away from the wrong crowd."

"Keep him away from Sonny Taylor?"

No smile on Sister Rita's face at the mention of Sonny Taylor's name. "That one." She shook her head. "He was well-known in the convent. I never believed in striking a child but some of the older sisters wore out their rulers on him and then sent him to the principal's office where Mother Superior used her yardstick to drive home whatever point needed to be made. He just did not know how to stay out of trouble." She gazed into my eyes with an intensity that begged for understanding. "You do know that was another time and corporal punishment is no longer permitted in our schools. It hasn't been in a very long time."

I nodded with an exaggerated motion. It seemed very important to her that I understand.

"But back then . . ." she shook her head with regret. "Poor Sonny kept putting himself in harm's way. I felt sympathy. He had a horror-show for a mother. She tried to put on a good face but I doubt she fooled many people. At least for very long. The kid was terrified of her. I guess she bullied him, so her son bullied others. I tried to get Sonny to confide in me, but he would barely speak unless he was ranting about something." She let out a sharp breath. "I wish I could forget *him*."

"Did you happen to teach Linda Lockwood?"

"Linda Lockwood." I could see the nun's brain working. "Was she the little girl who was at the party with Seth that last night?"

I nodded.

"She was in my class. A very nice girl." Again, she

smiled remembering her student.

"Did she tell you anything about the night Seth died?"

"No. I don't recall that we ever spoke about what happened to Seth. My memory says Linda and I only spoke about schoolwork."

It had been worth a shot. Alex would be disappointed but what did he expect? I didn't believe a 1964 girl would talk to a nun about what well may have been her first kiss, but I'd hoped.

Chapter 26

"New term starting already? It looks like someone has been working hard." Alex affected the tone of approval generally directed at two-year-olds.

"I thought a short term would be easier but three nights a week? Monday, Wednesday, Friday." I repeated Friday. "That explains why I am sitting here on a Saturday morning reading my students' character profiles."

"Did you sleep down here?"

The evidence, my pillow's imprint on my face, yesterday's clothes on my body, and students' papers on the floor around me, suggested that I did. "I have to give fewer assignments."

"Did you make coffee yet?" He sniffed as he swiveled his head around searching for the scent of coffee.

"I haven't moved."

"Since I'm up . . ." he disappeared into the kitchen and I dozed until he returned with a *Hostess with the Mostest* mug for me and a *Party Party Party* mug for him.

"Is that pile of papers the reason you haven't mentioned your investigation lately? Nothing new?"

"Nothing. I hoped Sonny Taylor would call sooner. It's been a month."

"Maybe he doesn't smoke."

I called for an explanation.

"Smokers run through their commissary money quickly. If he doesn't smoke he might not feel the same urgency."

"Or he doesn't want to talk to me."

"Very possible but don't take it personally. Maybe he just doesn't need anything yet. Wait until he runs out of junk food."

"I must say he did not look like a smoker, a caffeine lover or a junk-food addict what with the obvious body-building and all." I didn't sound hopeful.

"He looked clean. You know, like he used a lot of soap." Alex offered. "Do they have to buy their own toiletries?"

I didn't know but I assumed so. "It isn't as if their cells are stocked. He's not living in a suite at the Four Seasons."

"Maybe he'll call when he runs out of deodorant." Alex sounded cheerful.

I was doubting Sonny would ever call. "Maybe, when I said I would deposit something in his commissary account, I should have mentioned a dollar amount, a big dollar amount."

"He might still call." Alex sounded supportive but not convinced.

I doubted it. "So, Alex, do you have something special on for today?"

"Free as a bird."

"How would you feel about a ride in the country and a stop for lunch? I'll drive."

He stared.

"I just had my car tuned up. It's fine."

Alex always found my old car acceptable when he wanted a ride to the beach, but the vehicle's age became an issue if he wasn't sure he liked the destination.

"It's thirteen years old and has two hundred thousand miles on it." He protested.

"That is never a problem for you when we head to the ocean. Come on. I'll buy lunch."

"I'll put on some shoes." He disappeared up the staircase.

Alex and I had a leisurely lunch in a quiet restaurant in the quaint town of Skippack. The conversation was about our travel histories. I did not raise the topic of my project, even once. Then, as we walked out of the restaurant, I suggested a ride on the back roads.

"I want to look in some of the shops." Alex protested.

We compromised. After we'd walked in and out of what felt like a dozen stores, Alex bought a painting for the condo he was still searching for. Then we got into the car and headed west on Route 73 into the country. We hadn't gone far when Alex spun in his seat to look past me.

"What are you up to?"

"Me." I played dumb. "Nothing."

"Did you happen to notice the rather impressive structure on our left, the one with the tall walls and the guard towers?" He challenged me.

"It's hard to see with those trees."

"You are unaware that we are riding by Graterford Prison, the current residence of Sonny Taylor?"

"Well, I guess I realized the prison was around here somewhere."

"You guess? You knew exactly where to find the big house, but what is the point of coming here? We can't just drop by to say hi, you know."

"Don't be ridiculous." I tried to get a look at the prison.

"Do you really believe you'll spot Sonny out for a weekend stroll? That's not how these places work. See those high walls. They're thick and there are no doors in them. And if someone—let's say Sonny—did get a hankering for a walk in the sunshine, the guards in those towers would shoot him. So, I'm figuring not a lot of inmates just step outside because it's a gorgeous day."

"Are you finished?"

"Probably not, but I'm taking a break."

I thanked him and made a left turn. After a while, the residential area turned into woodlands that I presumed adjoined the prison.

Alex eyed one of the few houses along the road. "Oooooo. I don't think I'd want to be here in the middle of the night. Alone in my house. Surrounded by darkness. And then I hear a creak on the steps to the porch and I say to myself, 'Did the guards remember to lock all the cells tonight?'"

"Don't creep me out," I begged Alex. I could envision the scenario on the lonely road and wished I had put up the top. I stepped on the gas to get us to a crossroads.

"Don't even think about turning left." Alex strained to read the signage. "No thoroughfare. When the Department of Corrections speaks, I listen."

"I am not going to go up to the prison gates." I drove straight ahead and made a left to continue our circle around the penitentiary grounds.

"You know you've had a guard on your tail since we passed the entrance."

I glanced at the SUV in my rear-view mirror. "How do you know it's a guard?"

"Well, who else would be driving the lone car out of a prison, alone, in the middle of the afternoon? And, he's still on your tail."

"Alex, it could be any kind of person. A lawyer. A social worker. A lawyer." I ran out of ideas. "Don't freak me out. We turned at a dead end. We had two choices: right or left. There was a fifty-percent chance that car would follow us."

"Especially after the cameras detected your car circling the big house." He looked ahead. "Wow, now I know why they call it that. That's a really large complex and it looks like they're making it bigger. I wouldn't want to disappear inside those walls." He forced some phony concern into his voice. "You haven't seen any of those movies where you get yourself thrown inside so you can break someone out, have you? Because if you're considering that approach I would like to make it clear that method only works in Hollywood. And not that well, if you take into account that the movie may only take two hours but will always include one or more sequences where calendar pages fly into the air. You know January, February, March then 1947, 1948, 1949 . . ."

"Okay. Okay. I get the message." I told him not to worry. I wasn't planning to trespass with or without him.

"I hope not because, if I am not mistaking, the sign says *no picnicking*. He paused and forced a theatrically pensive look onto this face. "Do you think they have a significant problem with picnickers?"

"Well, they won't have one with me. I just wanted a nice ride in the country."

He sat quietly for a full minute. "This is about your alleged psychic powers, isn't it?"

"I don't claim to have psychic powers. You tell me that I do."

"Number one, you should know better than to listen to anything I say. Number two, circling Graterford Prison, even with the top down, will not make Sonny call you, no matter how hard you focus. Your powers will not work here. The walls are too thick."

Turns out Alex was wrong. My powers did work, albeit after a five-day delay and after I had despaired of hearing from Sonny Taylor. The call came on a Thursday morning.

After I accepted the charges for the call, the robotic voice was replaced by a human voice. "You didn't send a picture." Despite his words, the caller sounded angry, not flirtatious.

"I didn't know I was supposed to." After all, I wasn't looking for a date.

"I like to know what kind of chick I'm talking to."

"What do you want me to look like?" I wanted to sound friendly, not seductive. I might have failed.

"What? Did I call a sex-line?" He chuckled.

I said nothing.

"Okay, I want you to be tall, tan, twenty-two and blond. I like blonds. But not too skinny. I like voluptuous."

"You hit the nail on the head." One nail. I wasn't too skinny. Technically if I dressed right and posed appropriately, I might even look voluptuous. As far as the other nails went? I'd never be tall but, in summer, I might have had a few blond highlights in my brown hair. And tan? I did have pink cheeks from a recent walk along the Schuylkill. As far as age went, I'd been twenty-two once. Why clarify? Who was Sonny to quibble?

He chuckled. In truth, he grunted but I decided to consider the noise a laugh. "What do you want?"

"My call is not about me. I'm just researching a 1964 crime, Seth Timmons's murder."

"Oh," he dragged the word out. "It would still be nice to know who I'm talking to." His tone gave no indication he was upset because I mentioned Seth. I had violated some basic protocol of prison correspondence by failing to include a photo.

"I can send you one, but since you called I hope we can talk today."

"I don't know what I can tell you about the Timmons kid. We told everything we knew to Mikey's dad."

Yeah. That must have been one tough grilling.

"We were a bunch of seventh-graders watching baseball. That's all. Mikey Sawyer saw it as a tragedy. The game. To the rest of us losing that game was just one more bum deal."

"You had no other issues that night?"

"I was what, twelve, thirteen. I didn't have issues. Issues! You're beginning to sound like my mother."

"I talked to your mother."

"My mom? She married yet?" He seemed amused by his question.

"You don't keep in touch?"

The amused tone vanished from his voice. "My mother thinks I ruined her life."

"How so?"

"She believes I destroyed her relationship with her one true love." I heard a snort. "My mother had a new love of her life every week. But John Lockwood had the most money. He was there the night Seth died."

"Did you ruin the relationship?"

"I didn't mean to but I did. I had a mean temper in those days."

"And you took it out on John Lockwood?"

The silence lasted an uncomfortably long time. I fought hard to keep from breaking it.

Finally, Sonny did. "How much money you gonna put in my commissary account?"

I upped the ante and repeated the question.

"Not on John Lockwood. In front of John Lockwood."

****Sonny Taylor****
September 30, 1964

The party would have been okay if his mother hadn't invited Seth. The new kid in school was a pain. He didn't care about the game, about the Phillies. He only cared about Linda. Little creep. Why did girls like those puny little kids with pretty faces? They didn't seem to like him that much. He didn't understand. His mother said he was handsome. She called him my handsome boy. *But he knew not to trust what she said. She told everyone their house was spectacular, but he knew theirs was smaller than most of the houses in the neighborhood, and that the neighborhood was nothing special.*

But his mother liked to pretend everything was always perfect. Like now when she plastered a smile on her face as she led Mr. Grady down the stairs into the rec room.

154

"Mikey, your dad is here." Her voice sounded sickeningly sweet.

Mr. Grady said hello and then told Mikey to get his things together. *"You too, Seth. We're neighbors. I can walk you home."*

Thank God. He could get rid of Seth, although it was kind of a shame Mikey had to leave—even if he was a pain about the Phillies. Mikey was his best friend. His only friend.

"But Mr. Grady will stay and have a drink, won't you, Jack." His mother continued to use that syrupy voice she used whenever a man was around.

"Sure."

Damn it. The game was over. When your dream of a pennant in your town has just been crushed, who wants company? Who wants to listen to Mikey go on and on about how even though the Phillies didn't clinch the pennant the team could still get to the World Series? What did it matter? They would still lose there. He wanted to move on, think about football. Not that he cared about the Eagles. Why should he? Tonight proved he could never count on anything good happening. It proved you could count on something bad happening.

At least Mr. Grady was nice. He said hello to every kid in the room. A lot of parents ignored Sonny but Mikey's father never did.

Mr. Lockwood stood to shake Mr. Grady's hand. Sonny knew that was what gentlemen did. His mom was always telling him what a gentleman Mr. Lockwood was. She always had a goofy smile on her face when she talked about Mr. Lockwood. But Sonny didn't mind. He liked Mr. Lockwood.

"Sad night. Did you watch the game?" Mr. Lockwood asked Mr. Grady.

"Yeah. Phils can still tie for first and maybe get into the Series."

Now Sonny knew where Mikey got his idea about how they could pull it off. Mikey's father went on and on about some results over the next few days that would have to happen including the Mets, the new loser team from New York, beating the Cards. "If the Phillies make it, Mikey and I have tickets lined up."

While Sonny tried to figure out an angle on how to tag along, Mr. Lockwood's reaction revealed less self-interest. "I hope you get to use them. Let me get you a drink."

Sonny's mom patted Lockwood's arm. "You sit down, John. I'll take care of Jack." She grabbed Mr. Grady's arm as if they were going to walk down the aisle at a wedding or something. "Let me get you something nice." She led him to the small room where she'd jerry-rigged a tiny bar. Sonny figured so she could drink while she was doing the laundry. For someone who wasn't very interested in housework, his mother sure did a lot of wash.

Sonny leaned over and whispered in Mikey's ear. "We all need a little something. I'll go in to get us cokes. After my mom gets your dad his drink, I'll put some Vodka in ours."

Sonny waited a couple of minutes but his mother didn't come out from behind the folding doors she always kept closed as if he didn't know she kept more than detergent in the locked cabinet. He slid the folding door aside and stopped dead. He couldn't believe it. His mom was kissing Mr. Grady. Her arms were wrapped around his neck and his hands were moving all over her. Right there. Not a first down away from Mr. Lockwood. He felt his fists clench and his face grow red.

*****

"I came out of that room a raving maniac." He sounded exhausted by his recollections.

I felt sympathy for the kid that Sonny had been. "Did you tell anyone why?"

"My mother and Grady had to know. They must have heard me slam the door. It was one of those cheap pleated things, only plastic, but, man, I gave it one hard push. I guess making so much noise wasn't smart but I wanted that door shut. I didn't want Mr. Lockwood to know what my mother was up to. It worked. No one saw."

"And you didn't tell anyone, even Mikey."

"Funny. I wasn't real mature but I knew telling him would ruin everything. He'd hate me. He'd hate my mother. Plus, even then, I appreciated the value of having info to hold over someone's head. I was probably smarter than I gave myself credit for. I was sure I was smarter than other people gave me credit for."

"So you didn't tell Seth?"

"Why the hell would I tell him? I didn't tell anyone. I couldn't risk that. I believed Mr. Lockwood could replace the father that disappeared out of my life. I liked Mr. Lockwood more than my mother did."

"Did Lockwood know how you felt?"

I detected bitterness in his laugh. "The way I acted? He never would have guessed."

"Did he say anything to you about the way you acted?"

"No. He cleared out of there like a bat out of hell."

"And he broke up with your mom that night?"

"He didn't say so, but I never saw him again. My mom tried to hold on but he didn't want a woman with a maniac son. I played it all wrong."

"So it wasn't Seth Timmons you were angry with?"

I began to doubt that he would ever answer when he finally spoke. "I wasn't mad at him but when he showed up that night, I didn't like it. I didn't like him. I gave him grief, stupid, kid stuff but the worst I could manage. I know what you are thinking but at twelve, I didn't have my own gun so I couldn't have shot him even if I wanted to, which I didn't."

I was interested in what he did do, not what he didn't do. "What variety of grief did you give him?"

"Kid stuff. But I didn't hurt him if that's what you're getting at. I was a kid, not a creep."

Nothing said he couldn't be both.

"Don't look my way, lady. The perv did it."

"Did you see anything that night? Did you see Ralphie Barker?"

He hadn't. "How could I? I didn't go outside, but I know he did it. Not just because he had a thing for little boys like everyone says but because Seth was mean to him. Seth laughed at him with the rest of us."

The incident Sister Rita told me about.

"Ralphie had a reason to hate little Sethie Timmons." He paused. "So what are you wearing?"

I sputtered.

"Just a little joke, unless you send a picture. Then? Who knows?"

I was pretty sure I knew. I thanked Sonny and said good-bye. After I hung up, I realized I'd never asked about the kiss. It just never seemed like the right moment.

Chapter 27

Standing in the rundown hallway of Grady's low-rent apartment building, I was too scared to knock. Not that I was afraid of Grady. I was reluctant to see the place he called home, to become a witness to his decline. How did Jack Grady descend from middle-class comfort to this?

I raised a fist but before I could knock, the ex-cop opened the door, wide until he saw me. Then he yanked it close to his body. He was dressed to go outside with a straw fedora on his head. "You know it works better if you actually touch the door with your knuckle."

I chuckled. Even I recognized the sound as insincere and nervous.

"To what do I owe this honor?" His sarcastic tone indicated he viewed my visit as anything but an honor. He slipped through the narrow opening he'd left and made a great show of locking the door behind him. He said, "I didn't think I'd be seeing you again." I heard, "I was hoping I wouldn't be seeing you again."

"I checked the *Biding Time* first."

"I'm late getting to the office today. Some days I just find it hard to get out of the house and start drinking on time." He raised his eyebrows to appear playful but I detected no joy in his eyes. "Walk with me. I don't want to lose my seat at the bar."

I followed him down the stairs and out the door onto the sidewalk. Luckinbill Lane matched the image that I, as a suburban kid, had of city streets. Narrow and flat. No lawns. No shrubs. No trees. No vegetation unless I counted the ragged knee-high hedge of weeds in the crevice where the road met the curb. The only other adornment was litter, graffiti and a visible layer of dust. The gray sky with dark, hanging clouds completed the drab image. One more time I asked myself how Grady had come to this.

We walked slowly down the street, but age wasn't holding Grady back. He just didn't seem anxious to get where he was going.

"I assume you have another question about Seth Timmons." The prospect seemed to tire him.

"I wanted to ask you about Marcia Taylor."

"I hoped I'd never hear that name again. What about her?"

"Sonny Taylor told me he saw you kissing Marcia Taylor the night of the party."

He stopped and stared at me. His mouth was smiling. His eyes were not. "Why would my kissing Marcia Taylor have anything to do with Seth Timmons's murder?" He tried to sound casual and amused but I sensed he felt neither.

"I don't know. I hoped you could tell me."

"The answer is it doesn't." He took a few steps and stopped again. "What are you doing, Ms. Shaw? I know you told me about your class and the students' need-to-know, but why would they need to know that I kissed Marcia Taylor?"

"I have them write character profiles. I give them a few facts about Victim, Victim's Parents, Classmate 1, Classmate 2, etc. They take it from there assigning personalities, pasts, motivations—all from the same point. Most importantly, they develop a character who lives in that place and time. I could present them with a character, a nameless abstract, who is based on Sonny and his perception of the night. And, Sonny told me he went nuts when he saw you two together." I didn't expect Grady to buy my explanation, but, despite a lack of confidence, I tried to sell it.

Grady began moving again at an even slower gait. "I didn't know he saw us together. I wondered why he blew. And trust me, he blew. A major tantrum. When I saw Sonny explode, I got my son and the Timmons kid out of there right away. So, there's no way Sonny killed him."

"While we're talking about characters, I had heard Marcia Taylor was involved with John Lockwood. I was surprised to hear you had a relationship with Marcia Taylor."

"Relationship? Give me a break. I had nothing in common with that freak. Not that it's any of your business and don't give me that character development crap."

"So why . . . ?" I got part of my question out.

"Was I was kissing her?

I nodded.

"Maybe I wasn't. Maybe she was kissing me." He tried to change the mood by forcing a flirtatious expression onto his face.

"Sonny didn't see it that way."

"Look I was a guy. I was a jerk. Maybe I didn't resist the way I should have. She was a widow, she was hot and she was game. Not like the other wives in the neighborhood."

I got the picture. I wanted to say, *See, that's sociological context*, but I was afraid to interrupt.

"I loved my wife, been faithful for almost ten years. My life was routine, boring and when I looked ahead I saw forty. So Marcia looked appealing. I was kind of young and very stupid. Believe me, I never kissed her again after that fiasco. Never saw her again for that matter. Not that she could see me, anyway. She and the kid moved away the year Seth died."

He paused but he wasn't finished. I waited.

"I spotted her once. I was sure the woman was Marcia. I have no idea where she lived, but she was playing a slot machine in an Atlantic City casino. She was maybe fifty, and not a good fifty. That age didn't look the same on my generation as it does today, but on Marcia it looked worse. Tight pants. Low cut blouse. Gobs of makeup. She was still working it. I watched her for a couple of minutes and couldn't believe I had ever seen anything appealing about her, but my amazement had nothing to do with her failing looks. I've come to understand what a phony, what a manipulator she was." From the look on his face, it appeared the memory of the woman who had threatened his marriage caused him pain, although it might have been his own behavior that was the root of his discomfort.

We had arrived at the Biding Time Tavern. He stopped and turned to face me.

"Listen to me, Ms. Shaw. You are out of your league. Go ahead. Give your students *some basic facts*. Then, let them make up what they will, but you're not a detective, let alone a cop. It's okay when you're dealing with me. Appearances to the contrary, I'm a stand-up guy. Others might not brush off your insinuations so easily. You could end up in trouble."

Grady did not invite me to join him in his office.

Chapter 28

Grady's warning didn't make me feel intimidated. It made me feel energized.

On Friday morning, I found Alex in the basement, in the space where the homeowners had created a gym that he and I generally ignored. He was on the treadmill. "Oh my God. I thought I was awake but I must be asleep. I am dreaming I see Tracy Shaw in the exercise area."

I ignored him and climbed on the stationary bike with a level of unease that suggested I'd never taken that action before.

"What brings you to the gym so early in the morning?"

I explained why my talks with Sonny and Grady had inspired me. When I finished Alex put his feet on either side of the belt and let it pass between them. "What evidence do you think you have?"

I summarized the night's events. "The party was not a simple get-together. There was intrigue."

"None of which had a thing to do with Seth. He left with Jack Grady."

"Yes, but so much had gone on."

"So much that had nothing to do with Seth."

"But why didn't Grady tell me about it when I first met him."

"Because it had nothing to do with Seth."

I understood the exasperation in Alex's voice but I couldn't let go of the thought that I was onto something. My speed dropped to a leisurely pace; I saw the register drop below 10 mph and head downward. "I just feel there is more there. Grady and Lockwood after the same woman."

163

Alex started walking again. "Nothing to do with Seth."

"Sonny's rage had to do with Seth."

"He took it out on Seth but he was angry with the adults. Besides Seth had left with Grady, and Sonny said he never went out."

"*He* would, wouldn't he?"

"What do you think? Sonny sneaked out of his house, found a gun, ran to Seth's, knocked on the door, without waking up Seth's mother who was asleep in the living room, talked Seth into taking a walk, and then killed and violated him because he was mad at his mother and Jack Grady?"

"When you put it that way." I pedaled harder. "But there is something there. I cannot believe the incident is as simple as it appeared. I think Ralphie was railroaded."

"That may be true, but that doesn't mean it had anything to do with the get-together at the Taylors'."

Alex was right. At least, it was possible he was.

"You, yourself, said it could be a crime of opportunity by a stranger. Or maybe, just maybe, Ralphie was guilty. While you've been running around investigating what people did the night of the party, have you ever tried to find out what Ralphie did? Maybe he was home watching porn getting himself worked up so he did become capable of the crime."

"Sitting home watching porn in 1964 wasn't that easy to do. No VCRs. No DVDs. No Internet."

"That is not my point. His sister says he didn't have any prurient interests. Even if he had a twelve-year-old's mind, he had a twenty-something-year-old body. You don't really know what he was like." Alex shook his head as he increased his pace.

I didn't argue. "All I can say is I am feeling inspired." Not so inspired that I rushed into taking the next step in my investigation. Friday I was busy with class preparation and Saturday was busy with self-preparation. I had a hot date. Hard to believe but 6 PM had come and gone and Marcus had not begged off. As I headed downtime, I felt confident that this time he would show and Alex would have to eat humble pie.

I was humming "You'll Never Walk Alone," Ralphie's favorite, as I turned the corner from Juniper Street onto Drury, a thoroughfare bearing the name *street* that could more appropriately be called an alley. Not only was Marcus walking from the opposite end, he had a bouquet of bright yellow flowers in his hand and a big smile on his face.

I remembered why I'd agreed to meet him after all the excuses and delays. He was very cute. Not classically handsome. Cute. The eyes were a little too wide apart, the nose was a little too small, and the mouth was a little too big which explained why the smile seemed so broad. He'd dressed for the occasion, better than I had I expected. I could see him more clearly as I stopped in front of McGillin's and waited. He raised his hand and waved, tentatively. I read the gesture as saying *Can you believe I am here at last?*

I'm not sure if I noticed his fading smile or the passing van first. Drury Street is barely wide enough to handle cars and, although the vehicle got by me without incident, I saw the concern on Marcus's face. Concern and puzzlement. His smile had vanished. His friendly wave changed and seemed to be saying, run for your life or something similar. He was pulled into the grip of two men in black so quickly that I didn't hear what he yelled at me as he disappeared into the van's wide side door. I'd like to say I ran behind the car waving frantically screaming "Stop that car." I did not for a couple of reasons. One, I did not expect a vehicle that had just been part of an abduction to stop at my command and drop the victim off. For another, I appeared to have lost the ability to move. My feet were glued to the ground by fear. In my defense,

I did have the presence of mind to check the license plate or would have if there had been one.

"Are you okay?" Ellie Shields materialized beside me.

"How? Why? Here?" I waved my hand at her with actions supporting the confusion in my mind.

"How did I get here? I'm a regular. Remember?"

"Sure," I said but I wasn't convinced.

"We'd better call this in." Ellie pulled out a mobile phone and called 911 and I heard sirens heading our way within a minute.

"Are you going to put this online?" Maybe that shouldn't have been my first question, but my immediate reaction was fear of being exposed as the idiot who showed up for a date after constant rejection by some sort of disreputable character who disappeared before the nachos hit the table.

"You bet I am, but don't worry I will not tie it into your research on the Seth Timmons case. Why would I? You dragged it out so long, I assumed nothing was going to come of it."

Consumed by what had just happened, I didn't have any energy to focus on being insulted. I considered wandering down the street to collect my bouquet but figured the cops might consider the pile of flowers evidence, at least a marker of exactly where Marcus was grabbed. They wouldn't care about my need to get something out of this date. Alleged date.

Chapter 29

Alex, claiming I should not drive myself home, met me at the police station with a tight hug. "And to think you went to all the trouble of taking down your ponytail." He stroked the hair hanging loose to my shoulders.

"It's not a ponytail," I protested.

"It's not?"

"No. It's kind of an updo." I defended my usual hairstyle. Okay, my usual ponytail.

"Well, whatever you call it, it is certainly serviceable, but this hairdo is really lovely."

"Yep. Definitely worth the trouble for a trip to the police station." I eyed the cops, criminals, victims and witnesses swirling around us.

"There. There." He said the words as if comforting a baby. "Tell me what happened."

I told him the story, how my rendition of "You'll Never Walk Alone" was interrupted shortly after I turned the corner. He gave me another hug.

"For now it appears I will, despite Ralphie's inspirational musical preferences, be walking alone."

"But clearly that is much better than walking with Marcus." He released me from his arms. "I hate to say *I told you so*. Actually, I don't. I love saying it, but only because I know there is someone better right around the next corner."

I glared at him.

"Too soon for that analogy?" He grimaced.

Luckily for Alex, the cop who had interviewed me appeared from behind the locked doors and told me I was free to go. He thanked me for being a good citizen.

167

"You have my number if you need anything," I offered.

"Thank you. I don't think that will be necessary. We can take it from here." He flashed a perfunctory smile to dismiss us.

"Does my friend need some sort of protection? She was a witness."

The cop shook his head at Alex. "The perps had a chance to grab her. If they wanted her, they would have taken her. She's got nothing to worry about." His fake smile dismissed us.

The sky was dark when we set out to hail a cab back to my car. "You know, Alex, I still don't buy the theory you forced on the police. I don't accept that Marcus faked the entire incident to get out of the date."

"Yeah. They didn't buy it either." Alex waved down a passing taxi and we climbed in the back.

"Ellie Shields will write the truth."

"Does she know the truth?"

"She'll write what she witnessed and whatever she wormed out of the police. She promised not to use my name."

"You know," Alex defended himself, "the idea that he faked his own abduction is not necessarily a negative interpretation. Maybe he is a spy and maybe he realized by seeing you he was putting you in danger and maybe he did care for you and maybe that's why he needed to break up with you."

"He didn't need to break up with me. We never went out."

Alex glanced at the driver, held a finger to my lips and nodded towards the front of the taxi. Apparently, he found it possible that the cab driver worked with Marcus at the CIA or even worse for a foreign enemy. He waited until we were in my car to express his concerns. "Are you sure you're safe? There is the possibility he really was abducted."

"Do you think?" I used my best sarcastic tone.

"I'm really worried about you." Alex sounded sincere.

"Don't be. The cops aren't. That detective offered a persuasive argument. If the perps wanted me, they could have grabbed me at the same time. They didn't want me. The police officer who took my statement told me they'd call me if they needed a witness. And, given the send-off he gave us, I get the feeling I won't be hearing from them."

"And we'll never know the truth about Marcus."

"That will give me time to find the truth about Ralphie."

"After we eat." He patted my knee. "I'll buy you dinner. You know, to keep up your strength."

I understood the real reason. He wanted to make up for the dinner I missed with Marcus. "That guy is costing you a fortune."

"It is money I am very willing to spend." Once more he patted my knee as my grandfather might have if I had ever met him.

Alex drove my car to Chestnut Hill where we ate in one of our regular places and didn't say one word about Marcus or Seth Timmons. While Alex checked the bill, I pulled out my phone. "Ellie said she assumed I had given up on helping Ralphie Barker and maybe on some level, I have. I can't let that happen. Let me see what she put on her blog. I hope she kept her promise to keep my name out of it."

"What? You look stricken." Alex showed genuine concern. "Don't tell me Ellie Shields went ahead and put your name in. I hope only about this incident."

"No. She didn't mention me."

"That's what you wanted."

"She hasn't put anything up about this incident."

"Maybe she hasn't gotten around to it."

"She's updated her blog twice this evening about stories that just happened. I mean just within the past hour."

"Check tomorrow. She'll have put something up."

But I didn't think so. I didn't think Ellie was ever going to write about Marcus. "You know, Alex, I suspect Marcus might work for the CIA."

"Not necessarily. I never really discounted a drug cartel or organized crime. I just didn't want to scare you."

"That is not what frightens me. What I'm worried about is what was Ellie Shields doing there and who is she working for?"

Chapter 30

I had trouble falling asleep because I was worrying, not about Marcus, but about Ellie Shields. Was she at McGillin's simply by chance? What could she gain from following me? What was Ellie's angle? Was she trying to scoop me? I speculated that she believed my theory was correct but didn't trust me to prove it.

Energized by a competitive urge, I reactivated my investigation early. I figured I'd try to reach another attendee at the party, John Lockwood. I reached the correct John Lockwood on the eighth Florida number I tried. Turned out I'd called a cell phone. Lockwood explained he had already made his seasonal move from his condo in West Palm Beach to his condo at the Jersey Shore and then added it didn't matter because he didn't want to talk to me at either location.

Since he had basically told me to get lost, I didn't think slipping in a question about the possibility of his daughter kissing Seth would be appropriate or successful. I felt dejected as I ended the call.

"Well, you were on a winning streak if we discount the episode with Marcus and that was personal. I wouldn't feel bad because one person turned you down. Until now your success rate was incredible." Alex only stopped trying to cheer me up when my phone rang.

I heard John Lockwood's voice. "Does Susan Timmons know you are doing this?'

"She does."

"And she supports what you are doing?"

"Yes."

"Why? What is left to be said at this point? The boy is

dead. His killer is dead."

"I think she is interested in the truth."

"And you believe there is a different truth than the one we all accept?"

"I don't know. That is what I'm trying to discover."

"Do you feel I can help you find the truth?"

"I do."

"I'll call you back."

I turned to Alex. "Lockwood said he'd call me back."

"Sonny did. Eventually." He tried to sound encouraging.

The phone rang ten minutes later. I didn't hesitate. When John Lockwood asked me to schedule a meeting, I asked if he was free that afternoon. I was out of the house within a half-hour and headed for New Jersey.

I had never even heard of the town where Lockwood's retirement community was located and when I got a look at Seaside Meadows, I had a feeling the development had put the town on the map or at least provided the town with a reason for visitors to look for it on the map. I identified only a dozen buildings that were not part of the sprawling complex.

Ten miles from the nearest body of water, the gated community was as landlocked as possible for a town called Seaside anything. Seaside Meadows was full of mini-Taras, shortened to one floor but widened by two-car garages. Instead of hoop skirts and tails, the residents wore outfits in shades that made me crave sherbet: banana, raspberry, lime, blueberry. Every color looked great against deep tans and silver hair. My visible preference to wear black and my invisible need to work differentiated me from the residents.

I didn't know which house belonged to John Lockwood and never would. The guard gave me directions to the clubhouse at the end of a long, elegant driveway where my host would meet me. I parked near the entrance and made the trek to the plaza in front of a gleaming white antebellum mansion. Not long after I arrived, a tall, tan man parked his golf cart in one of the mini-spaces and, identifying me as the outsider, approached with long, easy strides. "Tracy Shaw?" He offered a bright smile.

"Yes."

"John Lockwood." This time he offered a warm handshake.

Based on appearances Lockwood was enjoying the type of retirement I could not look forward to—even if I ever found a full-time job to retire from. I calculated Lockwood was north of eighty but didn't figure on his being so handsome. The tall silver-haired man appeared distinguished in spite of his clothes in the required palate of pastels generally found in baby clothes. On him, the look worked. The pale blue shirt that matched his eyes flattered his skin tone.

"Ms. Shaw. Nice to meet you although I am a bit unsettled by the circumstances. After all these years, I still find it embarrassing to say I dated Marcia Taylor. And I am sure you realize that was why I was at her house that night." The blush visible through his tan confirmed he was telling the truth. "And, of course, it is upsetting to revisit the tragedy of Seth Timmons's death." He brushed off the sad memories quickly and wore a big smile as he led me to the clubhouse, all the while listing the benefits of living in the fifty-five plus community. He stopped dead at the building entrance and ceased his nervous chatter. His tone grew serious and more than a little melancholy.

"Maybe because I heard talk of the 1964 season on the radio, I have been thinking about Susan Timmons a lot lately and feeling guilty about letting her drift out of my life when her son died. I guess I was involved in my own issues. I didn't have room in my life for her problems too."

I believed him only because his face grew flushed yet again. He held the door open for me and I stepped into an elegant interior that reminded me of Independence Hall but with comfortable seating and piped-in music.

"You and Susan had been friends?" I asked as we strolled down a gallery with windows overlooking a formal garden.

"I was friends with her husband. Susan was quiet, almost timid but we got along. We did, however, have very little in common. I enjoyed seeing her with Bob, but after he passed away—my wife had died long before—I found it hard to make conversation. And after Seth was killed . . . ." His voice trailed off. He pointed outside to a stream of water rising and falling in time to some rhythm I couldn't figure out. "They try to make this place as pleasant as possible."

I suspected he wanted to add *but* . . . but he didn't. He stopped and gazed into the dancing waters.

"Bob Timmons was a great guy. Now, I'm used to losing friends but back then his death was such a shock I didn't know how to act, how to handle the situation, how to deal with Susan. You'd think I, of all people, would have known. I'd lost my wife. She died in childbirth when our only . . . when Linda was born, but I don't remember much about those days except that Bob was there for me. I should have been there for Susan. You've seen her?"

I nodded.

"How did she fare in life?"

I didn't offer an opinion. I stated facts.

He didn't hide his dismay or concern. "Still in the same house? Is that neighborhood safe?"

"I find Germantown to be a wonderfully diverse neighborhood." I defended my adopted hometown. "The block where she lives is beautiful. Not every block is."

"I picture her keeping her house as a memorial to the

few happy years in her life." His eyes asked if he was right, and begged to hear he was wrong.

I simply nodded.

"I should have been there for Susan. I have no excuse. Maybe I was afraid she expected me to step in when Bob died. Not so much for her, but for Seth. I knew that would have been the right thing to do. But I had my hands full with my daughter." I saw tears congregating in the rims of his eyes. "It was just the two of us." He straightened up, pulled himself together, and pointed at a second fountain. "Looks a little too much like Versailles for my taste."

As we strolled, he lapsed back into his sentimental recollections. "I didn't know what to do when Seth died. Such hardship. First Bob and then her only child. Two tragedies so close together. Seth seemed like a nice boy. I didn't see him often because he was so young when they moved away, but I kept in touch with Bob. He was worried because Seth was shy. Bob was working with him, building his confidence, playing sports with him."

Without a glance my way, Lockwood began to walk again and I followed.

"Seth was little, like Susan, and when he started school he was always the last to be picked for any sport. By sixth grade, Bob had turned him into a relatively decent baseball player, small but competent. Not long before he found out about his illness, Bob called about something— I can't remember what—and we talked a bit about Seth. He was excited that the kid was building up some strength in his shoulders and I saw it, that last night, at the Taylor house. He was. Bob thought Seth was going to have a great season and I think he might have, but by then Bob was sick."

We reached the entrance to an elegant room where Lockwood asked a very attentive hostess for a seat on the patio. She led us through an overdone dining room to a flagstone terrace with a striped awning protecting two dozen dining tables from the midday sun. The hostess offered us the spot closest to the fairway.

Lockwood made pleasant chit-chat with the waitress before we ordered drinks. He then explained the house specialties and his favorite items in excruciating detail before putting the menu aside and returning, unprompted, to the topic of Seth Timmons.

"When Susan and Seth came back to Philadelphia, I should have done something, anything. Susan's parents invited me over for a barbecue. I went and took my daughter, but I felt uncomfortable without Bob there. I sensed that seeing me made the family feel his loss even more. Except for marveling at what a brave front he put up at his father's funeral, I barely knew Seth at that age. All I can say for sure is that he was shy although Linda seemed to get along with him that night at the Taylor house. Of course, Linda got along with everyone." He smiled.

The waitress appeared with a gin and tonic for Lockwood and, for me, a fruity concoction with cherry, orange slice, and tiny umbrella but no alcohol.

I waited until Lockwood finished fending off the attentions of two female versions of himself before I followed up on his opening statement. "Any particular reason you're embarrassed about your relationship with Marcia Taylor?"

"Have you met her?"

I smiled and nodded.

"Then, I'm sure you understand. I haven't laid eyes on her in over thirty, forty years, but leopards don't change their spots. And, Marcia spent a lot of time in leopard spots." He chuckled at his own joke. "I must say I'm surprised Marcia's still alive. She lived hard. She is alive, right? You just met her?"

I nodded.

"Was she wearing leopard spots?"

I nodded. "So was her dog."

His expression said that was exactly what he expected. "In 1964, there weren't many single parents around. The divorce rate might have started its climb, but not in my neighborhood. I tried to meet women. Now, I realize I should have been reading the obituaries to find a nice widow. I was a widower, the only single man I knew. I was lonely. After my wife died, I saw a few women for a short time. It never worked out. Maybe because I was so devoted to Linda. Eventually, I gave up. I hadn't had a date in three years until Marcia came on to me. I chose not to see what she was like."

"What was she like? Aside from her clothing." I could pretty much guess the basics.

"Cheap. Aggressive. Manipulative. Frightening temper. No wonder her kid was a horror."

Lockwood took a long drink and smacked his lips. "I needed that." His smile disappeared quickly.

I was afraid he would change the subject but he didn't.

****John Lockwood****
September 30, 1964

Sonny Taylor came into the rec room in a sullen mood. John hadn't even noticed that he was gone, but the kid certainly made sure everyone knew he was back. After slamming the folding door to make sure everyone noted his entrance, he stomped across the room and yanked his baseball bat out of a tall box, tipping it over, and spilling gloves and balls onto the rug. He didn't stop to pick the items up. He began to swing the bat. Fast and hard and too close to the other kids in the room.

"Hey, Sport, you're going to break something." Not to mention kill someone if he wasn't careful. "Put the bat down." John tried to speak in a calm tone. Marcia went

nuts if he sounded at all disapproving of her son. He didn't want to listen to another sob story about how she was a single mother, who did her best etc., etc., etc.

Sonny took a wide swing and slammed the bat onto the coffee table. Potato chips scattered and onion dip splattered across the surface. Glasses flew onto the floor, but the table survived, which, given its quality, John considered both a miraculous event and a sad development.

He rose to his feet slowly. "Hey, Sonny." He used a soothing tone and smooth motions to place himself between the bat and his daughter.

Mikey moved fast, closer to the television to save himself and to make sure he could hear every word said about the game. Mikey took care of all his own needs, but not Seth. Still seated the boy slid between Sonny and Linda to protect her. Wondering how on earth he was going to stop this rampage without anyone getting hurt, John stepped toward the raging boy. He didn't get far before Marcia ran into the room and laid a hand on his chest.

"I'll take care of it, John." She moved towards her son slowly. "Sonny." Her voice was sweet. "You know why you can't do this."

Apparently, Sonny didn't know because he used the bat to smash a lamp and a small table John figured would not be missed.

He moved to his right slowly. He didn't want to rattle Sonny but he needed to get himself between Sonny and Seth, behind whom Linda cowered.

"Sonny, Mr. Grady is a policeman." Marcia didn't use a threatening tone, just informed.

John glanced over his shoulder and saw Grady standing in the doorway to the laundry room. Sonny, however, didn't care who was in the room. Wielding his bat to keep his mother at a distance he reached out with

*his left hand and grabbed Seth's Phillies hat off his head.
He held it higher than the smaller boy could reach but
Seth didn't even stand up. He was more interested in
protecting Linda.*

*Sonny, however, was not to be ignored. "Want your
hat, Seth? Come get it."*

"Please, give it back."

*"Maybe I will, if you come and get it. Come and get
it."*

*Seth obeyed but only after he crossed the room to turn
Sonny away from Linda. John moved quickly and pulled
her to safety behind him. Seth grabbed for his hat, but the
bully swung a bat at Seth with his other hand.*

*Behind him, Grady did not appear interested in
subduing Sonny. Like John, he seemed interested in
getting out. "Seth. Forget the hat. Let's go. Mikey, move
it. Seth, you too. Let's go."*

*"Who wants your crummy hat anyway?" Sonny tossed
the baseball cap across the room. Mikey caught it and
slipped it behind his back, out of Sonny's view.*

*"Now get out you little creep." Sonny took a final
swing at Seth with his bat.*

*****

"I'd seen Sonny get agitated before but never like that.
I saw an uncontrollable rage growing in that boy. I may
talk as if I stayed calm but, to tell you the truth, I was
frightened. I got Linda out of that house as fast as I could,
before Sonny exploded. We were step-in-step with Grady
and the boys heading for the door."

"What did you think when you heard Seth Timmons
got killed?"

"Given the sequence of your questions, I believe you
meant to ask, did I think Sonny killed him?" He shrugged.
"It occurred to me, but Seth had gotten out of the house.

Sonny could have followed him but Seth was with Grady. It made sense that a neighbor snatched the kid at his front door."

"Did you tell the cops about Sonny's behavior?"

"No need. Grady witnessed the same episode I did."

"No one else interviewed you?"

Mr. Lockwood shook his head. "I didn't expect that anyone would. Grady had it covered." He took a long drink of his gin and tonic and used the heavy linen napkin to wipe his lips with motions I found both amazingly precise and annoyingly slow. "I never saw Sonny again. I didn't want to see Marcia but I had trouble getting rid of her until I told her I knew why Sonny went nuts."

"Why did he?"

He took a carefully measured sip. "I told her that Sonny saw her with Jack Grady, that she was kissing him. I made it clear I did not like being played for a fool. After that, I never heard from her again."

"How did you find out what happened?"

"Linda told me. She was talking to Seth, so that made her the only one looking in that direction when Sonny opened the door. She saw what was going on and figured out what made him fly off the handle."

"Can I talk to Linda?"

"Not unless you have special powers." He tried to smile but tears coated his eyes. "Linda died in a car accident at twenty-three." His tone was soft as if comforting me for my blunder. "Her funeral was the last time I saw anyone from the neighborhood. The only person I spoke to was Mikey Sawyer. He came to apologize for his behavior."

"His behavior?"

"Sooner or later Mikey had to figure out there was more to life than sports. When he did, he decided that something was Linda."

"They dated?"

"Briefly. Kid stuff. After that, he stalked."

"When did this happen?"

"The stalking happened twice. First time on a bicycle not long after Seth died. It began again after we moved away and Mikey learned to drive. He drove by our house just about every hour."

"How did you get Mikey to stop?"

"Linda went to college and graduate school in California." He paused and took a deep breath before making his next statement. "She died out there." The breath didn't help. The memory overwhelmed him.

I had more questions but I couldn't ask them of the sobbing father. I glanced and saw women shooting daggers at me. A pastel wave headed in our direction.

"John, what's wrong." Visions in pink and blue and yellow huddled around the man.

"I didn't mean. I am so sorry." I stuttered.

"No, no. Don't worry." Lockwood touched his napkin to his eyes. "It's always been this way, I have always been this way when I tell the story to someone who doesn't know. All the time that has passed never made it easier." He waved the solicitous neighbors away. "Sometimes it feels so freeing to talk about it, to let the pain come to the surface." Nonetheless, he changed the subject. His expression suggested the next topic would not be a happier one. "There's one other thing I've never allowed myself to say aloud but I wake up in the middle of the night thinking about. I could be responsible for Seth's death."

I held my breath. I couldn't imagine what I was about to hear.

"If I hadn't been lonely and weak and responded to Marcia's cheap tricks, maybe she would never have invited Seth. And even if Marcia had invited him, Susan would have thought twice about letting him go if I hadn't been going."

I guessed that, with the exception of Marcia Taylor, every adult at the Taylor house that night was living with some feeling of guilt over their inability to save Seth. I didn't know what to say, but Lockwood changed the mood.

"Why are you doing this? Are you trying to prove that Ralphie Barker was innocent?"

"No. I don't have anything to prove. I'm just interested in the truth." I told him a little more about my class. "Telling my students about real people helps them understand the era. Except for the victim, I don't use real names. If anyone does enough research, they might locate some, but I don't reveal or confirm the identities of anyone I interview. I use real situations, personalities, motives. Then we do a session on naming characters based on the era and family history. After that, I set the kids loose."

"So you're interested in the truth so your students can deal with untruths?"

I laughed. "No one ever repeated my strategy back to me in quite that way. What I want is for them to get a feel for living in another time, to feel the constraints of a different era, to see how those differences might motivate the characters. I see if they got it when I read their stories."

"And? Do they get it?"

"Some do. Most shed their modern-day mindset but every term so far at least one student puts an iPhone in the hands of someone from the rotary phone era."

He laughed.

"Do you put this much effort into every case?"

"No," I admitted.

"But you didn't talk to me because you're trying to prove that Ralphie was innocent?" He was tricky, rephrasing his earlier question.

I shook my head. "I told you. I never try to prove anything." I didn't add that I often *hope* to prove something. "I start out just looking for a story. As time goes on, I become interested in the true story."

"So you must think Ralphie might be innocent."

"Why? Do you think he might be innocent?"

"No. I don't, although I did always wonder how someone so slow even figured out that hanging himself might be a good idea." He shrugged. "And then to figure out how to do it. I'd only seen him around the parish but, from what I observed, Ralphie didn't seem smart enough."

"Maybe he saw someone do it on television or in a movie."

"Maybe. As I said, I really didn't know him. Or his family. I would see his sister at church sometimes. I was mildly acquainted with her because of the volunteer work she did. She looked sophisticated but she was timid. Pretty girl. I guess that was why I noticed her. I thought she was afraid of her husband. He was a very unpleasant man. Handsome in a tough-guy way. I don't see how the two of them ever got together. And she seemed grateful to have him."

"When I met her, she alluded to his disposition. He's no longer around. He left town but where he went, I have no idea."

"Hmmh." John Lockwood had something he wanted to say but he was not going to say it.

"What?"

"I have a theory. It's really far out there."

"If you read my students' papers you wouldn't call anything far out there."

"Well," he paused but this time I knew he would go on. "Just suppose I was kind of tough guy, not the humanitarian type. Suppose I married a woman with looks good enough to feed my ego who lets me do just about anything I want and who caters to my every need. I might feel she was just grateful to have someone like me."

"Ok. I'm with you."

"So, I'm living the good life when all of sudden I've got some mouse of a man, my wife's brother living in the basement. Her disabled brother. I wouldn't be too happy."

"Why not leave?"

"Remember my little wife might not be exciting but she lets me run the show while she caters to my every need. I don't want to get rid of her. I want to get rid of him."

Helen had practically said as much.

"So if that brother gets accused of a horrible crime, I see a way to get rid of him. So I tell everyone how depressed he is."

I did recall a statement where Helen's husband had claimed that his brother-in-law was horribly depressed.

"I set the scene and then. . ." Mr. Lockwood did a pantomime of hanging Ralphie Barker. A refined pantomime but I got his point.

"But Ralphie would have been going to jail."

"After an embarrassing trial that would have cost them more money than they could afford. That woman loved her brother. She would want him to have a decent lawyer."

"But her husband could have left her and he did leave her not long after . . . after."

"Right away?"

"Soon."

"Well, it was only a theory."

But if it were true and Ralphie Barker did not kill himself, his suicide could no longer be considered a confession.

I found the theory crazy for about fifteen minutes. Then it began to sound more and more reasonable. By the time I crossed the Walt Whitman Bridge to Pennsylvania, the idea that Ralphie Barker had been murdered seemed rather plausible.

Chapter 31

How was I ever going to get back into Mikey Sawyer's office? The answer was simple. I wasn't. An *accidental* meeting was required and that kind of accident required research and planning. When I didn't find the information I needed online, I took another trip to the library where I located an article from a recently defunct sports magazine that discussed major agents including Mikey Sawyer.

I was in Aunt Julia's neighborhood—if I used a broad definition of neighborhood, which I did. So, I gave her a call. She met me at a tea shop near her apartment and, always supportive of my projects, joined me in ordering pie a la mode in Ralphie's honor. "I'm trusting your intuition that he is innocent. If you're wrong, we are sitting here honoring a child killer."

"Don't worry. I have no idea who is guilty but I am relatively certain that it isn't Ralphie Barker." I raised my fork in a toast to Ralphie. "I don't know why celebrities aren't more cautious about the information they give to the press."

"Something in particular cause this sudden shift in conversation?" She asked.

"If you tell a reporter that, during the week, you jog daily along the East River Drive, all some crackpot has to do is go to the East River Drive and wait."

"Are you the crackpot in this scenario?" She sounded worried.

"Of course not. I'm just saying it might take a day or two, but sooner or later the celebrity jogs by, providing the crackpot full access."

Understanding, despite my protests, that I was the

crackpot in my story, she said only, "Be careful. I mean it."

If being careful meant *watch for Mikey daily*, I was. Dressed in rarely donned jogging gear and barely worn running shoes, I managed to drop by his morning route three times in a week. The third time was not the charm, but the fourth day at the beginning of the next week was.

I spotted him easily. Sawyer stood out from the other runners, even the overdressed. He was ostentatiously overdressed. Not that he wore too many clothes. His clothes were too flashy, too obviously expensive like his fluorescent running shoes and his wrap-around sunglasses. I had to make those observations quickly. Sawyer got by me before I could get myself together and follow. By the time I was on my feet, there was no way I could catch up with him. My only hope was that he would not make a circle and cross the river to come down the West River Drive, but would return down the east side of the river where I could approach him.

I picked a bench and watched until he did come back towards me, but he veered away and ran up the hill to the Art Museum.

On my next visit I concluded that his driver dropped Sawyer off and picked him up in front of the Art Museum steps, not so he could begin his run with, as most Rocky impersonators did, a run *up* the iconic stairs but so he could end his jog with a run *down* the steps. So the next day, I sat along the edge of the stairs and he ran right by me. No jogger would stop mid-descent. So, for my next effort two days later, I took a position near the spot where the Lincoln Town Car would come to pick him up. My heart fluttered when I saw Sawyer coming down the iconic staircase. When he reached the bottom he pulled up his shirt to wipe the sweat from his brow and strolled the last few steps to his waiting car. At last, he was moving at my speed.

"Hi." I chirped as I came alongside him and jogged in place as if interrupted mid-run. "I can't believe I bumped into you." Given the time of the morning, I felt ridiculously cheerful but I figured Sawyer's endorphins had kicked even if mine hadn't. I tried to simulate a runner's high.

He made it clear he had no idea who I was and no desire to find out.

"Tracy Shaw." I smiled.

He didn't respond but I suspected he recognized the name. Even an innocent man would recall the name of a woman who practically accused him of murder.

I stopped my running motions and took some deep breaths. Anyone watching would have wondered how fifteen seconds of in-place jogging could exhaust anyone under forty. "I came to your office about Seth Timmons."

He blanched. Again, he pulled up his shirt and wiped his brow. I imagined he wanted to hide under the cloth. I'd already seen him wipe his face dry.

"You look different. I didn't recognize you," he said when he reappeared.

"No problem. I am happy to see you. I talked to John Lockwood." If a way to approach this topic casually existed, I hadn't identified it. "He was with you and Seth that night."

"If you say so."

"With Linda."

"That makes sense."

"He said you were interested in Linda."

"Did he say *too interested*?" He was exasperated but not visibly apprehensive. "I don't get you. Why do we have to talk about this? It's old news. God, it's ancient history. I've lived an entire lifetime since then. I had a crush. Maybe I came on a little strong. Hey." He flung his arms wide open. "I'm a competitive guy."

"And the night he died Seth was your competition."

"You're kidding, right? I was twelve years old. I wasn't about to kill someone over a woman. A Mickey Mantle rookie season baseball card, maybe. A woman, no way."

"This isn't a joke, Mikey."

"I know. Believe me. You've dredged up all sorts of memories. I'm still haunted by the last sight of Seth. Thanks for that."

"When did you last see him?" I responded to what appeared to be true emotion.

"When I stopped on our front steps and watched my Dad see him home."

"That haunts you?"

"Wouldn't it haunt you? Wouldn't you wonder if there was something you did, something you didn't do, something you could have done? I was only a kid and was annoyed because Seth didn't care that the Phillies lost. He was just happy because he got to lock lips with Linda."

Okay, my first reaction was to pull out a phone and call Susan Timmons to tell her the good news about the kiss, but that wasn't what this meeting was about.

"I was so rotten to him. I thought it served him right that he left his hat at the Taylors'."

"He didn't have his hat?"

"I dropped it on the floor at the Taylors' but I didn't tell Seth. I did that on purpose. I knew Sonny would never give him his hat back." He shook his head. "The last thing I did to that poor little kid was be mean." He stared down the Parkway towards Center City. "I know I didn't appear very cooperative with what you're trying to do, but you have to understand what a sensitive issue this is for me. That memory has stayed with me all these years, and not just me. I feel certain that night helped set Grady on his downhill slide. He didn't say it but I know he felt responsible he didn't get the kid all the way home. If he had only taken a few more steps, he might have seen the perv or the perv might have seen him and run. I used to hear him mumbling sometimes. 'If I hadn't been in such a goddam rush to get home.'" Sawyer wiped his face and I wondered if this time he was wiping traces of tears.

"Look, I still believe the perv did it, but I want to help. If you need anything call me." He pulled a business card out of a small pocket in his jogging pants. "My secretary's name is Celeste. Tell her you are a Code Blue." He returned to his hotshot persona. "That means approved caller. Not a hot chick, that's Code Red. Not a personal friend, that's Code Green."

Was he was telling me the truth? If I called would I discover that Code Blue identified me as someone to block? I hoped I didn't have to find out. Especially after what happened with Marcus, I wasn't in a place where I could handle rejection all that well.

Chapter 32

After a quick stop at home to change into my version of business clothes, I drove to the Biding Time Tavern. It was early but I suspected some of the clientele liked to drink their breakfast. And I was right. There were a few customers scattered along the bar including Grady in his usual spot. He did not appear surprised to see me. Nor did he appear happy. "You're not one of the regulars. You don't fit the profile."

He was right. I was female and sober. That made me different from the other customers. "I don't usually hit the bars this early. It would be easier if you gave me your cell phone number." I climbed onto the stool beside his. "Although I have no right to complain. I appreciate your willingness to help me," I said although he had done nothing to indicate he wanted to be of any assistance.

"Is that what I'm doing? Helping you?" He took a long slug of his beer.

"You have so far. It would be a help if you tell me about the Phillies cap."

I sensed the slightest hesitation in his movement and, from my previous observations, Grady had never before faltered getting a glass to his lips. He took a gulp before he spoke. "What about the cap?"

"It was with the body."

"Who told you that?"

"Seth's mother. She wanted it back but the police said they needed it as evidence."

"I don't remember that."

"But your stepson says Seth didn't have it with him when he walked away from the two of you."

"Mikey's wrong." He took another drink.

"He felt bad because he knew the Phillies cap was still at Sonny's and Sonny would never give it back."

"He's confused. That was over fifty years ago."

"But Mrs. Timmons remembers."

"Maybe she remembers wrong. She never talked to me about the hat."

"I don't think that is something a mother is likely to get confused about."

"She's old like me. We get confused."

"I couldn't find any mention of the hat in the newspaper. Did you choose to withhold that one piece of evidence, the hat?"

"You took the class. Common procedure. If I have to tell you that, you really were a bad student."

"Why the hat?" I asked.

"Why not the hat?" He stared at me, studied me. "What are you thinking? That I murdered the kid?"

I had never considered that option until he raised the possibility. "I'm thinking I need to clarify how the hat last seen in the Taylor basement got to the body."

Grady dismissed my concerns with a wave. "Mikey was a kid. All this happened a long time ago."

"If your son had this strong memory of the last instant he saw this boy, if he couldn't forget the last cruel action he took, wouldn't he share that story with his father?"

"I guess not."

"And wouldn't his father, the cop hearing this, the cop who was on the scene found the body, question how and when did the kid get his hat back?"

"Not if his son never told him."

Grady slammed a twenty down on the bar, slid off his stool and headed out the door. I followed him onto the city street.

He turned on me, angry. "How do you even know the hat was his? Maybe he found it on the street. Maybe it

191

belonged to the perv."

"Highly unlikely." I refused to concede the point.

"But possible."

"Possible but not probable."

I stepped in front of him. "All I want is some help in figuring out how Seth got his hat back?"

After a long pause, he didn't give me an answer. He asked a question. "Did you like my class?"

"I did." Or, I'm sure I would have if I'd actually been in it.

"I was a good teacher wasn't I?"

"I saw you were a good teacher. I heard you were a good cop."

"That's what I thought."

"That's why you're going to tell me about the hat." I stared at Grady but couldn't catch his gaze. He was seeing something I couldn't see, a time before I was even born.

"I was on a winning streak until I met Marcia. Loving wife, great stepson, new house, job I enjoyed and excelled at."

"But?"

"I had a roving eye and Marcia was always on the lookout for any man who even glanced her way." Grady guided me back to the bar, but I had no idea where our conversation was going. I let Grady lead me.

*****Jack Grady*****
September 30, 1964

Marcia's basement was even more of a mess than when he'd fled an hour earlier. He stopped on the bottom step and surveyed the domestic devastation. Magazines were strewn across the floor. Tables lay on their sides. The kid had really done a job on the rec room. A lamp was broken, damaged beyond repair. Not that its demise was a tragedy. Marcia had some of the ugliest stuff he had ever seen. Potato chips snapped under his feet and onion dip oozed over his shoes as he stepped onto the carpet. "This better be good, Marcia. I had a hard time getting out of the house." He lied. He'd slipped away while his wife was sleeping, but he didn't know how he'd explain his absence if she woke up while he was gone.

Marcia turned and hissed at him. "Don't give me that. You're a cop. You must get calls at all times of the night. I told you. I need help."

"What the hell happened here?" His eyes had seen the room but his brain could not take in all the damage.

"Sonny went nuts on the Timmons boy. I tried to stop him but I'm no match for Sonny."

"How could that be? I left at the same time as the kid." He eyed the destruction. "Things were not half this bad when we left. What happened?"

"I told you. He went after Seth."

"But I walked Seth home."

"He came back."

"Why?"

"I don't know. I came down when I heard him fighting with Sonny."

"Where is he now? Did he get home okay?"

Marcia didn't say a word. She pointed to the blue couch turned 45 degrees from its usual position. Grady stepped forward and looked over the back. "My God. Marcia. What the hell happened to him?" Grady leaped into action. He pushed the sofa aside and knelt beside the boy's bloody body. "Call an ambulance," he said although he knew before he felt for Seth's pulse that summoning help would be futile. He tried to breathe life into the lifeless child. Even though the body was starting to grow cold, he had to try. He felt sick when he sat back on his heels. He saw that Marcia hadn't moved.

"You called an ambulance?" He asked although he knew the answer was no.

"I didn't know what to do."

"I told you what to do." He snapped. "Not that it matters now. He's dead. He's been shot. I'm right, aren't I? Sonny shot him." He climbed to his feet. "I've got to call this in." He moved slowly under the weight of the news. "Where's your phone?" He headed towards the stairs.

Marcia jumped in front of him and grabbed both his arms. The hands that had felt so soft and gentle hours before held him with surprising strength. "You can't. That would ruin me. Sonny's my only son, my only child."

"Marcia, your boy killed someone." He grabbed her by two arms and pushed her aside.

"He didn't intend to." She tried to soften her voice but not her grip. "He gets so angry sometimes. He doesn't mean to hurt anyone and when it's over he feels horrible."

"He didn't hurt someone. He killed a boy."

"But I know he feels bad."

Right. He feels real bad when it comes time to face the music. "Where is he now?" He pulled loose from her grasp.

"He's hiding upstairs. He ran when he saw me on the phone. He's just a little boy. He was so frightened by what happened."

"You mean by what he did."

Marcia crossed her arms tight across her chest. "It was an accident."

Grady didn't argue. "Where's the gun?"

Marsha nodded at a cushion on the sofa. "You've got to help me."

Grady lifted the couch pillow and found a Smith and Wesson. He leaned down and sniffed the gun. As he expected, it had been recently fired. "This isn't a matter of choice, Marcia. I'm a cop. I have responsibilities."

"Yeah, you're a husband too. You didn't take those responsibilities that seriously." Marcia snarled.

Grady turned and stared at her. The expression on her face scared him. Some might say hers was the look of a mother lion protecting her cub, but Grady knew better. What he saw was evil. He felt as if a demon lived inside her and was observing him through her eyes.

"You help me out here, Jack, and I don't talk to your wife."

"I can't help you out. Obstruction is a felony." He spoke the truth, plain facts.

"It's your choice, Jack." Her eyes were narrow and stared at him with an intensity he found frightening—and he faced criminal cop-haters all the time without fear. "I want you to help me, to help Sonny. If you say no, your wife reads in the newspaper why I called you not the precinct. Why I expected you to help me."

"Marcia, you don't understand. I have no choice. I am a cop. I know the law."

"Wait." She feigned surprise. "I just remembered. Your son can read too. I forgot." She slapped her hand against the side of her face to emphasize her amazement. "And wait, I forgot something else. He's not your son. He's your stepson. You got no parental rights. You won't be seeing him again. Not once his mother finds out what a cad you are."

*****

At last Jack Grady looked his age. His hands shook. He could barely lift the beer to his lips. When he did, a small stream ran down the side of his chin. He didn't bother to wipe it away. "I had not one iota of doubt that she would do what she threatened. Mikey was the best thing in my life. He worshipped me. I couldn't lose that."

"So you helped her?"

As he nodded, I saw every one of his eighty-plus years on his face. "What else could I do?"

I couldn't agree but didn't see any point in arguing. The devoted stepfather had done what he believed he had to do. "What did you do with the gun?"

Grady replied with a question. "Do you have children?"

I shook my head.

"Too bad. You don't know how much you love them, that you would do anything to keep your kid's love."

I am sure he was telling the truth but he hadn't told me what I wanted to know. "You got rid of the gun?"

"I didn't want that nutcase to have a weapon. God knows where she got it in the first place. I took it that night and after a week or so, I claimed the stress of the case had been too much for me and I had to get away on a fishing trip down the shore. I dropped it in the bay."

"And you moved the body from the Taylor house?"

"The body. And," he shook his head, "the cap." He paused while the impact of that statement sunk in. "I picked up the hat with all his stuff. I never noticed he didn't have it earlier. Mikey hadn't said anything about it."

He drifted into quiet contemplation of the night so long ago. I waited in silence for him to go on.

"It was dumb luck I caught the case. In a way taking the call frightened me, but I realized I had to. Being on the scene was the best way to cover any mistakes. At first, I was the spokesperson. Just because I was there, at the scene, I talked to the press. I just didn't mention the hat." He paused and I was afraid he wouldn't continue but it turned out he was just gathering his strength or as much as he could muster. His voice still quavered when he spoke. "When I got home from . . . when I got back from Marcia's and the Wissahickon I couldn't sleep. I couldn't imagine I would ever sleep again. I was in the dining room, listening to my police scanner when Mikey came downstairs. Turned out he couldn't sleep either. Even before he knew anything bad had happened to Seth, Mikey told me how bad he felt, how he had dropped Seth's hat, how he was going to make Sonny give him the cap so he could return it to Seth along with an apology. I told him how proud I was of him, how I thought that was the right thing to do, how I was sure it would mean a lot to Seth. Of course, Mikey being Mikey he went on to talk about how sad he was about the Phillies. I couldn't hear a word he said. All I could think about was that hat lying beside Seth on the trail.

He tried to pick up his beer but his hands shook too badly. He grabbed onto the edge of the bar to keep them still.

"I sent Mikey back to bed knowing that I had to catch that call, that I couldn't let Mikey read about the hat in the papers. Trying to come up with an explanation about how it got there would have been too complicated, and I would have had to lie to him. I didn't want to lie to my son."

I controlled the urge to scream about the other things he was willing to do.

"As soon as I heard the call over the radio, I was out of the house, but the uniforms beat me there. I couldn't pocket the hat. So, I didn't mention it and defended the decision to withhold the information. I said it would be a great way to trip up the perp. I came up with some garbage that we didn't want any potential witnesses thinking only about a Phillies cap. There were a million identical ones out there. Besides, we didn't know if he was wearing it or not. We were certain about the pants, shirt and jacket he had on. I described those."

"And when you put the body on the path, you were the one who . . ." I couldn't bring myself to be specific. "You staged the crime scene to misdirect the investigation?" I tried to sound matter-of-fact and nonjudgmental, but how could he not know what I was thinking?

He shrank before my eyes. "You remember how much

simpler framing a suspect was before DNA. All I had to do was make it look like a sex crime. I disgusted myself but I did what I had to." He gripped his beer tight to try to still his shaking hands. "I didn't plan to defile him that way, but there was this bottle and I knew . . . ."

He didn't have to tell me what he knew. I understood he would see how easy diverting the investigation would be. What I didn't understand was how he could have done such things.

"Seth was already dead. I couldn't help him, but I could help my family, myself."

I saw no such excuse when it came to Ralphie Barker. "So when the cops went searching for a perp, you made sure Barker popped up."

"I didn't finger him." He shook his head with a force that matched his tone. "I didn't have to." His chin dropped to his chest. He closed his eyes and for a moment I feared he had drifted off. Actually, I was afraid he had drifted off forever, but he wasn't dead. He was tearing up. "Barker was like a gift from heaven."

An even better gift when he committed suicide. I didn't speak. I didn't want to further upset Grady who was sitting beside me with his face in his hands, sobbing.

Chapter 33

"I believe him." I finished dinner, home-cooked by Alex, about the same time I finished telling him the story of my visit with Jack Grady.

"So what do you do now?"

"I don't know. I'm not about to hire a lawyer to help me because I was doing a good deed."

"You know the saying about good deeds. Did you expect yours to go unpunished?"

"I've been on the web. I suspect the statute of limitations for an accessory in Pennsylvania is the same as for murder itself." I paused for dramatic effect.

"So you have to turn him in or you become an accessory, yourself?"

"At least I'd be guilty of obstruction." I nodded, a forlorn gesture. "Tomorrow, I can call the police and find the right person to speak to about a cold case."

"Aren't cold cases unsolved? As far as the police are concerned, this case is solved."

"They'll tell me what to do." I sat in silence for a moment. "I feel guilty. Grady just told me and didn't ask what I was going to do with the information. He's an old man. Because of me, he's going to die in prison."

"Because of what *he* did, he *might* die in prison. He didn't kill Seth. Deals are made every day. He's a cop. He knows the game. You didn't string him up and torture him. He told you of his own free will. Confession was good for his soul. He wouldn't have revealed a thing if he didn't want the truth out in the open."

"I guess you're right," I said without conviction.

"Unless he's senile. Maybe he's confused. Or at least

his lawyer can claim he was."

"I detected absolutely no sign of infirmity in the man. He's strong enough to make me consider taking up drinking."

"You do drink."

"Not enough if I want to meet Grady's standards." I raised my wine glass in a toast.

"That's Coca Cola."

"I have to stand up and teach in class tonight," I explained with a shrug.

"You know," he dragged out the phrase. "If you don't tell, no one will ask."

"No, I can't do *that*." I paused. "I'll sleep on it."

"You won't sleep. Come dancing with me after your class."

"I'm not really in a dancing mood." I sighed deeply to summarize my confusion, disappointment, and anxiety. A lot of emotion to ask of one sigh. I made it a long one. "I didn't think I'd be turning in someone who helped me and who volunteered the information."

"What did you expect would happen?"

"At the beginning, I believed I would find out Ralphie Barker was guilty. If not, I thought I would discover that someone I didn't know or grew to despise killed Seth. Alone, without an accomplice."

"Tracy, Honey, I am so sorry you were so successful. I know you'll fail next time."

"Thanks." I grasped his hand. "I feel much better."

"At least Sonny is already locked up. So he can't hurt you. Of course, if they try him as a juvenile which he was back then . . ."

"He will get out and hurt me." I finished Alex's thought.

He made a dismissive wave. "We can worry about that when it happens. I mean if it happens."

"It's Grady's responsibility to tell them about Sonny.

I only know what Grady told me."

"In the meantime, you should relish your success."

Technically I'd scored a victory but not the kind to celebrate.

Alex disappeared upstairs to dress for a night on the dance floor. I headed for class but looked forward to rushing home so I could settle in for an evening's rest enjoying mindless TV and cool breezes wafting through the windows.

By 10 PM, I was on the couch but although my body was relaxing, my mind didn't rest. What would Grady think when he realized what he had revealed? What would he decide to do to the person to whom he confessed? How long would it be before he decided to take action? I shut the windows, secured the locks, and closed the shutters, just in case he was ready to act. Yes, Jack Grady was over eighty but he was a strong octogenarian. It didn't occur to me that he, an ex-cop from another era, probably possessed picklocks, weapons and a contact who could find addresses, especially since I'd told him I lived next door to Harry.

Chapter 34

"I'm not drunk."

Just my luck. After years in a fog, the guy sobers up in time to figure out two things. One, how careless he'd been. And, two, where I lived.

"I'm generally drunk." Grady's tone was apologetic.

"So you said."

"Don't you want to know why I am usually drunk?"

"Of course. I'm concerned about you." Maybe that was why, against my better judgment, I'd opened the door to the ex-cop, even though I had locked the windows specifically to keep him out. "If you keep drinking the way you are, it will kill you."

"The drink will never finish me off. I've given liquor every chance, but it looks like I'm going to have to shoot myself." He pulled out a small revolver, at least it looked like a revolver to me. It was definitely a gun. "Do you mind if I come in?"

I found it hard to say no to a man with a weapon pointed at me. I'd like to say I stayed calm figuring, given the 11 PM hour, Grady would soon fall asleep and I could steal the weapon out of his hand. I wasn't that cool. I was shaking as I backed away from the door, letting him into the living room.

As Grady slumped onto the couch, I realized the only real danger his firearm presented was slipping from his loose grip and firing accidentally.

"Why don't I hold your gun?" I moved towards him.

"No." He shouted. "I need it. I don't know how I lived this long. I don't know why I lived this long." He waved the barrel at me like a parent wagging a finger at a

202

misbehaving child. "Not that I was really living. I have not had one happy day since the night Seth died. Not one. That's a long time to live so damn unhappy." He sat and stared at the floor. I waited for him to doze off. But he didn't. He let his gaze meet mine. "There's more to my story. And although it's hard to believe, it's worse. I bet you can't believe that I sank lower, but I did." He closed his eyes and shook his head.

I contemplated grabbing for the gun for too long. By the time I felt confident enough to make a move his eyes were open.

"Marcia Taylor called me on the Sunday after Seth died. Mikey and I had watched the Phillies game. They won big but we knew it might be too late. We had to wait for news from St. Louis and when it came it wasn't good. Not for Phillies fans. I knew Mikey would be upset so the last thing I wanted to do was go out, but Marcia said it would be in my best interest. So, I told my wife something came up with Seth's case and I had to go. She wouldn't have stopped me. Not when it had to do with Seth, and in a way it did."

*****Jack Grady*****
October 4, 1964

"I told you, Jack, this is our only chance." They were sitting in Marcia's car around the corner from the Mitchells' house where Ralphie Barker lived in the basement.

"Marcia, this is crazy. I cannot be part of this."

"You can't not be part of this." She sneered. "You are already part of this."

"Marcia, I understand your concern for your son, I do, but even if I wanted to do this I would have to tell you: we cannot get away with it."

"We can. I've got everything we need, and a plan."

"But his sister will be home. Everybody is home on Sunday night. That's what people do. They sit home and watch The Ed Sullivan Show. It's what we should be doing. Wait until tomorrow night. The Mitchells both work." Maybe time would calm her down or maybe time would allow him to calm her down.

"Jack, give me some credit. Once I saw those clues in the paper about the identity of Seth's killer, the plan just fell into place. I'm not like you, Jack. I don't let things happen to me. I take charge. I was at the seven o'clock mass this morning."

"You went to church?" He thought that when someone like her went into a church something happened. Something bad. Wasn't it supposed to get struck by lightning or something?

"Of course, I would go to church. Wouldn't I be so upset by what happened to Seth so soon after I last saw him that only prayer would comfort me?" Her toned mocked the tragedy. "I was thinking I might even have to stay for the later masses but she came to the first one, probably to stay out of sight."

"She?"

"Helen Mitchell, the perp's sister. I figured she'd be praying for that brother of hers. I guessed she might come early to avoid stares. And, I was right. There she was, that little mouse of a woman, sitting on the side aisle praying her heart out. I thought she might crush her rosaries." Marcia snickered. "As if that would help her. Anyway, so after communion I slipped in the pew beside her, near the aisle so she couldn't leave without squeezing by me."

"You didn't go to communion?" He didn't even attempt to keep the horror out of his voice at thought of Marcia receiving a sacrament.

"Of course, I did. Right after I saw her going. I went up there and stuck my tongue out and received the body of Christ."

"Don't be sacrilegious, Marcia. You've got enough problems with the Man Upstairs."

"I wasn't being sacrilegious. I was being practical. I told her I wanted her to know that no matter what other people said, or how they talked, I was on her side. I told her how well Sonny spoke of Ralphie and how he could not believe that he would do such a thing. She bought my story—hook, line and sinker. And then, and this is the best part, she tells me how worried she is about Ralphie, how she wants to take off work to be with him and how her husband says absolutely not. He won't even stay home from a family dinner tonight. Or let her stay home. And she is torn because she worries about him too. If she lets him go alone, he will drink too much and drive home drunk. She feels she should go with him." Elated, she punched his arm. *"I told her she was absolutely right."*

"But they could be back any minute."

"Dinner was at 6:30. One of the things she hates is that the night drags on while her husband and his brothers get drunk and she's stuck cleaning up with the mother and her sisters-in-law."

"How long did you sit with her?"

"Long enough to figure out that Ralphie is home alone until close to ten tonight."

"You don't know that. It's too risky. That will not be a routine family gathering tonight. Let's get out of here. We can come back."

"No. We might not get another chance. On the one hand, I was thrilled to see the newspaper talked about Ralphie today—even if they didn't mention his name. On the other hand, I realized our time was limited."

"We don't know that. Let's go. No one will ever know we were here. It's dark. No one has seen us."

"All the more reason to act now."

He made a grab for her but she was out of the car before his hand caught hold. He didn't want to follow but

205

what choice did he have? He hurried to catch up. "Tomorrow would be better." He begged.

"Tomorrow may be too late. What if the cops arrest him? What if they keep investigating? What if they buy some story that he's innocent? Then what?"

"Marcia, he is innocent."

"What's this bleeding heart sensitivity? We can't stand here all night. You're too drunk to see it now but this is the only way. I'll do my part. Then you come in."

Wishing he was too drunk to understand what was happening, he followed the click-clack of Marcia's high heels down the common driveway behind the houses and into a narrow alley that separated the Mitchell house from the one next door. Grady was worried. "What if someone saw us come down the driveway?"

"How? It's nighttime." She dismissed his concern with disdain. "If there were any street lights they'd be on. Besides, you live on the next block. You could say you were walking the dog or something. So if you don't have a dog, you might want to think about picking one up in the morning." She laughed, but the sound was evil, not happy.

"What if someone in the house next door hears us?"

"Them?" Marcia did not appear to be worried about anything. She sounded amused. "Elderly couple lives there. I checked. They are old and deaf. She spoke as if she were whispering but her voice sounded so loud it pushed him towards the neighbor's wall. The rough edges of the rocks hurt but not enough to propel him back towards Marcia. He pressed against the rough stone surface as if he could force his way through it.

"Come here." She crooked her finger for him to join her at that window.

Like a browbeaten schoolboy, he obeyed her command and gazed over her shoulder through a crack in the curtains. Inside his basement apartment, Ralphie was sitting on his couch, with his back to them, guffawing at

My Favorite Martian.

"Just like him to laugh at that stupid show." Disgusted, she shook her head. *"I knew this retard would be alone."*

He cringed at her use of retard. *He hated that word.*

"He has no friends. We're doing him a favor." Her tone was confident and completely devoid of regret.

"Marcia, think about what we are doing here."

"You think, Jack. Think about Mikey. Think about what it will be like when he knows you for what you are."

What he was? What would he be if he helped Marcia with her plan?

"Well, we can't stand here all night. We have a lot to do and that sister of his will have to drag her drunken husband home sometime. You know your part." Marcia raised her fist. Grady grabbed it but she wrested it free and banged on Ralphie's door.

Certainly, his sister had warned him that this day of all days, a knock at the door could present a threat. Grady stepped back under the stairs that lead to the Mitchells' kitchen and prayed that Ralphie would not answer. But he did. Marcia plastered a phony smile on her face and began the spiel she'd prepared to explain why she had stopped by. Grady wouldn't have bought Marcia's incoherent and contradictory story, but its complexity worked in her favor. Ralphie was too confused to understand and too polite to refuse. He let Marcia into his apartment.

Marcia stepped inside but, as planned, didn't pull the door all the way closed. The path to his damnation was now cleared. The scheme was moving ahead. Instead of giving in to the urge to run, Grady stepped to the window and watched as much as he could see between the dark drapes. The side of Marcia's face was visible and showed she was carrying through with her campaign to engage and distract Ralphie. Sitting beside her prey on the couch, she appeared not at all conflicted as she flirted with him. The woman had a heart of stone.

This was his chance to flee. He took only a few steps away from the window before he stopped. Where would he go? Could he run home and wait for his family to collapse around him, for the police to come for him? Marcia threatened to ruin his life and he had no doubt she would. He moved back to the window. Grady couldn't see Ralphie's face but knew he would have appeared confused if not downright frightened. He tried to distance himself from Marcia, but there was no getting away from that woman. For Ralphie or for him.

Marcia was not used to a reaction like Ralphie's, but she soldiered on, working her plan. He appeared to be polite to his unexpected guest, even when the commercials started and Grady knew she was asking for something to drink. Grady edged towards the door. He couldn't hear Ralphie's words but his tone suggested that he was apologizing for why he could not be a good host. Marcia was willing to instruct him. She followed him into the alcove that served as his kitchen and blocked his view of the apartment door.

That was Grady's cue. He counted to three, but his feet didn't move. He did a quick review of his options and decided he didn't have any. He started the count again. This time on three he pushed the door open. Inside he found an unexpected bonus, a closet along the wall to his left. He slipped inside. Marcia's happy conversation combined with the noise from the Ed Sullivan *theme covered any noise he made. He peered through the slats in the door. Marcia had a glass of water in her hand as she led Ralphie back into the room. Grady knew she could not see him when she glanced in his direction but she assumed he was there.*

"So, Ralphie, do you have a girlfriend?" She slipped onto the couch with seductive moves.

Ralphie's tone confirmed how shy he was. "No."

"A cute guy like you?"

Through the slots in the louvered door, Grady read the confusion on Ralphie's face. He didn't know how to answer or what to do.

"Would you like to be with a girl?"

Poor Ralphie appeared more and more puzzled. "I don't understand."

Marcia leaned forward seductively. "Here, sit beside me." She patted the cushion and Ralphie took the spot that fit Marcia's plan.

Grady could see his face until he sat down and turned towards the TV. He appeared obedient, not interested. Undaunted, Marcia fought to hold his attention as together they watched The Ed Sullivan Show.

The time for the next step in the plan had come, but no signal came from Marcia. Was she enjoying this? The thought disgusted but didn't surprise him. Maybe she was getting cold feet. He hoped so, but what would happen if the police did a thorough investigation? What if the cops decided to talk to the boys and they told them about the hat? What if he couldn't convince them it didn't belong to Seth? What if they found some other piece of evidence out there that would exonerate Ralphie? Grady had no problem with the guy, but maybe Marcia was right. Maybe Ralphie would be better off. What kind of life was he living? Working at a boring dead-end job, sweeping up for kids who mocked him, going home to stare at the TV in a dark basement barely furnished with luckier people's cast-offs. Every day filled with sadness and loneliness. Grady had a lot to lose if the truth came out, but Ralphie? Grady tried to convince himself that he was doing Ralphie a favor. The guy had nothing to lose. For a moment, Grady believed it.

On the couch, Marcia worked her plan without hesitation. "Ralphie, you know in the movies when you see a man and a woman kissing?

Ralphie shook his head. "I don't go to the movies."

"But you watch TV, don't you?"

He shrugged.

"You must like Peyton Place. *Have you seen it? It's a brand new show but already everyone likes* Peyton Place. *I bet you'd see some kissing on that show."*

Marcia maneuvered Ralphie into a position where he would not see Grady moving towards him.

Grady had killed a man before. He'd had no choice. The guy had him in his sights. Kill or be killed. He never felt he had any other option but everyone told him that would not matter, he would suffer, need therapy. He never did. How could he feel bad about killing a man who victimized his ten-year-old daughter? He had no regrets. Ever. But he could tell already this was going to be different. Grady could not believe the sad man-child in front of him could hurt anyone.

Marcia glanced his way. The look in her eyes was a command that he obeyed. Grady pulled a rope from under his jacket and clutched it in his hand. Marcia expected him to put that rope around Ralphie's neck and pull it tight until he could no longer breathe. Grady hid the rope in his hand and stepped out of the closet. "Marcia, let's go. This I cannot do."

Ralphie turned, appearing more bewildered than scared, probably wondering why this strange man was in the room and how he got in there.

"I should never have trusted you." Marcia glared over the back of the couch. "It's too late to back out now. I told you what would happen if you didn't go through with this."

"I'll face the music." He moved towards the couch. "Ralphie, sorry we bothered you." He glanced at the coffee table and the half-eaten piece of pie. "You got ice cream melting there, Ralphie. Go back to enjoying your

pie a la mode. Come on, Marcia." He grabbed her arm and tried to pull her off the sofa.

Behind him, Marcia hissed. "You'll lose everything. I will see to it." She wrested herself from his grasp.

"I'm done, Marcia. Let's go." He headed for the door. When he heard the grunting sounds, he turned and saw that Marcia had pushed Ralphie back on the cushions. She was on top of him, holding one of his Atlantic City pillows over his face with one knee and both hands. Her other knee was digging into Ralphie's neck. He tried to push the pillow away but for a large man, he wasn't very strong. Grady did nothing as he watched the fight drain out of him.

Grady took a few long strides and pulled Marcia off the crying man. She kept screaming. "We have to do this. You have to do this. Or else."

*****

"It's strange. I stopped hearing her yelling. All I heard was Louis Armstrong singing this song called 'So Long Dearie.'" He looked to me for recognition. "It's from *Hello Dolly*. I looked it up—not then but a few years later when it kept playing in my head. Still does when I try to go to sleep. Ironic, wasn't it?"

He dropped his head into his hands and I heard him humming. I didn't know what to say or do. I sat in silence. After all, the man still had a gun hanging from his index finger.

"I knew Marcia would make good on all her threats. And I grew angrier. I was desperate." He took a few short breaths. "Ralphie was coughing and crying and then he began making this wheezing, whistling noise. It was so loud. It drowned out the music." Grady shook his head in amazement. "I'd heard that sound before, but never from anyone who lived to explain it. I understood that there was

211

no turning back. Marcia had done so much damage when she knelt on his neck. He might not have lived until we could get him to the hospital, and if we did manage to save his life, my life would be over."

He shook his head. In wonderment or disgust? I wasn't sure.

"When I slipped the noose over his head, the poor schmuck didn't know what was happening—I don't think I did either. I had the rope around *his* neck but it was Marcia that I was trying to kill. I don't remember what happened. I recall Marcia yelling. And I discovered I had been wrong about his lack of strength. He didn't seem able to raise his arms but he struggled so long." Grady dropped his head into his hands. "I made him suffer. He was so scared."

"And you rigged his body so it looked like he killed himself." I tried to keep any emotion—shock, disapproval, revulsion, all of which I felt—out of my voice.

"Marcia and I did. That was her plan and we executed it. Once I moved Seth's body, she had me. The press always talks about the Phillies's September swoon. Their downward spiral was nothing compared to mine. Until the night the Phillies lost the pennant, I was convinced I was one of the good guys. And then step by step I lost it all. I believed I could get away with it and hold onto my family and my job. I rationalized everything I did. How could a cop like me go to jail? What could I do?"

I had a litany of alternate responses he could have made at many points during the series of mistakes he made, of crimes he committed.

He lifted his gun and pointed it into the dining room. "I'm not going to hurt you. I came here to tell you the whole story. I want you to tell the truth for me. My life was really over that night. Everything else has been ridiculous. These bullets are for me."

212

"But you can't kill yourself."

"I can't stand the grief I caused myself and others. Not anymore."

"If you shoot yourself, you will end your own pain, but you'll do nothing to lessen the pain of the other people you hurt."

"You can. I told *you* the truth."

"I have no proof. No tape. You have to tell the authorities. You have to clear Ralphie Barker's name. You have to make sure his sister knows he did not kill himself."

"She'll believe you." He waved the gun in my direction.

"But nobody else will." I heard myself begging.

He scratched his head with the gun.

"Seth's mother will believe you too. She would want to know the truth. All these years, she worried that Seth had suffered so horribly. It would make such a difference to her."

He wasn't convinced.

"Only the authorities can clear Ralphie's name. You know that. They will only listen to you." I realized I had moved closer—an unconscious move that my brain, still aware of the gun, did not endorse but couldn't stop. "You said you wanted to do something your son can be proud of?"

"Oh yeah. Mikey will love the press he gets on this one. He'll come running back into my life."

"He'll understand why he lost the father he loved. He'll see the courage you had to do the right thing."

"And forgive me for fifty years of doing the wrong thing?"

"Now you will have done the right thing." Even as I said the words, I knew Grady's expectation was more realistic, but my issue was not analyzing Sawyer's reaction. My problem was getting myself out of this situation. I spoke even more softly. "It's been a long time since you've done the right thing."

Chapter 35

I drove Grady to the local precinct and explained to the officer on duty that he had a confession to make. "No, not for public drunkenness. He told me his head is clearing and he wants to talk to you about something considerably more serious."

When he interrupted, Grady did not speak in the manner of a man with a clear head, but his words were easily understood. "She is telling the truth and so will I."

The cop didn't seem interested in what a drunken Grady had to say, but called a detective that I was sure would be. I turned Grady's gun over with only a brief description of the night's events. Eventually the police would have more questions for me, but I made a quick exit before they could figure that out. Back at home, I tried to sleep, but my mind kept trying to imagine the chain reaction Grady's confession would set off. I didn't expect to have an inside track and figured I would have to wait for any news coverage before I found out what dominos had fallen.

I dozed off about 6 AM and awoke just after noon. I was still exhausted. I had news to spread but wasn't feeling up to it.

"Finally," Alex greeted me when I staggered downstairs.

I told him about my late-night visitor and my trip to the police precinct.

"Congratulations. Now that you've done all this good work shouldn't you let everyone know? They've been waiting for 50 years."

This wasn't the type of information to deliver over the

phone, but I needed to make sure I beat any press coverage. For all I knew, I was already too late. I made the calls. First, Helen Mitchell. "Jack Grady has gone to the police to tell the truth about what happened to Seth and to Ralphie. He knows that Ralphie did not kill Seth." I did not provide details. That was up to Grady and the police. She did not press mainly because simply saying thank you put a strain on her voice. I could hear her gasping and holding back tears, but could barely hear her good-bye.

Then I called Susan Timmons. "Jack Grady has gone to the police with evidence that Ralphie Barker did not kill Seth and that your son did not suffer the way you feared." Again, I did not provide the details, only the news that the truth was coming out.

I was still telling Ellie Shields the story when I heard her fingers on the keyboard.

"Grady went to the precinct late last night to give evidence in the Seth Timmons case. Ralphie Barker did not kill him. You can call me back after you talk to the police but please don't use my name. I am an unnamed source."

"An unnamed source close to the investigation." The sound of keystrokes did not stop. "I've got to go confirm." But before she hung up she asked if I was still seeing that undercover cop. I didn't let on that she was solving a mystery for me even as I solved a mystery for her. I told her no. Marcus was gone from my life, but knowing his true profession made me feel a little better about the episode and more hopeful about his situation.

Next, I called Aunt Julia.

"I'd say we should celebrate but it is a sad situation all around." She offered. "I'll bring takeout."

She did. Chinese. Alex contributed the wine. Then, over Kung Pao Chicken and Sesame Shrimp, we speculated. What would happen to Grady? To Marcia? To all the people who had been victims of Sonny Taylor's crime now that they knew the truth? We had reached no conclusions when Aunt Julia headed home, Alex headed for the clubs and I headed for the couch and the quiet night in front of the TV that had been interrupted the night before. I fell asleep before I made it through one half-hour sitcom.

When I woke up, a *Friends* rerun was playing on the TV. Or so I heard; I could not see the screen. A figure was standing in front of it. I squinted but I felt fairly certain I was not looking at Alex. Despite a surfeit of spots, I ruled out a leopard escaped from the zoo; leopards didn't stand erect on two feet but if one did it would tower over my five-foot-tall visitor. As my vision cleared, I realized Marcia Taylor was standing in front of me and she was holding the remote.

"What did Jack Grady tell you?"

Definitely Marcia. I recognized her raspy voice. I sputtered in response. Not fully awake, I couldn't quite make sense of what was going on, but I had a feeling it wasn't good.

"Did that bastard rat out my Sonny? No one can hold Sonny responsible. Sonny was only a baby."

Even after pulling myself to an upright position, I was still getting my bearings.

"How did you find me?"

"You think because I'm old that I can't use a computer?"

I thought *I am only housesitting* but I said, "How did you get in here?"

"The window was open."

Now it was. The screen was gone. Where was Harry when I needed him?

"Why did you do this? I know it's your fault. Don't even try to tell me it isn't."

I wasn't about to tell the woman that I was proud to

take the blame, at least not while she was in ranting mode.

"Years, I hear nothing. And now you start nosing around. How could you do this? We didn't do anything wrong. We were only trying to help Sonny, but the cops don't understand that." Her eyes were full of disbelief. She could not grasp that they did not see the situation her way, that they would not see it her way. "Grady told them the whole story and he's going to get some sort of deal. You should have come to me first. I could have told the cops everything they wanted to know, but I know they are going to charge me with being an accessory in that kid's murder. They didn't say it, but I know they are going to try. They will believe everything Grady tells them just because he was a cop."

Or just because it's true? Why wasn't she talking about Ralphie's death? Why was she in my living room and not in a jail cell? Shouldn't the cops have her in custody for Ralphie's murder? Had Grady failed to tell the cops the whole story? Did he think he could tell me the truth and then hope I would hold back when the cops came to me? Grady knew they would. But if Grady never confessed, it would simply be my word against his. No one could ever prove what really happened. No one would bother. And Marcia Taylor would get away with murder.

"Grady." She spat the word. "The way he lived, I can't believe he lasted this long. Why didn't he just die? I should have helped him along. I used to check up on him once in a while. We couldn't be seen together. 'Never again.' That's what he told me back in '64. But I always knew in the back of my head that he could hurt me. I mean my Sonny. When the years went by and I saw what a mess he became I stopped worrying that he'd blow the whistle, but then you came along. You." She said the word with the same force she accorded the word *Grady*. "You . . . you . . ." When she couldn't find the right descriptive phrase she screeched. I had no trouble filling in the blank.

The rage in her voice faded to exhaustion. "I know I shouldn't have helped Sonny. But what would you have done? I was his mother. What mother would not have done what I did?"

I reached for the remote and turned off the television. As if with a five-second delay, I realized Marcia was not holding the remote in her hand. I checked once more with clear eyes. She was holding a gun.

Not again. The odds of my talking myself out of the same predicament two nights in a row were slim. I tried to remember if Alex was home, but with a gun pointed my way, my brain was not working at full-tilt. Part of me hoped Alex would save me, the other part knew he would be safer if he remained oblivious to what was going on in the living room. I had to count on myself.

"Marcia, put the gun down."

She ignored me. "That horrible man betrayed my son."

She would see the situation that way.

"My poor little boy."

Only she would see the situation that way.

"I tried so hard with that child."

"I'm sure you did, Marcia. Why don't you sit down and we'll have a drink? We can talk about it." I pulled myself to a sitting position. "Here, let me take your gun."

She waved the weapon at me. "What, do you think because I'm old I'm stupid? I am so sick of young people treating me like I'm an idiot."

It occurred to me the reason people treated Marcia like an idiot had nothing to do with her age.

"I'm not that old. I still look pretty hot, don't I? I do, don't I?"

"You look great, Marcia." I didn't add *for your age* fearing that comment would earn me a bullet in the chest.

"I have so much trouble finding dates these days. I haven't had a date this month."

This month? I hadn't had a date this year—if you

discounted the thirty seconds I had Marcus in my sights.

"A woman needs men, you know."

I noted what she did not say *a woman needs a man*. She wanted them all.

"I . . ." she elongated the word and bounced her gun for emphasis, "I used to be able to get any man I wanted." A dark cloud passed over her face. "And then they would meet that son of mine. I should have given him away when he was still young enough to be cute. He's no looker now. You know?"

I had to agree, but then again I'd only seen him on the prisoner website.

"What a pain in the ass that boy turned out to be. You got kids?"

I shook my head.

"Oh, that's right. You told me. I forgot. I'm tired. I had a rough day. Spent the afternoon at the police station thanks to you. I gotta sit down."

I could have taken the gun from her while she settled herself into the chair, but I didn't figure that out until I saw the difficulty the usually spry Marcia had getting seated. By then it was too late. She rested her thin arm along the chair's wide arm and pointed the weapon my way. "This thing is heavy. I don't remember any of my guns being so heavy."

That comment caused some concern. Just how many weapons had she owned and what had she used them for?

"Well, you could put it down."

She laughed, a loud bawdy cackle. "That's a good one." She grew suddenly serious. "I can't put it down. Everyone is against me. I have to defend myself." She shook her head to show me she was amazed. "The cops believe everything that Grady says. I know they do. So what if I did try to help my boy? The cops, they think I did a bad thing by protecting him. How could that be wrong? A mother protects her son, right? That's what I'm supposed to do. Ain't it?"

I nodded. "Absolutely. Any mother would have done, no, should have done, what you did. I am sure the jury will realize that."

"Jury! I ain't goin' before no jury."

I didn't argue with her, but I was pretty sure that was exactly where she was going. She didn't seem like the type to confess her guilt and accept a plea bargain. Images of her yelling "I am innocent" as they dragged her out of the courtroom played in the back of my mind. The front of my mind had bigger problems.

"It isn't my fault that I have to tell the cops the truth. I'm no fool. That's the only way I am going to get immunity." Marcia rubbed her forehead with her free hand. "Oh God, I knew that boy would be the ruin of me. His father was no good and he was no good. Wouldn't even nurse, the little shit. Had to go buy formula. Formula's expensive. I couldn't afford that, but I did. You know why?"

"Because you're a good mother, Marcia."

"You're damn right I am and I could not stand that crying." She put the real reason she paid for the formula on the table. "Cry, cry, cry. That was all that kid did." She scratched her head with the tip of the gun.

I didn't move. Another opportunity lost. I'd better formulate a plan. Rushing her would not be part of it. This woman was just crazy enough to shoot me.

"Do you have any cigarettes?" She glanced around the room as if searching for signs of smoking.

"Sorry."

"I quit years ago, but I need to pick that old habit up again."

I could understand why this might be the moment. "How about a drink?" I offered another form of comfort.

"Got any beer?"

"I'll have to go in the kitchen."

"I'll come with you."

Now, I had her. Watching how difficult getting into the chair was for her, I realized she'd have a harder time getting out. I stood up and got into position, ready to lunge but I didn't have to execute my plan.

The front door flung open and two uniformed policemen burst into the living room. The two worked together and, in a flash, they had the gun out of Marcia's hand and Marcia out of the chair. As they struggled to get her into handcuffs, they were forced to abandon any thoughts of treating her gingerly because of her age. They needed the help of two more cops who appeared from the kitchen to subdue her. Now, I understood Marcia's penchant for animal prints. In those few moments, she earned the right to wear tiger stripes.

Alex came running down the stairs. "Thank you, gentlemen." He turned to me. "I feared I was going to have to save you myself, and let's face it, physical rescues are not my specialty, although I have done it before." He turned to the cops. "She seems to need saving a lot."

They didn't ask why. They had their hands full with Marcia Taylor. Literally. To stop her kicking and screaming each of the first two officers to arrive had grabbed a leg and a third held her by the shoulders as they carried her out the door.

"I want a deal. You creeps, don't manhandle me. I want a deal. I can't help it if that jerk of a kid was a killer."

The police appeared confused. They'd answered a trespassing call. Beside me, Alex shook his head as he watched Marcia disappear outside. "I wonder how a kid could go bad with a sweet mom like that."

I glanced at the sole remaining police officer who produced a notebook, I explained. "I'll fill you in on her son."

Chapter 36

The memory of awakening with Marcia Taylor standing over me did little to promote a sound night's sleep but by 6 AM exhaustion made it impossible for me to stay fully awake. I was lost in a dream but not a deep sleep when the phone awoke me. Before I could reach for it, my bedroom door flew open. I saw two figures revealed by the hall light. Both rushed into the room and leaped into action. Alex grabbed my phone. Aunt Julia wrapped an arm around me.

"Who is it?" Aunt Julia asked.

Alex didn't answer. "Oh." He sounded concerned. "Ah, yes." He listened for a moment and then repeated "Yes" in a voice that was stronger and louder. "This is Tracy Shaw's line." Again, he listened. "Not if you're going to talk to her like that."

"Who is it?" I asked.

"Whoever it is, you don't have to talk to them." Aunt Julia whispered.

"I don't know what the police told you but you have to calm down."

"Sonny?" I asked.

Alex nodded. He held the phone away from his ear and I heard a loud male voice.

"I'll talk." I pried the phone from Alex's hand.

"What the hell is going on? What did you do? Cops came to visit me and accused me of killing Seth Timmons."

"Your mother gave you up, Sonny. She admitted you killed Seth."

"No, she didn't."

223

"She did. And Jack Grady confessed how he fixed it for you."

"Is that what she told Grady? That I killed Seth?"

"Their stories matched."

"Don't try to trick me. You're bluffing. My mother would never say I killed Seth."

"She wanted to clear her conscience." Even as I said the words, I realized I was describing Grady, not Marcia.

"Now I know you're lying." Sonny's quick response quashed my attempt to clarify. "My mother doesn't have a conscience."

"She going to testify against you if the cops offer her immunity." This was true, although I didn't reveal that Grady got there first.

Sadness replaced disbelief in Sonny's voice. "Now that sounds like my mom. She always knew how to figure the angles. But in this case, she's got nothing to barter. I didn't kill Seth."

"Are you saying your killing Seth in a fit of anger is not how it went down?" I waited but heard no sound on the other end. "If you don't tell a different story, all the cops have is what your mother told Grady." I listened to thirty seconds of silence. "We don't have unlimited time. If you are going to tell me a story, tell me now." I waited and heard only breathing. I fought the urge to speak.

At last, he spoke. "I told you I got mad when I saw her making out with Jack Grady. I was a jerk and I took it out on Seth."

And killed him? I didn't think it was a smart time to interrupt with a question. I listened.

"I picked on him in front of everyone. He was such an easy target. The new kid who wanted to be liked. I held his cap so the little guy couldn't get it. Kid stuff. I swung a bat at him. I just wanted to scare him."

"What did your mother do?" I asked.

"She tried to calm me down. Probably afraid I'd say

224

something in front of Mr. Lockwood. She still tried to keep the party going, but Mr. Grady got Mikey and Seth out of there fast. Mr. Lockwood was right behind them. When everyone was gone, she just let me act out. I know that's what they call it now."

"So how did Seth end up dead?"

"In a way I blame myself. If I hadn't grabbed that stupid hat he wouldn't have come back for it. But I swear to you. I didn't kill him. Do you believe me?"

I didn't, but why share? "Who did?"

Sonny answered with a very long pause. I worried that he had hung up.

"After everyone left, I was alone with my mother. She was really angry at me because I had driven Mr. Lockwood away. I was upset and she had this way of calming me down." His voice sounded odd, strangely calm, as he told his story.

*****Sonny Taylor*****
September 30, 1964

His mother stood at the foot of the stairs staring up at Mr. Lockwood, begging him to stay. She reached out and grabbed his arm. He stopped. He was always polite. Sonny liked that Mr. Lockwood was always courteous. That was a word Sister Rita Mary had on the bulletin board.

"Please. He'll calm down. You know I can calm him down."

Mr. Lockwood pulled his arm away and she lost her grip. "I'll call. This isn't the right time to talk."

Linda had already fled upstairs. Mr. Lockwood appeared anxious to follow but the scene with Sonny's mother repeated until he was beyond her reach. She begged. He moved away. She took a step and grabbed his arm. He wrested it free. She begged. He moved. She

225

grabbed. And, so on.

"John, it's okay. You can stay."

Sonny heard her trying to keep her tone light but Sonny knew. She was desperate.

Sonny thought Mr. Lockwood sounded desperate too, desperate to get away. "It's late." "Linda has school tomorrow." And finally in a kind voice that reminded him of Sister Rita, "Marcia, your son needs you."

"He's fine. He'll be fine. You're calm now aren't you, Sonny?" His mother turned to him with a smile on her lips and hatred in her eyes.

He remained in the same aggressive position, breathing heavily and holding his bat as a weapon. He didn't want Mr. Lockwood to leave, but he couldn't let go of his anger. Why should Mr. Lockwood stay? So his mother could play him for a fool?

She took a few steps up the stairs. "John, please. Come back."

The only response was the sound of a slamming door. Marcia, frozen in place, stared after him. "He won't be back, you know." She turned and moved down the steps slowly. She appeared calm, but Sonny recognized the tone. He had encountered this version of his mother before. He felt himself take a step backward.

"And it's all your fault."

His fault? "I like Mr. Lockwood more than you do."

"So why did you drive him away?"

His mother's tone was controlled, but Sonny understood the emotion lurking under the surface. He also understood that rage could burst through at any moment.

She grabbed some empty cups and a bowl that had once held the potato chips now strewn across the floor and headed upstairs. He still had the bat in his hand as he followed.

"Stay. I don't want to see you." She disappeared

through the doorway at the top of the stairs.

He told himself he was practicing his swing while he listened to her slam things around in the kitchen, but he knew the truth. He wanted the force of his swing to kill his feelings of fury, to somehow free him from the pain. Why couldn't his mother be like other mothers? All he wanted was a nice father to live with them. Why couldn't she see that? Why couldn't she see him? Why couldn't she love him? He stopped swinging, but couldn't stop trembling. He understood what caused the shaking: rage. He tightened his grip and resumed swinging at the air.

He didn't know for how long. When his mother returned, she ignored him. She spun around the room dumping all the cigarette butts into one ashtray. She never spoke, but he felt her rage.

"I wasn't the one all over Mikey's dad." He hissed.

His mother pitched the ashtray at the paneled walls and a cloud of ash floated to the carpet. She moved towards her son with measured paces, each coordinated with a carefully enunciated word. "I am your mother. Do not question what I do."

"But I don't understand. Why did you do that with Mr. Grady? I want you with Mr. Lockwood."

"Well now you've fixed that, haven't you?" She grabbed the end of his bat and wrestled it from his hand. He didn't resist. "We could have had both."

"Why do we need both?" He heard his voice cracking and fought to control himself. He didn't want to cry. Sonny Taylor didn't cry. Sonny Taylor was tough. "Mr. Lockwood is nice. He treats me real good. We don't need Mr. Grady."

"It's always wise to have a cop in your pocket, Sonny. Haven't I taught you that? We learned that when your father died, didn't we?"

"Yes." He felt defeated. He would always feel defeated. His mother always won.

"You could have gone to jail if Officer Donnelly hadn't come through for you, if he hadn't confirmed your father shot himself by accident." Her voice was shrill. She was outraged. She twisted the truth to be what she wanted.

"For me?"

"For us."

"No, Mom, for you. I know. I remember. I didn't shoot my father."

"Sonny, you were too young to remember." She leaned the bat against the wall as if finishing a routine housekeeping job.

"You say that but I do. You shot him. I do remember."

His mother pressed the heels of her hands against her head and massaged her scalp. He knew what she was thinking, what she was asking herself. She'd asked herself the question aloud, in front of him, many times. What could she do with this boy? She let out a deep sigh before she opened her eyes, but said nothing. She pulled a chair to a spot near the corner, climbed on it and pushed back a ceiling tile. "You may think you recall what happened, but you've had a dream. Sometimes dreams feel real."

He knew what she was reaching for and he was frightened. He needed to let her win one more time. "You're right. It must have been a dream." But this time changing his story didn't satisfy her.

"How often do I have to remind you?"

"I said I was wrong. What else can I do?"

His mother jumped down from the chair. When she turned around he saw exactly what he expected, what he feared. She was pointing a gun at him, the same weapon she used to shoot his father. "I knew the day would come when you would be too much of a liability. Just like your father. I suspect it may be time for you to join him."

He never doubted that she would shoot him—that his mother, his own mother, would kill her only son. He had worried about that for as long as he could remember but *he never told anyone. Who would believe a mother would shoot her child? He had understood for a long time that it wasn't a matter of if, but when.*

"Mommy, I'll be good. I promise."

"I can't depend on you. You cost me a lot tonight. No one will miss you, Sonny. No one will look for you and if they do, they would never question why I had to send you away to a military school."

Never moving the gun from her target, she backed to the TV. She glanced back, found the volume knob and turned up the sound.

"If that damn team of yours had won, there might have been fireworks. That would make this a lot easier."

Sonny never had the illusion that he could change his mother's mind. He would have to overwhelm her physically, restrain her until she calmed down. He'd done it before. What worried him was that at those times she had been screaming and crying, but tonight she was so calm. That scared him more than any yelling or ranting she had ever done before. He took tiny steps towards her but she backed away just as slowly. He followed as if caught in her magnetic field. He kept staring into her eyes, searching for any glimmer of love. She actually looked happy. She was enjoying this moment, holding a gun on him, her baby. How could that be?

He never heard Seth come down the basement stairs but as his mother moved to her left, there he was, standing on the steps behind her. Sonny felt so embarrassed. He didn't want that kid to see his mother treating him this way. He didn't want anyone to know his mother treated him this way. But Seth saw and he understood. Sonny could tell. The kid's eyes grew wide with fear. He nodded. Like he was telling Sonny that everything would be okay, that he would help him.

Sonny realized he was more afraid than embarrassed. Maybe the kid could help. He played for time. "Mom, I learned my lesson. You can put the gun down." He threw one of her favorite phrases back of her. "You're going too far this time."

"No, Sonny. You went too far. I knew you would. Sooner or later you would. God knows I tried with you, but it was hopeless. You were hopeless. You are hopeless, Sonny. Just like that loser father of yours."

He felt such shame at his mother's words but not for himself, for her. It was bad enough he realized what she was really like, but now Seth would know and the world would know.

Marcia raised the gun. He tried to tell himself she was just trying to teach him a lesson but he was afraid that this time she was serious.

Like a superhero, Seth flew off the stairs and landed on his mother's back. The force threw her off balance but didn't knock her down, or the gun from her hand.

"What the hell?" She screeched. "Who the hell?" She used her free hand to claw at Seth's hand.

Sonny wanted to move. He wanted to help Seth but he didn't know what to do. The gun swung back and forth as the two staggered across the room.

"Help me, you idiot. I'm your mother."

Help her? Why would he help her? He ran forward and charged into his mother. He tried to do karate chops like he'd seen on television to knock the gun out his mother's hand, but she held on. He saw Seth tighten his grip on his mother's neck and reach over her shoulder to make a grab for the gun. The maneuver didn't work. They spun away from Sonny and around the room as Seth slipped off his mother's back and the top of his body slid down her arm.

Sonny felt a moment of freedom when he heard the shot ring out. Just for an instant, he felt a weight lift from his shoulders. Not the real kind but the kind adults talked about when grown-up life got too hard. He felt so relieved. He might be free of her. He knew he shouldn't feel such joy at the prospect of life without his mother, but he couldn't help it, he did. The spinning twosome stopped. He waited for his mother's body to crumble, but it was Seth's that slumped to the floor. His mother stumbled backwards, and Sonny dropped onto the floor beside Seth. The kid's eyes, showing only shock, stared past him. Sonny could see the dark spot growing on the arm of his shirt, already red in honor of the Phillies. He wanted to stop the bleeding but he didn't know how. He looked from the wound to Seth's eyes. They were full of fear. "I'll call a doctor. You'll be fine. We'll take care of you. You'll be fine." He meant what he was saying. He believed what he was saying. He wanted to help Seth. Surely, his mother would help Seth. He felt awe at what the kid had done. For him. He had been so mean and the kid had saved his life. "I won't let anything bad happen to you. I'll go get help."

Seth was trying to tell him something. He opened his mouth but could not form any words. With eyes full of terror, he stared over Sonny's shoulder.

"I'll be right back. With help. I have to get up." Sonny stood, turned and started to run in one quick move, but stopped dead when he saw what Seth had been trying to tell him. Not only was his mother still holding the gun, she had it pointed at the two boys.

"Sonny, honey, what are we going to do about him?"

She said him, *but Sonny knew she meant* you. *The two of you.* You *and Seth. She still spoke in that eerily calm tone. "I think I know what happened. You shot him and I had no choice but to defend myself against you. After all, you shot that poor young boy."*

His fear turned to rage and propelled him forward. He expected to hear a shot but he reached his mother before she could fire. He grabbed for the gun but her grip was too powerful. She curled away from him to protect the

231

weapon. He wrapped an arm around her neck. "Drop it. Drop the gun." Even in the frenetic action, he heard himself say the words that seemed to come from a television show. Words that belonged in a television show, only in a television show.

"Let me go." His tight grip meant she could only croak the words. She still managed to make them sound harsh and mean. "Let go of me. I am your mother."

He didn't let go. He kept one arm around her neck and reached for the gun with the other. He felt his mother falling, pulling him down with her. He heard the gunshot before they hit the floor. When he knocked the gun out of her hand, he saw it land beside the overturned coffee table. He let go of his mother and crawled across the floor. She grasped his foot but he pulled away, snatched the gun and turned it on his mother. "Stop." He commanded her. "Stay where you are. You're not going to hurt us. We'll be okay now, Seth." He looked across the room to where his classmate still lay. The kid's eyes were still open. Staring. But Sonny knew they couldn't see. That was when he saw a second circle of blood. This one on Seth's chest, growing bigger and bigger.

*****

"I never forgot how quickly that circle grew until it wasn't a circle anymore. The kid's shirt was turning from bright red to a darker red. Almost black. Like death. I understood what was happening and I could not stop it." I heard a long sigh at the other end of the phone. "I hid upstairs, waiting for her to come and kill me but she never did. She told me not finishing me off when she had the chance was one of the biggest mistakes of her life. Instead, she got Mr. Grady to come over to help me, to save me. What a joke? She only wanted to save herself. That was my dear mom. So, you can believe her, if you want, but what I just told you? That, Ms. Shaw, is what really happened."

I took a deep breath. This time I knew exactly what to do. Since Sonny had called from the prison phone, I could suggest to the police they might want to listen to the recording.

Chapter 37

I took a shower as soon as I got off the phone, more to give myself a place to think than to get ready for the day. I was still wrapped in a towel when I called Ellie Shields to let her know she might want to check with the cops about potential developments in the Seth Timmons case, but she knew more than I did.

"More? You done good, kiddo. Grady confessed to killing Ralphie Barker this morning." She croaked with a voice straight out of a 1940s detective movie. "You know, Grady didn't cop to that murder until they brought that lunatic Taylor dame in from your house. She was hollering and yelling. The desk sergeant told me that right there in the lobby she screams, 'I guess he tried to tell you some cockamamie story about how we killed Ralphie Barker.'" The reporter chuckled. "Apparently, Grady hadn't gotten to that part yet. Maybe he thought better about telling that story but after that loony brought it up, he did. I only got the basics but he didn't try to deny anything. Let me go see what's happened now. I gotta go."

I felt relief. My work was done. Ellie Shields could take the investigation from there.

I was dressed but craving a nap when Alex knocked. "You decent? You have more company."

"Are they toting a gun?" I opened the door.

"Not that I can see but I didn't frisk her. She claims she's Ralphie Barker's sister."

"Here?"

"In the living room."

I'd be happy to see Helen but I had to wonder how she

and all my other unexpected guests found me.

"I guess they have access to the Internet. You're not the only one using it. Word got out."

"But I'm only housesitting at this address."

"Sorry. I'm not a documents expert but you *are* getting mail here. What should I tell her?"

"Tell her I'll be down, but I'll need a few minutes."

I struggled into my clothes. As I pulled my hair into a ponytail, my phone buzzed. I didn't recognize the number but I knew the signature. The text read: Heard the news. Nice work. Will contact you when I can. M.

I wasn't sure how Marcus heard. I guess it was through some sort of cop grapevine. I was fairly certain the time would never be right for romance with an undercover cop, but I typed a single letter, K, and hit Send.

When I came down the stairs, I found Mrs. Mitchell sitting on the sofa, chatting with Alex. As soon as she saw me, she grinned in a way I had not seen before. She wasn't smiling; she was beaming. "I came here because two very nice policemen came to see me this noon and told me they believe that he, Jack Grady, told the truth. He said Ralphie did not kill Seth or himself. Mr. Grady, Detective Grady, insisted the police tell me the news. I guess since he had been a policeman they respected his wishes."

I understood. "He felt a lot of guilt because of the pain he caused you. He told me that."

"I want to thank Detective Grady for the truth but they won't let me see him. It could not have been easy for him to own up to the things he'd done."

I could not understand why she didn't hate Grady. For killing the brother she loved. For hiding the truth all these years. For changing her life in so many negative ways.

She answered as if I'd spoken aloud. "I am just so happy to know the truth." Her smile confirmed that assertion. "No one can change what happened. But the truth . . ." Her eyes filled with tears and when she spoke her voice quavered. "That was all I wanted. All I could want."

She was kinder than I was, and wiser. I didn't tell her more information might be coming. I'd let the police decide on the truth of Sonny's story. Helen had gotten the news she wanted.

"And, I want to thank you too." She waved that I should come and sit by her side.

As soon as I sat she grabbed me in a hug.

The success of my investigation seemed inadequate. "I was happy to help although I know it doesn't bring Ralphie back."

She loosened her grip and patted my hand. "But it did. I can't say I won't have nightmares about the way Ralphie died. I will. When they gave me the good news today, I cried as hard as I did when he first passed, but I know how happy Ralphie would be that people know the truth."

It seemed like so little to have done. "I wish it had never been necessary. My investigation."

"We can't go back. I only learned that after I created dozens, maybe hundreds, of scenarios of how I could have protected Ralphie, saved my marriage, kept my baby. I can only deal with now. And, the future, however long that might be. Which brings me back to Detective Grady. I want him to know I forgive him and to understand what a difference he's made in my life. The life I live now. Promise me you will let him know."

"I don't think they'll let me see him. When all this is settled, you might be able to visit him. You could write him a letter."

"A letter." She sounded pensive. For a moment I thought she was composing the entire communication in her head, but she finally spoke. "I came for one other reason. I wanted to make sure you understand all this would not have happened without your help. I wanted you to know how much I appreciate all that you've done." She reached into her bag. "I don't know if you will want this or not. It may be silly. If you don't, I'll understand."

No one could accuse her of overselling.

"It's something that Ralphie loved."

I kept my expectant look optimistic although I couldn't fathom what Ralphie could have loved that I would like to have.

"It's not the original. I mean, no one has a turntable anymore. So I got some CDs made, but the sound is not high quality like a new disc. Ralphie made this for me at one of those booths they used to have where you could make a record. I'd like you to hear how beautifully he sang."

She handed me a package, carefully wrapped in loud yellow paper covered with bright red apples. I started to rip the paper but she asked me to wait. "Later when you are alone." She smiled. "You really won't get a full picture of what he was like. He stuttered and his speech was oddly paced but when he sang . . . ." A wider smile. "Well, you'll hear."

And I did hear. And I understood why Helen asked me to wait before I played it. No one wants to see a grown woman cry. Ralphie's tenor was slightly tentative at first. He didn't launch into "You'll Never Walk Alone." He crept up on it, his voice growing stronger and more confident as he hit the crescendo. My face was drenched with tears by the time he reached the final note. And, then I heard Ralphie. The Ralphie everyone saw. The Ralphie Seth saw. He chuckled nervously and spoke in a halting voice, "I hope I was okay."

You were okay, Ralphie. You were more than okay.

About 1964

For more information about the world that Seth Timmons and Ralphie Barker lived in and the 1964 Phillies go to: www.Pinterest.com/JaneKelly80.

Jane Kelly

For information about the Writing in Time and other series by Jane Kelly go to:

www.janekelly.net
www.facebook.com/janekellyauthor
www.amazon.com/author/janekellyauthor

BOOK CLUB DISCUSSION QUESTIONS

1.   What does your experience of the characters tell you about America in 1964? How do the characters reflect the social conventions of the times?

2.   Would events surrounding the crime have unfolded differently if the story took place in the current time period?

3.   Do you think any of the characters would have made different life choices if they were born fifty years later?

4.   The testimony given by the witnesses includes a lot of details about the times. Do you recognize any of them?

5.   In 1964, the United States was beginning an era of tremendous change. How do you see these changes reflected, or not reflected, in the behavior of the characters?

Jane Kelly

About the Author

Jane Kelly is the author of the Meg Daniels Mysteries, Writing in Time Mysteries and Widow Lady Mysteries. She holds an MS in Information Studies from Drexel University and an MPhil in Popular Literature from Trinity College, University of Dublin. She is a past-president of the Delaware Valley Sisters in Crime and has served on the board of the New York Chapter of Mystery Writers of America. Her fourth Meg Daniels mystery, Missing You in Atlantic City, won an Independent Publisher Book Award silver medal for mid-Atlantic fiction. She currently lives in the Philadelphia area.

Made in the USA
Middletown, DE
09 December 2021